T0326004

Strike of THE
COBRA

DRUG SMUGGLERS WHO WOULD CRUSH ANYONE IN THEIR PATH TO ESCAPE JUSTICE

BASED ON A TRUE LIFE EXPERIENCE

STEPHEN HEUBACH

STRIKE OF THE COBRA

DRUG SMUGGLERS WHO WOULD CRUSH ANYONE
IN THEIR PATH TO ESCAPE JUSTICE

MEREO
Cirencester

Published by Mereo

Mereo is an imprint of Memoirs Publishing

1A The Market Place Cirencester Gloucestershire GL7 2PR
info@memoirsbooks.co.uk | www.memoirspublishing.com

Strike of the Cobra

ISBN: 978-1-86151-076-1

To my dear mother Angie, whose selfless love, support
and dedication to her family and friends, along
with her strength and courage through adversity, are truly
admirable and inspiring.

FOREWORD

This book is based on an extraordinary sequence of events which took place a little over a decade ago, involving myself, my family and some of my colleagues and friends. While most of the narrative is based on fact, in fictionalising it I have changed names and some of the settings, as well as various other specific details to avoid embarrassment to those who were caught up in the story. Some passages are speculative, some are invented, and some characters have been created to represent others involved in the plot but with changed national identity. Whilst I have added to some of the peripheral detail, the core of this story is absolutely true.

I hope my story will make the reader aware of how easy it is for innocent people, to be caught up in serious crime through no fault of their own - other than, perhaps a willingness to trust their fellow human beings.

Stephen Heubach, October 2013

CHAPTER ONE

The 747 400 of Singapore Airlines flight SQ22 banked sharply to the left, steadied on her course and then after about five minutes, broke the cloud cover out of Heathrow. It was a glorious sight. No matter how frequently Daniel Cassidy flew, he could not help but glance out of the window and marvel at the contrast between the damp, dark, drizzly conditions below the cloud base and the brilliance of the deep blue sky above, with the sunshine reflecting off the tops of the clouds. The late hour of the flight, with the sun setting on the horizon, only added to the moment.

A young couple, both perhaps 25 years old, sat on the aisle and centre seats to his right, totally absorbed with each other. Since saying "Hello" on boarding they had not uttered another word in Daniel's direction, preferring to whisper and giggle quietly between themselves. This suited Daniel fine, as he was not in the mood for small talk and had dreaded the thought of being seated next to someone who would try to spend the entire 13-hour flight giving him his life history. Daniel remembered briefly a flight a few years before when he had been seated next to a middle-aged man who had not only had a severe body odour problem but had chain-smoked disgustingly strong cigarettes. He had also had verbal diarrhoea, which had become more and more slurred as the flight had progressed. Thank goodness all flights were now non-smoking.

The drinks trolley was heading slowly down the aisle with the stewardesses attending it handing out the complimentary drinks and peanuts. Daniel normally restricted his drinking of alcohol on an aircraft, as it tended to exacerbate the dehydration and the feeling of headiness. This was something which, at the age of 36, was taking longer and longer to get over.

However, today was different. As the trolley neared, he felt a distinct need to quell the worries that the last trip to London had generated.

"Would you like a drink?" came the soft 'Singlish' accented voice from the attractive young Singaporean stewardess dressed elegantly in her long dark blue sarong.

"Gin and tonic please."

"Ice and lemon?"

"Please."

Daniel reclined his seat for the full few inches of travel afforded in economy class, settled back with his drink and reflected back on the two-week business trip to London. It had been good to catch up with family and friends, and indeed without their support, advice and help, things could have been a damn site worse. His family home was in an outstandingly beautiful part of Dorset, and what a wonderful retreat that always was to go and get away from things and totally relax. Even under the strain of the last two weeks he had enjoyed walking the two black labradors along the banks of the river and had even found time for a touch of fly fishing, although the trout always seemed to avoid his lures.

His mind slowly refocused on the reality of the situation. Gordon Burrage, who had been the general manager for his company in the UK, had not been the trustworthy ally and employee that both Daniel and his co-owner and director Luke had thought. In fact completely the opposite had been true. Gordon had driven the company into the ground, and now Daniel was having to pull what was left of it out of the quagmire.

Daniel was a man of honour and naively judged most others by his own standards, something he realised was one of his weaknesses, but he would soon learn never to do this again.

Daniel had personally paid off all the debts Gordon Burrage had run up in the eight months he had been left in control of the company. Having only recently started a company in Singapore and the investment that that had taken, as well as the company investment that had been needed in the UK, this final betrayal by Gordon had been a devastating blow. Daniel had remortgaged his house in Sussex to pay off the debts in order to maintain the good names of his company, and his partner and himself.

Daniel upended the final peanuts from the small foil bag into his mouth and bit down hard as he thought with disgust how Gordon had been living like a lord for the past few months, travelling everywhere first class and running up huge expenses, something neither Daniel or Luke had ever done, choosing to do everything for themselves on a tight budget. They should have kept a closer eye on things. How wonderful was hindsight!

Daniel's thoughts turned more positive as he thought of his dear wife Linda, whom he had phoned just prior to leaving the house. She had offered to collect him from Changi airport when he arrived there the following day. Daniel had insisted that it was easier to get a taxi and see her at about 7 pm, in time for drinks on the veranda, and possibly a dip in the pool before dinner.

Daniel pulled the handset from his seat arm and flicked on the television screen in the backrest of the seat in front. He looked at the in-flight guide, *Silverkris*, for any films of note that might be showing during the flight. He spotted two he would like to watch, although he knew from experience that about halfway through the first film a wave of tiredness would kick in, and the chances of him making it awake through both were pretty remote.

He prioritised a Bruce Willis movie as the first one to watch straight after dinner had been served. He studied the menu and decided upon the chicken for dinner. It duly arrived about an hour later and, it had to be said, was exceptionally good for an aircraft meal. It was good to eat these days with a proper metal knife and fork rather than the ones Daniel remembered on aircraft when he had flown as a child, which were plastic, cheap and nasty and almost unusable. Within ten minutes of the film starting, true to form, Daniel was asleep with his head propped up against the window pillar.

The next thing Daniel knew was a soft voice asking if he would like breakfast. The lights brightened in the cabin. About an hour later the Captain announced their imminent descent into Singapore's Changi International Airport.

About five rows in front of Daniel on the far side of the

centre block of seats, a nondescript but very fit Chinese Malay gentleman in his mid forties had just finished watching one of the Mandarin movies which had been showing on the flight. He removed his blanket, set aside his headphones, stood, and politely asked the passenger next to him if he could allow him access from his seat to go to the toilet. His name was Xu Xiang. As he shuffled out of his seat and wandered back towards the aft toilets he glanced momentarily to the other side of the aircraft and noted Daniel absorbed in a book. It was the Wilbur Smith novel *Monsoon*. Xu had already seen Daniel reading it in the departure lounge at Terminal 3.

It was not the first time Xu had checked up on Daniel during the flight, although even he had smiled as he wondered why, because there was nowhere Daniel could have disappeared to at 37,000 feet.

Xu had been following Daniel since he had alighted from the Jetlink bus at Heathrow's bus terminal. Daniel had followed his normal routine of taking a taxi from his house in Sussex to Gatwick airport and the bus from there to Heathrow. Xu mused at how perfect Daniel and his company set up were for the job he and his colleagues had in mind.

On the descent, Daniel put his book back into the pocket in front of him and reminisced about the number of times he had done this flight. He thought of the first time he had landed in Singapore, this strange distant land, with his parents some 25 years earlier. It had all been a big upheaval back then, completely uprooting from their farmhouse in

Surrey and moving 7000 miles to the unknown. Daniel had endured this with less than full enthusiasm at the time, having had to leave all his schoolmates back in the UK, but he'd soon settled into it. Now all these years later he was living here with his wife, out of choice.

Daniel's father had been an airline pilot who had joined Singapore Airlines back in the mid seventies as a captain of one of the new DC10 aircraft that were being added to the fleet. During that first year they had spent a considerable amount of time in Long Beach, California, while his father had done various refresher courses for the new model of DC 10. All of this had been a tremendous adventure, and at that age Disneyland, Universal Studios, Knotts Berry farm and Magic Mountain theme parks had all been beyond the wildest comprehension of Daniel and his two younger brothers. He remembered thinking that perhaps travelling was not so bad after all.

Upon settling in Singapore for the first time they had lived at the Raffles Hotel for the first three months while they were house hunting. This had been great fun, travelling to and from his new school, the United World College of South East Asia, in a taxi from the Raffles Hotel, without a financial worry or responsibility in the world.

How easy and carefree life had been then, and yet at the time, like most kids, he had always found something to worry about!

After much searching they had settled for a beautiful old colonial house not far from Daniel's school, in a park inhabited entirely by other expatriates. Rochester Park had been built originally for British Army Officers and the houses were of good proportions and very sturdy construction with full length verandas and balconies. They had an amah's quarters in a separate bungalow in the garden, and even a small plantation of banana trees. For a growing child, it was paradise.

Daniel's parents had continued to live in Singapore until the early nineties, and the majority of Daniel and Linda's Christmases and New Years had been spent in Singapore, a place he had grown to love dearly.

Landing approached and the stewardesses made their final round for a last check on seat belts, asking the lady next to Daniel to please put her seat in the upright position, which she duly did. An electric whine and rumble came from the depths of the 747 as the landing gear was lowered. The couple next to Daniel craned forward to look out of the window to his left, and the woman cheerily asked Daniel if it was his first visit.

"No, I've spent a bit of time here. How about you?"

"Oh, it's our first time. We're here for a couple of days before we go on to see Todd's uncle and aunt in Sydney. It's our first time out of Europe."

The view coming in to land had been fairly obscured by cloud cover, and no sooner had Daniel answered a few of their questions on shopping on Orchard Road when the aircraft touched down. It was a landing Daniel's father would have been proud of. The rain lashed against the aircraft windows as they were taxiing into the bay, and the severity of it reminded Daniel that this would soon be a daily afternoon occurrence when the monsoon winds set in again.

As soon as the pilot applied the aircraft brakes and brought it to a final halt, everyone was struggling to stand in the aisles and grab their luggage from the overhead lockers. Daniel had only his briefcase at his feet, and would stay seated until the rush subsided.

As the queue started to move, he wished the couple who had been sitting next to him a good stay and onward trip, then collected his book from the seat pocket, opened his case and organised himself for disembarkation.

Daniel always marvelled at the splendour and cleanliness of Changi Airport, a place he had been coming through since the second day it had officially opened, when it had taken over from the old Paya Labar Airport in the eighties. The rows of bougainvillea hanging from the balconied areas gave such a welcoming feel.

As he walked onto the moving walkway towards the arrivals hall, Xu was only about three people behind him. Daniel was completely oblivious.

Daniel gave the immigration official a friendly "good evening", but was met with the usual hostile, suspicious and unfriendly blank look. From this Daniel concluded that all immigration officials worldwide must be trained at the same place, with a complete courtesy bypass. As he stood at the counter he did remember one incident with an immigration official in Newark, New York who had actually smiled and bid Daniel a good day. What a memorable occasion that was.

CHAPTER TWO

Daniel stood casually at the carousel and waited for his case to come round. As he did so he glanced beyond the customs tables through the clear glass to where a crowd of loved ones was forming to meet the flight. He was looking for Linda. Although he had told her he would get a taxi, if she had nothing better to do she had this knack of occasionally just turning up to meet him, which was always a welcome surprise. However today he was fairly sure that Linda would not appear, as she had been playing tennis at the club that evening, and unless it had been rained off she would not have the time.

He concentrated his attentions on the baggage belt, which was now a solid stream of cases. He saw his case travelling down the far side. He had always made sure that his tatty case was easily identifiable, with a large security strap in bright colours round it, to save any confusion.

He moved forward to pick his case off the carousel when it reached him, but as he did so a Chinese man moved to pick another case off the line just in front of Daniel's, knocking into Daniel in the process and forcing him to move further down the carousel to retrieve his case.

"I'm sorry" Xu said as Daniel finally retrieved his case. "It wasn't mine anyway".

"Not to worry" Daniel replied with a short smile. Then he made his way towards the customs and exit.

As expected Linda was not there, so Daniel made his way to the taxi rank. As he stepped into the warm humid air, the pleasant scented smell he had become so accustomed to entered his lungs. He suddenly felt very clammy, and could not wait to get home and change into some shorts and a T shirt. The 94-degree heat was certainly too much when you were dressed in the thick clothes you needed in England.

The Black and Yellow taxis were waiting by their dozens, as this was a particularly busy time of the day at Changi with all the European flights landing. Daniel joined the queue and within minutes was seated in the back of a Toyota Crown taxi while its cheery Chinese driver put his case in the boot.

"You go where?" came the voice from the front, once the driver had switched on the meter.

"You go Holland Village, then I show you."

"Ah, Horrand Virrage!"

Daniel had become accustomed to the idiosyncrasies of the Singlish dialect and embarrassed as he was, he slipped straight into the same tongue when talking with average street traders, taxi drivers or similar folk whose English left something to be desired.

Dusk was falling over Singapore as the driver set off down the East Coast Parkway. Even in the light from the street lights, the central reservation and roadsides looked quite simply stunning with the abundance of various colours of bougainvillea and the magnificent fan palms lining the route.

True to form, the taxi driver could not apply a steady throttle. Instead he pumped the accelerator pedal repeatedly by applying three seconds of acceleration, followed by a similar period of deceleration, for the entire journey.

As they approached Holland Village, Daniel directed the driver in the direction of Dover Road. They then turned into Medway Park and towards Daniel's home.

With many of the roads and parks in that area being named after British towns, Daniel often felt the names stirring the emotions and an overwhelming sense of patriotism and pride at being British. After all when, these houses had been built Britain had been respected round the world as the epitome of responsibility and high standards.

It was approximately 7.30 pm when Daniel paid and tipped the driver. As the taxi reversed out of the drive, the porch light illuminated and the front door of the house opened to reveal Linda's beaming smile. At that moment it seemed to fill the doorway.

Their home in Medway Park was of similar construction to the one in Rochester Park in which Daniel had enjoyed his childhood. It was a large three-bedroomed detached house built originally for the British Forces serving there. It was of a less colonial style than the others, with glass windows rather than just shutters, but it was a substantial home with its own garden and a separate Amah's quarters. Gardens were becoming less and less common as time moved on with the development of all the condominium complexes, but Daniel and Linda had felt that with a child and the possibility of more on the way, a garden would be an asset. The other feature which had swayed them was a beautiful swimming pool in the back garden sitting in the shade of a fan palm, and with the garden backing on to a golf course, they were not overlooked at all.

As he trolleyed his case towards her, Linda held on to Skipper, their Alsatian, by his collar as he wagged, moaned and pulled with anticipation. He wanted to greet Daniel first, and the same ritual was followed every time Daniel returned from a trip.

Linda looked stunning. She was slim and her tan was accentuated by her off-white dockers and her white and navy shirt. Daniel's heart missed a beat as she stood there. He realised yet again how lucky he was to have such a wonderful wife, one who was not only very attractive but completely selfless, fair and honest. Linda was very like Daniel's dear mother. She did not have a bad word to say about anyone, and Daniel often wondered what he had done to deserve her.

"Hi hon" Linda greeted him. "Good flight?"

"Not too bad sweetheart, how have you been?"

As Daniel reached the door, Linda let Skipper go, and he made the usual fuss. He was not happy until he had been patted, stroked and talked to for at least two minutes as he whined with happiness, almost as if trying to tell Daniel in great detail what had been happening over the past couple of weeks. As Daniel embraced Linda, Skipper would barge between them insisting that he should not be left out. Skipper eventually calmed down and they made their way through the hall, where Daniel abandoned his case and went on into the sitting room and through to the veranda.

"What would you like to drink, honey?" Linda said over her shoulder as she disappeared from the veranda through the dining room and into the kitchen.

"I could slaughter a cold beer. What are you having?"

"I'm having a vodka."

As Linda prepared the drinks, Salvia, their Malay Amah, appeared round the side of the house to greet her master back.

"Good evening master" she said as she approached the veranda area. "You have good trip?"

"Yes thank you Salvia, is all well at this end?"

"Yes Master, although Salim very naughty."

"Oh dear, is he still messing you around? What has he done this time?"

"He has been very bad to me master, but is OK now."

"So long as it is OK now, that is the main thing."

"Yes master, you want me to take case up?"

"Please, Salvia."

Linda appeared back from the kitchen with the ice clinking in the vodka as Salvia disappeared upstairs to unpack Daniel's case. They sat down and Daniel asked how Sam was. Sam was their two-year-old son and a true treasure to both of them.

"He's in bed, absolutely exhausted following his swim this evening" she said. "He just loves the water."

"I shouldn't think it will be long before he's out of armbands, the rate he's going."

"How tired are you, honey?" asked Linda.

"Pretty shattered, it was not the easiest of trips. You sound as if you have something in mind?"

"Well Tom and Mary are in town. It's only one of their whistle stops, so they have only got tonight and Colin is off, so it's been suggested that we all go for a cheap and cheerful meal at Ghim Moh. Luke and Michelle are going."

Cheap and Cheerful, as it had become known, was a very basic Chinese eating house at the base of one of the housing development board flat complexes. Being completely off the tourist beat, it had become known among many of the expats for its superb but inexpensive Chinese cuisine. It was a favourite haunt for Daniel, Linda and their close friends and was always a must for Daniel's parents when they were back in town.

"Well that'll put pay to any thoughts I had for this evening" Daniel said with a cheeky lift of his eyebrow. "I'd love to see them, although I don't want to be too late. What time should we meet them?"

"About 8.30."

"I'd better get my skates on then, I'll go and shower. I assume Salvia's around?"

"Yes, of course, or I wouldn't have suggested it."

Daniel downed the rest of his ice-cold Anchor beer and headed up to shower and change. Linda sat on the end of the bed as he dried off and changed and brought him up to date with some of the gossip and events during his absence. After Linda had finished explaining some of the antics of Salvia's supposed boyfriend, Daniel suddenly felt less than happy about leaving young Sam in her care, in case Salim was about and started to misbehave and mistreat Salvia. This was a problem that had been steadily getting worse over the past few months, and whether Salvia had asked for it or not, it was something that both Daniel and Linda had tried to stay out of. However, it sounded as if it would soon be time for some intervention.

Linda assured Daniel that Salim would not be about this evening, as he was working.

CHAPTER THREE

They told Salvia they were off, advised her that they would not be late, and walked to their Mitsubishi Galant. Daniel got into the passenger side as Linda unlocked the doors. Linda reversed out of the drive and they headed off for the five-minute journey in the direction of Holland Village and Ghim Moh.

"How's the car going?" asked Daniel.

"Fine, although I think it's due for a service shortly."

"I'll book it in in the next few days."

Daniel was still reeling from the purchase of his car. In the UK it would have cost about £15,000, while in Singapore it had cost him the equivalent of over £40,000. He fully understood the reasons behind the enormous taxes placed on motoring in Singapore, but this didn't ease the burden when he had had to put his hand in his pocket to buy it. The car was actually on finance over a five-year period, and even at that it was a hefty amount to find each month.

Daniel started to think about the problems they were now facing in the UK with the business there, and the fact that they would soon have to start propping it up personally. Every outgoing was now beginning to play on his mind.

There was a lot to think about. They would have to find the new products they were after for the UK business, and now with Gordon Burrage sacked it was going to take life back a few steps. Anyhow as they approached Ghim Moh Daniel tried to reign back that train of thought, as it would only depress him, which he knew from experience would be made all the worse for being tired as well.

He was cheered immediately they rounded the corner and saw Mary, Tom, Colin, Luke and Michelle all having a good laugh at one of Mary's many jokes.

Daniel and Linda sat down and began to join in with the banter and jollities of the evening.

Luke had kept the seat next to him for Daniel, with whom he had talked just prior to leaving London, but even so he was dying to get a full rundown on the situation. "All OK?" he asked.

"Good as can be expected under the circumstances."

Daniel gave Luke a brief rundown on the conversation he had had with Gordon just before he had sacked him, and gave him a little more insight into just how little Gordon had achieved for his enormous salary and the expenses he had drawn. Neither Luke nor Daniel could understand the man's thinking.

"It was as if he was only in it for the short term and wanted to take us for as much as he could, while he could" Luke commented.

"Yes" Daniel agreed. "That has been through my mind, but it is not as if he had another job to go to, or as if he was well heeled enough to be able to throw away a £60,000-a-year job. I simply don't understand it."

"Have you changed the locks to the offices and warehouse?"

"Yes, and I've told Louise that if he shows up at the office for anything at all, he is not to be let in under any circumstances. I told her to get the warehouse manager to help her if she has any trouble."

"Do you think he's likely to create a scene then?"

"Well let's say he took his dismissal less than honourably. He said it would be the end of him and asked if we wanted that on our consciences."

"Surely he could get another job tomorrow – what's he on about? He surely can't be that financially hard up. Looking at his CV and his previous salaries, he could probably almost retire by now."

"Yes, I totally agree, and as I pointed out to him, if we let him run the company for any longer it would be the end of us. I don't know Luke. It does make you wonder what we're doing it for. Just when things are finally heading in the right direction, along comes another bloody great spanner and jams up the works."

"Come on chaps, I hope you're not talking shop" came Michelle's bright voice from the other side of the round table.

"Wow, I think this chilli crab is your favourite isn't it Mary?" Daniel said.

"I've been salivating at the thought of this for months" came the reply.

Daniel turned back to Luke briefly. "I'll be having a lie-in in the morning, but are you in the office tomorrow afternoon?"

"No, I've got a meeting at 2 pm at the Pan Pacific with the Shanghai factory rep."

"How about the Tanglin Club at six?"

"Yeah, fine."

"I'll reserve a table in the Churchill Room for dinner."

Colin sat to Luke's right. He had been a family friend of Daniel and Linda's as well as Daniel's parents for many years. He was also a pilot and had lived in Singapore for more years than he cared to remember. Daniel remembered most Christmas and New Year parties where Colin had been present, since before Daniel had left school.

Colin was responsible for putting Daniel in touch with Luke. Both Daniel and Luke had been living in Singapore working for other companies, but on meeting at one of Colin's parties they had started to discuss the future. They had uncannily similar views and shared the ambition of running their own business. They had turned this ambition into a reality only two years previously, both handing in their notice to their respective companies on the same days.

Both Michelle and Linda had had their reservations and worries about what Daniel and Luke were about to undertake, but knew they were both determined. They realised that they both knew their business well, and that it had to be worth a shot while they were still young enough. This decision had only been taken after a lot of discussion and with mutual backing from both their wives. Their leisure and marine business had in fact turned in better figures than expected during its first eighteen months of trading, but equally the costs had been higher than anticipated. All in all however, things for that period were not far off track.

They turned their attentions back to the table.

"How's the credit card Tom, is it in meltdown yet?" Luke asked. "Or hasn't Mary been here long enough to give it a good pasting?"

The response came from Mary. "I came with great expectations and I've been out today to do a 'shop till you drop', but I simply couldn't find anything I liked" she said. "Tom couldn't believe it."

"Still managed to spend over a thousand dollars though" came the wry response from Tom.

"But Tom's promised to buy me the most beautiful pair of earrings. I saw them during our stopover in Dubai on the way out. He's going to treat me to them on the way home, aren't you Thomas? I saw a similar pair in London before coming out and they were about twice the price of the ones in Dubai's duty free, so with that sort of saving he just couldn't afford not to! They are to be Christmas and birthday presents combined though".

"What's on the cards for tomorrow Mary?" Daniel asked.

"Well we'd like to go and see our old house in Rochester Park, then do a trip to Holland Village before preparing for tomorrow evening's flight."

"I'm planning to collect them from the Shangri La at about 9.30, then we'll see how the day takes us" said Linda helpfully. "We'll probably all go back home about tea time before taking them to the airport tomorrow evening."

"OK honey, but I won't be able to make the airport trip,

because I've just got to catch up with Luke on everything."

As they finished their meal, Daniel turned to Linda and gave her a look that said he was tired and wanted to make a move. She recognised it immediately and knew how exhausted he must be, so she suggested running Tom and Mary back to the Shangri La before making their way home.

On arrival at the Shangri La Tom offered Linda and Daniel a nightcap, more out of courtesy than anything else, as they had noticed that Daniel had been nearly asleep in the back of the car.

Linda waved goodbye to Tom and Mary and headed home. She would almost need to carry her husband to bed.

CHAPTER FOUR

Giang Xu had followed Daniel through passport control and seen him get into a taxi. He was watching more out of curiosity than anything else, as he knew only too well where he was going. Xu and his colleagues had learned everything there was to know about Daniel Cassidy and his family, and indeed Luke Oakley and his family. They had been doing their homework since they had first targeted them six months earlier.

Xu then made his way along to the car pick-up point and Han Atima, as he was known, drew up in Xu's White Mercedes S280. Xu saw him coming, picked up his bag and without a smile or a thank you got into the passenger seat of the Merc. Han took off, not irresponsibly, but with some verve, forcing an unsuspecting taxi driver to brake heavily as he did so. This was not the first time Han's extravagant driving style had caused trouble. Only a few weeks before he had tried an impossible manoeuvre and ended up with a long deep gouge down the right hand side of the car, something that had still not been fixed.

They passed the control tower and were heading down the East Coast Parkway before Han said "How's it been left?"

"They have sacked the stupid bastard."

"Justified?"

"Oh Yes, it was justified all right, he was getting greedy and trying to do them up like a kipper. I'd have done the same in their position."

They continued to their office in the Shaw Centre on the corner of Orchard and Scotts Road, where they parked in the multi-storey and made their way up to the 12th floor and to their office. The heading above the door read 'United European Marine Ltd'. It was a single large room with a small individual office made entirely of glass in one corner.

UEM Ltd had rented the office for a six-month period only two weeks previously. They had had decorators in continuously since then and had turned an ordinary room into a very plush and decadent office with thick Wilton carpeting, leather suite, expensive coffee tables and a solid rosewood desk. Even the receptionist's desk was brand new and of the highest quality available. The photocopier and fax machine were in the small glass office in the corner along with newly-printed headed paper and business cards, but very little else. The copier had not even been switched on yet, but they had mastered the fax machine and used that a couple of times.

Han unlocked the door, flicked the light switch and went to sit down. Xu broke open a bottle of Courvoisier from the under-lit wall cabinet and joined Han in another of the luxurious leather armchairs.

"Looks good" Han remarked.

"It'll do the job" Xu commented as he handed a cognac to Han.

"Just needs some pictures now."

"Have you brought them with you?"

"Yes, I'll take them down town for framing tomorrow."

All the pictures Han had rolled up in his case were general photos of an assortment of sports boats from various manufacturers. They had doctored the pictures by computer in Turkey to eliminate any manufacturers' markings or names that might have shown, and to make detail changes. The results were not perfect, but they would do the job that was required.

"Yes if you do that, I'll collect them when they're ready" said Xu. "If you give me the negatives I'll also get the brochure completed."

Han was a Turk. He had arrived on the Turkish Airlines flight from Istanbul only hours before Xu. He had anyhow planned to visit Singapore to discuss the next stage of their business, but following an urgent call from Xu in London, he had caught the next flight out to Singapore. It was now apparent that a new crisis loomed which was going to need immediate attention. Time was not on their side for major problems to crop up at this stage.

"In the light of the situation with Gordon Burrage I am going to try and make contact with Daniel or Luke in the next day or so" said Xu. "You need to go to London and deal with Burrage. He's claiming his fee for what he's done so far, and he's going to talk to Daniel and the authorities if he doesn't get it."

"I agree" said Han. "I think that idiot has just pushed his luck too far. I'll try and get a flight out tomorrow."

They spoke for another half an hour on the next steps to

be taken, then decided to call it a day. They locked the office, got the lift down to the car park and set off to Xu's home in Clementi.

Xu treated his Amah like something he had trodden in. He woke her the moment he got into the apartment, demanding she make them both a meal and make the guest room up for Han. The frail-looking Philippina duly jumped up and obeyed her boss.

CHAPTER FIVE

The advertisement in the *Daily Telegraph* had read: *General Sales Manager required for expanding Marine Leisure company based in Surrey. Friendly team, good benefits. £60,000 p.a. + car + expenses. Candidate must have previous marine experience, be a good communicator and able to lead. In the first instance please send your CV to Louise at…….*

Gordon Burrage had seen the ad, and having seen the writing on the wall in his current company he had decided to apply. He knew he was on the shortlist for the chop, as he had been unable to hide his drinking problem from them for long. They had put up with it for some time without mentioning anything, but it was getting worse, and was now affecting not only his performance at work but also attendance. He knew it was only a matter of time.

He had sent his CV off, and before long had a response inviting him to the company's office for an interview. He had been interviewed initially by both Daniel and Luke, who had been in the UK for the purpose.

The UK arm of their company had expanded to a stage where it could no longer be run remotely by Luke or Daniel commuting in turn every couple of months. Their sales staff and office administrators did a fine job, but it needed a consistent leader who was there all the time. They had interviewed five possible candidates, but Gordon had presented an impressive CV and he had been the one they had settled on. Gordon knew he would be able to start immediately, as his other company would ask him to leave straight away if he was going to another company in the same industry.

Gordon had been very keen on the thought of being left solely in charge, with nobody looking over his shoulder every day, and with his bosses on the other side of the globe most of the time his drinking could surely remain undiscovered. His successful application was good justification for him to celebrate with a drink.

Gordon's wife had left him a year or so earlier; his drinking had been the worsening addiction that had finally pushed her over the edge. Their marriage had already been on pretty rocky ground, following the discovery that her husband had been seen with a prostitute on one of his business trips to Amsterdam. He had finally admitted it, as it was impossible for him to deny. It had been extremely unfortunate for him that one of his wife's colleagues had been in Amsterdam the same week, and happened to notice Gordon diving into a sleazehole with a woman of the night. Gordon's mates at the time had all agreed that this had been rotten luck and that it could not have been organised that way if he'd tried.

Gordon had been befriended about six months before, during one of his regular evening drink binges, by Han Atima. Han was of Middle Eastern origin, Gordon had thought, and had continued to bump into Gordon 'coincidentally' for several days afterwards.

Discussing the marine industry, Han reckoned he had an offer that would make Gordon a hero with his bosses. The profit this venture would surely generate enabled him to guarantee Gordon personally £100,000 in commissions to be paid in cash from Han's company in on the bargain.

Gordon had sobered up immediately at the thought of all this cash and had given Han his undivided attention. With the realisation of the easy money that would be coming his way in the near future, and the new product line-up that would be available, he had started to spend money, both personally and even more of the company's. He had become complacent in what he was doing and soon the drinking and a new happy-go-lucky attitude was showing to all who worked there.

Louise, after a few months of this, had voiced her concerns to Luke and had started to make notes. She would let Daniel know what was happening on his next visit in three weeks' time.

Daniel had been warned that there was trouble brewing, and on his return to the office he had had a lengthy meeting with Louise and the warehouse management, taking on board what they and some of the other employees had to say. Upon looking at the latest finances, he had been horrified at what he had seen. In the previous three-month period there had been no fewer than eight first-class flights to Germany, Italy, Spain and Portugal, all accompanied by further lavish expenses at five-star hotels.

That was when, after consulting Luke, Daniel had taken

issue with Gordon and sacked him. The whole meeting had taken only half an hour. Gordon had not taken it well and had begged to keep his job. It was a pitiful sight to see a man of that age dissolve in to such a state of distress so readily. Daniel was amazed at Gordon's apparent over-reaction to the situation, but he had to stick to the decision.

CHAPTER SIX

Han had managed to get a flight on Emirates back to London the day after the meeting with Xu. He'd had a couple of days now to think about how to handle Gordon and his blackmail, and had come up with the perfect answer.

Han got the hotel courtesy bus from Terminal 3 to the Forte hotel, where he started to put the plans in motion. His first call was to Chan, one of Xu's contacts in London. Xu had already sent a message to Chan to keep time free for Han, so when Han explained what had to be done, they had things arranged for the very next day.

Han then called Gordon, who had eagerly been awaiting the call, expecting his payout, or at least a proportion of it, as silencing money. Although Gordon did not know the full extent of Han's plans, he felt sure that for a commission of £100,000 he must have earned something for what he had done so far or at least for not disclosing the plans. He was deeply annoyed with himself for having allowed himself to be sacked, and consequently not being able to earn the full money, but what did he have to lose by requesting it?

"Gordon, it's Han."

"I wasn't expecting a reply so quickly."

"I've spoken to my boss about your money. They want me to meet you to talk it through."

"I wouldn't have expected less."

"I'll meet you tomorrow night at the Hatch pub on the outskirts of Dorking."

"What time?"

"About 9 pm, I have some other business to tidy up first."

"See you then."

Gordon rubbed his hands in anticipation as he started thinking about how he would spend his pay-off. After all Han's company would still most likely get the business; the mere fact that he would not be directly involved would surely not matter to Han or the others. The boat deal would still go through and everyone would be happy.

The following evening, after many phone calls during the day about the strategy to be taken, Chan pulled his rented Mondeo into the Forte hotel where Han was waiting for him. Han hopped in. They stopped near Leatherhead, at a restaurant that had been recommended to Chan where the two of them had a good meal and a chat about the job in hand. Han had already familiarised himself with the geography of the pub. They finalised their game plan.

Chan knew better than to ask what all this was about, and as it was a direct instruction from Xu, there would be no hesitation. Chan had telephoned Xu in Singapore during the day and had been asked to cooperate fully with the Turk. That was all Chan needed to know.

They arrived at the rendezvous at exactly 8.45 pm, parked the Mondeo in a dark corner of the car park and waited. At 9.10 Gordon arrived, late as always, and probably half pissed already. Certainly from the way he swung his Jaguar into the parking slot it appeared that way. They sat and watched as he entered the bar. They would leave him there, knowing he would keep drinking, particularly as he would be nervous about this particular meeting.

Gordon looked around as he entered the bar, but could see no sign of Han. His first priority was to order a whisky, to fortify his nerves and his resolve to stand up for what he wanted. In truth he had already been drinking heavily all afternoon and by the time he had downed his fourth double whisky, even by his standards he was becoming drunk.

Chan went into the bar at about 9.30 pm and noted that Gordon was propped up on one of the bar stools. As it was a weekday, there were very few people in the pub; only a few gaggles of people at the tables around the edge. Gordon was the only person who was actually sitting at the bar, in conversation with the barman. Chan went up to the bar only a pace or so away from where he sat and ordered a pint of Tennants. As he approached, he could gather the gist of the conversation with the barman, a sob story of his current life status. Chan smiled to himself. Perfect.

One of the other customers came up to the far end of the bar at that moment to order a round of drinks for his friends. It was at that moment, when the barman left his end of the bar, that Gordon decided to head out to the gents'. Chan could see by the way he walked that he was nearly at saturation point. While the barman's back was turned Chan seized his opportunity and emptied a minuscule quantity of powder into Gordon's glass. He knew that in the state Gordon was in, he would not need much to knock him out.

Gordon returned and regained his stance at the bar. Within a couple of minutes the barman had finished with the other order and headed back in his direction. Chan moved away to a side table to sit and observe.

True to form, Gordon emptied his glass in minutes and was ordering another.

"Shall I book you a taxi?" the barman had asked Gordon.

"If my friends don't turn up you might have to" admitted Gordon.

Chan used his mobile to text Han in the car park with a report of the Gordon situation and the layout of people in the pub. Within a few moments Han put his head round the door and addressed, as if in a hurry, one of the tables of people near the door. He could not be seen by the barman or Gordon.

"Any of you people got a Jaguar in the car park, because if so you've left your lights on." With that he departed back outside and waited.

One of the guys at the table got up and walked towards the bar, stopping by Chan on the way, asking him if he had a Jag in the car park. "No, but thank you for asking" had been Chan's reply. The man continued to the bar, where he informed the barman that a Jaguar was sitting in the car park with its lights on.

"It's not by any chance yours is it?" the barman asked, looking in Gordon's direction.

"What's not mine?" Gordon was by now lost in the depths of alcohol-induced emotional thoughts, and was beginning to feel quite depressed and very tired.

"A Jaguar. In the car park."

"Oh yeah, why?"

The barman looked at the man who had informed him, raised his eyebrows, and thanked him. He looked back at Gordon.

"Your lights are on. Not that that will worry you tonight" he muttered, knowing he was going to have to call a taxi for this particular customer.

"I'll switch them off."

"OK sir, you do that and I'll phone for a taxi for you."

Gordon stumbled and swerved his way towards the door and out into the fresh air.

"Evening Gordon" Han greeted him just outside the door. "Follow me and we'll have our chat." Gordon was by now almost beyond knowing who Han was.

Han guided Gordon to the Mondeo, where he sat him in the passenger seat. Gordon was rapidly becoming more and more slurred, and within two minutes his head had lolled forwards and he was out cold. Han felt his pockets and with his gloves on, recovered his car keys. He got out of the Mondeo, leaving the keys in the door pocket, checked that there was nobody else around and walked to the Jaguar. He let himself in and fired the engine up, revving it unnecessarily. He put the automatic drive into reverse and planted his foot to the floor. The tyres screeched mercilessly as the Jaguar's rear wheels lost traction on the smooth car park surface. Han then engaged drive and gunned the engine to the exit onto the road. As he turned sharp left out of the car park he accelerated hard onto the main road, the inside wheel screeching loudly as it tried to gather traction on the tarmac. He passed the front of the pub and then backed off and drove sedately to the rendezvous.

The barman had been on the phone at the bar to the local taxi rank when he heard the shriek of burning rubber in the car park. "Cancel that booking, I'm sorry but he's just left" he said down the phone.

Chan left it three or four minutes before he made a point of thanking the barman and making his way to the car park. He got into the Mondeo, retrieved the keys from the door pocket, buckled Gordon into his seat, and without fuss headed off in the same direction as the Jaguar.

Chan caught up with Han in the car park they had agreed upon at the top of one of the local beauty spots, Leith Hill. The car park was fairly small with an unfinished gravel surface and it was dark and deserted, as expected. Han reversed the Jaguar into one of the corners where the back of the car was facing the trees and killed the lights. Chan drove up and parked next to the Jaguar.

Within four minutes Chan and Han were heading back to London in the Mondeo. They had not seen another soul.

CHAPTER SEVEN

Linda got up quietly the next morning, leaving Daniel in the land of nod. She went into Sam's room to find him playing quietly with his toys. His little face lit up as he saw Linda and he held his arms up to be picked up. Linda dressed him and took him downstairs where Salvia had laid out the breakfast on the marble veranda table. Sam's high chair stood alongside the main table next to Linda's normal seat.

Breakfast was a wonderful occasion in the Cassidy household, sitting in the fresh air with fresh honeydew melons, papaya and freshly-squeezed orange juice, as well as croissants and a fresh brew of tea. Linda's favourite was diced papaya with fresh lemon and a sprinkling of sugar. She had finished her own breakfast and was feeding Sam when she realised that she would have to go to collect Tom and Mary.

"Salvia, we're off now, but will be back for lunch with two friends" she said. "They will be here for the day before going to the airport tonight."

"OK two friends Mam... where Master?"

"He's still in bed, so don't disturb him, he's very tired"

"He have lunch too Mam?"

"Yes please. See you later."

"You take Sam?"

"Yes, Sam's coming with me this morning."

They drew up at the Shangri La, where Mary and Tom were waiting. "Do you mind if we pop into town first?" Mary asked. "There are a couple of things I would like to get at CK Tangs before we leave."

"Sure, you know me Mary, I would welcome the opportunity."

They parked in the Shaw Centre car park, as this was very central for most things. Shopping always took longer with a child in tow. Linda got the pushchair out of the boot, unbuckled Sam and fastened him in. Within minutes they had locked the car and were on their way.

They crossed Scotts Road and went into CK Tang. Tom had opted to go off on his own for a while, so they arranged to meet at a coffee shop on the corner next to the Dynasty Hotel main entrance at 11:30.

Linda was loving it. She enjoyed having friends from the UK around and as they approached the coffee shop she realised that neither of them had stopped gassing for the entire hour. Tom was duly waiting and when he saw them coming he got up and went to order three cappucinos and a selection of Danish pastries.

The three of them and Sam sat there as Linda told them how after all the hard work with Daniel and Luke starting the new business, life was at last beginning to take on a sense of normality and routine. It was a comforting feeling, but she admitted that she couldn't go through all that stress and worry again.

"I'm dying to show Tom where I used to live in Rochester Park" Mary commented.

"I'm not so sure that you'll appreciate what you find" Linda warned her, "But we'll go in now before we head back for lunch." With that they left the coffee shop and headed back to the car.

On this occasion they approached the Cassidy family house from the opposite direction from normal and Linda saw a large white Mercedes stopped in the road outside their neighbour's house. She only noticed it because of the awkward way it was parked on the verge and the fact that there was someone sitting at the wheel. She was sure it had been there when she had left to go and collect Mary and Tom earlier that morning. Probably someone's driver waiting while the mistress was out to a coffee morning or lunch, she thought.

Daniel was up when they arrived home. He had been working in his study on his laptop, but when the others arrived back he joined them as they all retired onto the veranda for a glass of wine before eating.

As soon as they had finished lunch, Daniel changed clothes and bid goodbye to Tom and Mary, who were going to spend the afternoon relaxing by the pool before going to the airport that evening.

"I'll run you to the office honey" he said.

"You sure? Why don't you relax here with Mary and Tom?"

"They'll be quite happy on their own for an hour or so, I'm sure."

As they reversed out of the drive, Linda caught a glimpse of the front corner of the white Mercedes still in the neighbour's drive. They drove off, and as they did so, the Mercedes edged out and started to follow.

With Han duly despatched to look after Gordon, Xu knew that he now had to move quickly. Without Gordon to help them by organising and assisting with the formalities of the deal, they were going to have to cajole Daniel or Luke in the right direction. Xu had to find a way of introducing himself and getting things under way, and promptly.

Xu followed the Mitsubishi to the entrance of Daniel and Luke's office in the Golden Mile tower on Beach Road, where he saw Daniel kiss Linda goodbye and head into the office. Xu parked in a public car park opposite the office complex and again sat down to wait. He sat at a table at a small old-fashioned shop house on Beach Road near Arab Street and had a sweet, thick coffee as he made conversation with the stereotypical old Chinese owner, who was dressed in a scruffy singlet type vest with shorts and flip flops. Xu also pretended to read a paper and followed the coffee with root beers, never taking his eyes off the main doors to the office block for more than a second or two at a time.

Daniel and Luke's office on the 23rd floor enjoyed beautiful panoramic views over the harbour. This had been the main selling point to them, particularly to Luke, who enjoyed the sea so much. He had insisted that as they spent so much time in the office it might as well be a pleasant environment. It was not lavishly or expensively furnished, but practical and comfortable.

As Daniel arrived, Vera, their secretary, greeted him and

thrust a handful of message notes in his direction, stating that the top three were urgent. Daniel settled himself at his desk and went through the messages, calling back those which were of immediate importance. Vera made him a tea and started to bring him up to date with the office events of the past couple of weeks.

At about 5.30 Xu saw Daniel leave the building and stand in the road to hail a taxi. He quickly left and made haste to his car. He fired up the Mercedes and edged it into the road so that he could follow as soon as Daniel succeeded in getting a taxi. They arrived at the Tanglin club at 5.56 and Daniel alighted from the taxi and headed straight for the bar. Xu passed the taxi as Daniel got out and followed the road to the back of the building and the car park.

When Daniel had first arrived in Singapore, The Tanglin Club had been a place of tremendous character, being an old colonial construction and built up on stilts, as most of the buildings of that era had been. As a child they had spent many an hour in the pool while parents had socialised at the pool bar. He remembered it being closed for the reconstruction and the impressive transformation. The club was now undeniably impressive and smart with its grand main entrance and elegant marble-clad lobby, but it had sadly lost some of its relaxed charm. It was, however, still a good watering hole and meeting place for the expatriate community.

Xu had recently joined the club as a temporary member. He would have to have been on the waiting list for years to become a full member, but temporary membership was all he needed to give him the short-term credibility required. Xu headed for the car park, from where he made his way to the bar.

Daniel had ordered a beer and was standing at the bar waiting for Luke when Xu walked in. Xu stood close to Daniel, and seeing what he was drinking he also ordered a beer. He looked quizzically in Daniel's direction for several moments, until Daniel looked up and caught his eye.

"Excuse me, but haven't you recently arrived from London?" Xu addressed Daniel.

Daniel looked at Xu with faint recognition and a slightly puzzled look on his face. "As a matter of fact I have" he said.

"I thought I recognised you. I'm embarrassed to admit it, but I bumped into you while I was trying to get my luggage from the conveyor."

"Oh, yes of course." Daniel said with a smile.

"I am Edward Lim" said Xu, offering a hand.

"Good to meet you Edward. Daniel Cassidy."

"I am sorry about that business at the airport. My case weighed a ton and getting it off the conveyor caught up among the other baggage was not easy."

"Don't worry Edward, no offence taken."

"Have you been in Singapore for a long time?"

"On and off for many years, how about you?"

"Yes, born and bred" lied Xu.

"I haven't seen you around at the club before, have you belonged for a long time?"

"Yes, quite a while, but I don't use it that often, as I spend a large portion of my time in Europe."

"Really, whereabouts in Europe?" asked Daniel.

"Well, I have a branch of my business in Istanbul, Turkey."

"What line of business are you in?"

"I actually have a number of interests, but my main interest in Europe is boat building."

"Really! What sort of boats are you involved with?"

"We manufacture small sports boats and Scarab style power boats. Do you know what I mean by Scarab style boats?"

"Well, what a coincidence, I do, because I am actually involved with boats of that type myself."

"Really?" Xu responded with a genuine look of surprise. "Do you manufacture yourselves?"

"We design and market, but we subcontract the manufacturing to various UK companies."

"Oh I see, so you sell in the UK?" said Xu, knowing perfectly well the set up of Daniels organisation.

"Yes the marine side of our business sells in the UK and continental Europe, while our other leisure business markets to both Asia and Europe."

"Oh I see, I see" remarked Xu. "This must be fate!"

"What is your set up?" Daniel inquired.

"My partner and I have a number of interests in Europe, including a boat manufacturing plant in Turkey. We decided to build there because of the labour costs. We can produce beautifully-finished boats for about a third of the cost of production in the UK. We design and develop new models all the time, as well as building to spec for customers like yourselves."

"That's very interesting. I must say you never know who you're going to bump into in this place. I thought I was pretty unique in that line here." remarked Daniel with a smile.

"Maybe we should get together and have a longer chat at some stage. Do you have a card?"

"Sure, I would be interested in doing that." Daniel dug a card out of his wallet. Xu duly produced a card from his introducing 'Mr Edward Lim, CEO United European Marine Ltd', and handed it to Daniel with both hands and a slight bow, something Daniel reciprocated. Daniel's card detailed both office addresses in the UK and Singapore.

At that moment Luke walked in to the bar and headed for where Daniel and Xu were standing. He wandered up between them and patted Daniel on the shoulder. "What can I get you?" he asked.

"Oh, hi mate, let me introduce you to Edward Lim. Believe it or not he's another boat manufacturer. Edward, this is my partner in crime, Luke Oakley."

"Pleased to meet you Luke" Xu said, as he went through the same ritual with the business card.

"Likewise."

Luke asked the barman for a beer and grabbed a handful of the complimentary nuts off the bar. "Shall we find a table?" he asked. "I think there's a lot we need to catch up on."

"Sure" said Daniel. "Would you excuse us Edward? I am afraid having been away, there is a lot we need to catch up on."

"Fine, it's been good to meet you, perhaps we can meet

in the near future to see if we have any common ground on which to do business."

"Fine, are you in town for a while?"

"Only this week. Could we meet towards the end of the week?"

"I am sure we can. If you can give me a bell in the office tomorrow we should be able to sort something out. If I'm not there Vera has my diary and I'll ask her to pencil something in."

"That would be fine. Have a good evening, nice to meet you too Mr Oakley." Daniel and Luke shook his hand and wandered to a table.

"What a coincidence bumping into another boat builder, and he was on my flight back from London as well" Daniel commented as they walked off.

Xu finished his drink and promptly left the club.

Daniel brought Luke up to date with all the happenings while he had been in the UK, including a detailed account of Gordon's dismissal.

"He took it far more badly than I had imagined" he said. "He was literally begging me not to dismiss him and to let him have a second chance. Anyone would have thought it was a matter of life and death."

"A second chance, after the way he'd behaved! He must have been joking."

"Our table will be ready in the Churchill room, shall we go and eat?"

They got up and walked across the beautiful marble lobby to the Churchill room, where they were greeted personally at the door and shown to their table. Once they were seated and had ordered their meals, Luke opened the business conversation again. "Have you any further ideas to keep the business in the UK on the straight and narrow, particularly in light of the Gordon situation?"

Daniel took a sip of the fine red house Merlot that had just been poured, and studied the liquid in the glass before responding.

"I don't think we have any option other than to view the lack of a general manager as just a temporary setback, and continue on the same tack and strategy as before."

"If that's the case, when should we think about the trip to the US to view that range of boats we're looking at?"

"Well, we're going to need to at least discuss things in greater detail with the manufacturers if we want to have an idea of what we're doing for the London Boat show in January. Perhaps we could go on to South Carolina after the boat show. Actually, do you know when exactly it is?"

"I'm fairly sure it starts on the 7th January. What about that guy you were just talking to, would it be worth seeing what he has to offer before we venture to the States?"

"If he rings tomorrow, we'll see him this week, but let's crack on with the US manufacturer anyhow. We've just got to expand the range with product that complements what we have already."

"OK I'll get that in motion tomorrow. It'll be good to be in the office for a while and crack on without a week full of meetings for a change."

The leisure side of their business was running fairly

smoothly with no major headaches at the moment, but they spent the rest of the meal discussing how it was performing and how to improve its productivity. Luke was in the middle of designing some new product along the lines of their previous discussions, and he brought Daniel up to date with the sample products that were currently being made for them.

They left together shortly after finishing their dessert of apple pie and ice cream, something for which Luke had a weakness, and had insisted upon. They shared a taxi to Daniel's house and Luke carried on home from there. They would continue their discussions in the office the following day.

CHAPTER EIGHT

Linda had returned from dropping Daniel at the office, and she joined Mary and Tom for a short while round the pool before they went to shower and change ready for the journey back to the UK. Once changed, they had a cup of tea on the veranda, with Mary lavishing much attention on Sam, while he made the most of all this undivided attention.

They left the house at about six and headed off to the airport. There was much chatter in the car en route; good as it had been to be away on holiday, it was always good to get home to your own four walls. Mary and Tom discussed all that they needed to get on with when they got home. It became obvious that Mary was angling for a new kitchen, something that Tom was less than enthusiastic about.

Linda did not go in to the airport terminal with them, as she hoped that Daniel wouldn't be too late home that night and she was looking forward to spending some time with him. As she stood outside the car at the drop-off point, Tom removed their cases from the boot and Linda reminded Mary that they would all be back in the UK for Christmas that year, and that as Daniel would be at the London Boat Show at Earls Court, they could perhaps go to the London sales in January. This was something Mary said she wouldn't miss for the world.

Linda was back in the house by 8 pm, where Salvia had the supper ready for her, having already put young Sam to bed. Linda tried ringing Daniel's mobile to find out what time he would be home, but when the automated voice announced that the cell phone was switched off, she realised that they were obviously still in the club - the use of mobiles there was banned.

Linda had supper and was nearly asleep in front of the television when Daniel finally arrived home at about 10:30. They sat up for a couple of hours and had a nightcap as Linda recounted the day's events. Daniel in turn told Linda of everything that had been going on, including the chance meeting with Edward Lim, who could well be of assistance to them in the manufacturing of boats in Turkey.

"Seems very coincidental" Linda remarked. "Particularly as you are looking for that type of boat at the moment."

"Yes, I thought so too" he acknowledged, "but life is full of coincidences, and if you don't make the most of these things you could well end up losing out."

Linda yawned and squeezed Daniel's hand "I think it's time for bed." He grinned. "I hope you're not thinking of sleep for a while!"

The following day life begun to get back to normal; getting up at seven, the morning cup of tea in bed, with Sam playing at their feet on the end of the bed. They chatted and both agreed that perhaps things were at last looking up, and that life might be a little less stressful from now on.

Following breakfast Daniel caught a taxi into work and

Linda started to go about her normal routine, which today would consist of a swim at the Polo Club pool, followed by coffee with some friends in Sunset Heights.

Daniel was sitting at his desk when Luke arrived and they both tucked in to their in-trays. Little was said for the first half an hour.

At about 10 am the phone rang and Vera answered it in the normal way.

"It's a Mr Lim for you Daniel, are you in?"

"Yes, fine Vera, thanks." He picked up the phone. "Good morning Edward, I hadn't expected to hear from you this early, thought you'd still be jet lagged."

Lim laughed. "I got used to feeling lousy from jet lag ages ago, now I just live with it."

"Anyhow, how about our meeting? Can you make it tomorrow? Only I have to leave town earlier than expected, and I'm sure you'll be interested in what we do."

"Sure, I can fit that in tomorrow, what sort of time had you in mind?"

"How about 2 pm? Can you make it to my office?"

"Shaw Centre isn't it? Yes I can be there for two." Daniel looked at Luke for confirmation that nothing else was on. Luke was nodding.

"Two o'clock it is then" said Lim. "I look forward to seeing you tomorrow Daniel, goodbye."

Luke then remembered that he had promised to take Michelle out to lunch the next day because they had some friends down for the day from Kuala Lumpur.

"That's OK" he said. "I'll go and report back, it's probably a wild goose chase anyway."

The pair spent the rest of the day sorting out the backlog of work that had built up, and it was not until Vera asked if there was anything else they would like her to do before she departed that they both realised how late it had become. Daniel did not want to be late home that night and left shortly afterwards. He wanted to have a swim with Sam before he went to bed, and to have a quiet and full evening at home with his family. Luke announced that he would stay on in the office for a short while, insisting that he had to finish a new specification to send to the material manufacturer in China before he left.

Daniel knew only too well that Luke's 'short while' would probably last until nearly midnight. He had been misled many times by Luke's "it will only take five minutes", usually at five o'clock when they planned to go for a drink. They would arrive at the bar just in time for last orders. He now knew better.

Michelle, who spent a lot of time with Linda, was always crying on her shoulder and becoming increasingly up tight with Luke's working hours and habits, something with which Daniel and Linda could sympathize. Rarely did Daniel interfere except for the odd occasion when Linda would say "Please ensure you get Luke to come home at a reasonable hour" or "Don't forget to remind Luke that it's our anniversary."

Linda's only reasoning was to remind Michelle that Luke was Australian and that 'not really thinking,' was just the way he was. She surely wouldn't want it any other way.

It had been pouring with rain again that afternoon and had only just stopped when Daniel arrived home in the taxi. As he got out he could hear the frogs croaking from somewhere in the large storm drains that ran round the houses. Steam rose off the driveway as the late evening sunlight evaporated the water on the tarmac.

It had been Salvia's afternoon off and Linda was preparing roast lamb for supper, while Sam was playing with his toys on the dining room floor. His face lit up as he saw his father walk in. Daniel picked him up, gave him a big kiss and suggested a swim. They swam and played in the pool while Linda finished preparing the supper, and Skipper lay flat out asleep under the ceiling fan on the veranda.

As they sat and ate and enjoyed their bottle of Barramundi, Daniel suggested that the following night they should go out to a favourite restaurant on the East Coast Parkway, Jumbo Seafood. Linda thought this was an excellent idea and it would make a change from the restaurants they had been frequenting on Boat Quay.

CHAPTER NINE

Daniel arrived at the offices of United European Marine Ltd on the 12th floor at 2.05 pm the next day, having spent the entire morning in the office. He had stopped briefly for a sandwich at the deli on Scotts Road on the way there. He pushed the button on the intercom to the left of the door. After a few seconds he heard the buzz and the latch releasing. He pushed open the door and went in. He was greeted by a young Chinese secretary/receptionist who welcomed Daniel and offered him a seat in one of the fine leather armchairs.

"Can I get you a coffee or green tea?"

"Green tea would be lovely, thank you."

Daniel stood and wandered round the room, looking at the pictures of the boats that adorned the walls. They certainly had an assortment of styles and models, although Daniel's initial thoughts were that those on show did not follow any particular theme. Usually with boat manufacturers there was a general trend in the styling, but these boats were all very different. If he had not been informed otherwise and was to put a professional opinion on them, he would have said that they were all manufactured by different companies. Some of the boats had flat sterns, some were canoe sterned, some with shaved-off sleek sterns. Again at the bows some had sleek cutting entries to the water with drooped bows, while others were blunt with raised bows.

Daniel guessed that these were probably a cross-section with one model from each range, each destined for different markets. If this was the case the firm must be a substantial manufacturer. There were certainly some models on the wall that Daniel was very interested in, models which fitted their requirements exactly. Maybe this was not a wild goose chase after all, and fate was giving a helping hand, Daniel thought to himself, his spirits lifting.

The secretary who had prepared the tea in a small office in the corner walked back in and advised Daniel that Mr Lim would only be a couple of minutes. Daniel sat back down with his mind already working overtime, thinking of what they could do with some of these products. Mr Lim's entry into Daniel and Luke's life could not have been timed better.

Edward Lim arrived shortly afterward. In reality he had been waiting round the corner to give his guest time to have a good look at the types of product they had on offer.

"Good afternoon Daniel, I see you found us all right."

"Yes thank you Edward."

"Welcome to our small and humble office, please do sit down."

"Very smart and tasteful" Daniel replied.

"Just like our boats!" Lim replied with a laugh.

Over coffee they chatted briefly about their respective businesses. Lim advised Daniel that he and his European partner produced about 2000 boats a year, most of which were models of their own design. He explained that they were looking for an importer into the UK for their boats and were keen to get the product moving by early the following season.

"Are you actively looking for new products to import?" asked Lim. "Or maybe we can be of assistance with manufacturing your current models in our factory? We can produce very cheaply, thanks to the low cost of labour in Turkey."

"Well, we are looking for product to complement our existing range of boats" replied Daniel. "We're mainly involved with the sailing side at the moment and we're keen to diversify into the power market, with 18 to say 28-foot sports boats initially, and see where it goes from there. I don't think transferring the building of our racing sailboats is really a feasible option, as the volume is not particularly high and the construction and weights are critical, but the importation of some models like this would certainly be of interest."

As Daniel said this he pointed at a particular model on the wall which had caught his eye. Daniel and Luke had done a lot of homework on the subject of their intended expansion and knew more or less what they were looking for, and how much they needed to spend for certain sized boats in order to make it viable.

"Of course the quality and price would determine our interest or otherwise" he commented.

"Yes, of course, of course" Lim acknowledged, smiling. "Prices, these I can give you a rough idea, but quality you will have to take our word for. You can talk to my partner Han on that side."

"OK. What sizes, for example, do you make that model?

And can you give me a rough idea in US dollars of the FOB and CIF Southampton prices on that model there?"

"What size do you want?"

"Well, do you make an eighteen foot version of that?"

Lim looked at the brochure he had been holding for the last 15 minutes and opened it to the relevant page for the model concerned. "Yes we make an eighteen-footer." He proceeded to quote a price in US dollars which seemed to Daniel to be extremely low, although Lim appeared to be a little confused at this point as to the difference between FOB and CIF pricing, which left Daniel feeling a little concerned. Sensing Daniel's unease, Lim hastily dismissed the misunderstanding by saying that he did not normally deal with any of that side of the business as it was all handled by Han in Europe.

"OK" said Daniel. "Do you have a brochure and specification sheet I could take with me now to show my partner and discuss the possibility of taking it a stage further?"

"Sure" said Lim. He spoke in Chinese to the secretary, who fetched a glossy new brochure from the room in the corner and handed it to Daniel.

He flicked through the pages until he found the range he was looking at.

"Are there no full specifications?" he asked. He was slightly bemused. No boat lengths were shown at all, so why Edward Lim had looked at the brochure for confirmation of the 18 footer? Perhaps Lim's brochure had his own notations in it.

"The specifications have recently changed, so they are on a separate insert for the brochure" explained Lim. "They're being sent from the factory in the next day or so."

"Could you get one to me as soon as you have it? The specifications and construction data are all important before we can give the boats serious consideration."

"Of course, I will get them to you. I am sorry I'm not more organised, but this is normally all handled from Europe and I don't have everything to hand here in Singapore."

"It's OK, I fully understand the difficulties of running two offices on opposite sides of the globe."

With that, Daniel got up and made his excuses. They shook hands and Daniel made his way back to Beach Road and his own office. It would not be long before Luke was back from lunch and they could discuss these new options now on the table.

The moment Daniel left, Xu was on the phone to Han's mobile. He told Han that he needed thorough specifications on all the boats, and he needed them yesterday. Things were not going to be quite as easy without Gordon, who would have taken things on without questioning everything.

CHAPTER TEN

Singapore

Luke arrived back at the office at about four o'clock, having obviously had a good and boozy lunch. Daniel could tell by the look on his face that not a lot of work was going to get done that afternoon. They sat and talked for a couple of hours, during which time Daniel commented on the surprising omissions in Lim's knowledge of boats in general considering it was their main business, particularly his lack of knowledge of their own product range.

Luke pointed out that perhaps, as with so many of these companies, Lim, being the Chinese partner, was in reality simply the money man with a controlling interest. They both agreed that they would need to get the bulk of the information necessary from the European connection, namely Han.

The next scheduled trip to the UK for them both was in late December, ready for Christmas and immediately after New Year, the London Boat Show.

They loosely discussed the possibility of Daniel going to see the factory in Turkey and Luke going on to meet the US company they were interested in.

"You could make a holiday of it in the US and take Michelle with you" Daniel suggested, as he knew this would be a good move for both of them and would certainly be a hit with Michelle. They agreed to leave that as the loose arrangement until they had more information to hand.

At 6:15 Daniel announced that he had to make a move, because they were going to Jumbo Seafood on the East Coast Parkway that evening. "Why don't you and Michelle join us, if you're not doing anything, Linda would love you to?" he said.

"That sounds great. I'm not that hungry having had a big lunch, but just the thought of those drunken prawns is making my mouth water, and we'll have to eat something this evening."

"See you there at eight thirty?"

"I'll just phone Michelle and check, but I'm sure she will want to."

Daniel hung on while Luke phoned home and when Luke gave him the thumbs up, Daniel just mimed a "see you later" and left.

Daniel arrived home just in time to have a quick swim with Sam and Linda before Sam's bed time. It was always a treat for Sam when Daniel read him his bedtime story, and tonight was no exception when the same episode of Thomas the Tank Engine had to be read not once, but twice. By halfway through the second reading, despite determined efforts, Sam finally fell asleep.

When Linda and Daniel had showered and changed they came downstairs and Linda went out to fetch Salvia and tell her they were off. Salvia was in tears, having had yet another bust up with her boyfriend, but assured them she was OK and that she would go in to the main house and watch television until they returned. Daniel made it clear to her that her boyfriend, Salim, was not welcome in the house; it was a discussion they had had before.

CHAPTER ELEVEN

Dorking, England

Maureen Marsh got up at 5.30 that morning, as she had done for years. She drove to the car park on the hill of the North Downs with Toby, her black Labrador, in the back of her Subaru Legacy at about seven. This was now part of her daily routine. She had to be in the office for nine, so she walked Toby early. She would walk him again that evening, and pop home at lunchtime to let him out in the garden.

As she approached the car park she had an uneasy feeling. She saw a blue Jaguar parked in the corner of the sandy car park, nose towards her. The windows were misted, and a plume of steam funnelled upwards in the still fresh morning air from the back of the car; the engine was obviously running. At first she assumed a couple were having a passionate time behind the steamy glass. This was unusual; in all the years she had been coming to this particular spot she had not encountered such a thing at this time of day before. She knew it happened during the dark evening hours, particularly at the weekend, but not at seven in the morning.

She opened the tailgate and let Toby out. He had his usual

excited, skittish bluster around the car for a moment as Maureen got the lead out and closed the car, but then, before she could get the lead on, he darted off towards the Jaguar. As he approached he started barking. Maureen ran after him, calling him, covered in confusion and embarrassment, in case the occupants appeared.

Toby darted around the back of the Jaguar, still making a lot of noise, and Maureen followed. It was only when she got around the back of the car that she noticed there was no plume of steam from the left hand exhaust pipe but a length of pipe attached to the exhaust, which trailed round and jammed in the far side window.

The reality of what she was witnessing suddenly hit her. She felt the shots of adrenalin hitting her stomach, and with amazing presence of mind darted round to the pull the pipe out of the window. She tried the doors, but all were locked. Looking around, she saw some small rocks along the edge of the car park perimeter. She gathered the largest she could find. On getting back to the Jaguar she peered in to the small opening where the pipe had been inserted. Seeing nobody on the back seat, she hurled the rock at the back window. The window erupted with the sound of a shotgun being fired, and immediately as the warm, damp, smoky air from inside the car escaped and hit the cold fresh air outside, a huge column of steam rose from the car.

Maureen put her head in through the window to unlock the door, but as she did so she nearly passed out with the appalling smell that assaulted her. She unlocked the door, letting more air in. When she saw the body slumped over the steering wheel, she turned and was promptly sick.

Toby, seeing her distress came up, to comfort her. Maureen went back to her car, pulled her mobile phone from the glove compartment and dialled 999.

The police took about ten minutes to get there and to seal off the area and go to work. It looked like a suicide. The driver was obviously intoxicated and had gassed himself. They took a statement from Maureen and asked if she had seen any other vehicles there that morning. She had not.

The slightly baffling thing as far as the police were concerned was that there had been rain the previous evening, and Gordon had obviously arrived after the rain as his tyre tracks showed in the sandy ground. There was however a second set of tyre impressions, so there had been another vehicle there at some time after the rain, probably someone who had thought, like Maureen, that the Jaguar was a passion wagon for the evening and had departed without looking more closely.

CHAPTER TWELVE

Singapore

As Daniel and Linda drove towards the restaurant, their main topic of conversation was Salvia and her jealous boyfriend, who was becoming increasingly abusive. As they approached the restaurant complex there were people all down the coast lighting barbecues on the purpose-built grills along the beach. They drove on and parked.

"I see Luke and Michelle are already here" Daniel muttered as they passed Luke's car in the car park. They parked and walked the short distance to the restaurant. The temperature was a wonderful 28 degrees with a light onshore breeze.

"I love it here." Linda commented as they walked arm in arm down the Palm lined walkway and neared Jumbo. "I can't wait for that black pepper crab."

"How did I know you were going for that?"

Luke and Michelle were already seated at one of the round tables outside. There was an air conditioned section inside, but unless it was raining, they all always preferred to eat in the open.

They joined the others and sat down. Luke immediately picked up the pitcher of beer that was in the centre of the table and poured one for Linda and Daniel.

"Have you ordered yet?" Daniel asked.

"No we were waiting for you" Michelle responded.

"I am sorry we're a few minutes late. Salvia's had another going over from that wretched boyfriend of hers" Linda told them both.

"Bad?" asked Michelle.

"Yes, she was in a bit of a state, but she still insists she is so in love, and that he really loves her."

Daniel turned to Luke. "It's when she's alone looking after Sam that it really worries me, I have told her he's banned from the house. It looks like I'm going to have to lay the law down to him yet again. I can't say I'm particularly looking forward to it."

"Do you want us to come back with you in case he creates?"

"No, thanks for the offer but I'm not even sure when he will next be there. I think he will be all right."

The waitress came over, literally dropped the menus on the table and wandered off. She was dressed in a T shirt and shorts covered with an apron, and her foot attire was simply thongs. It was a very casual restaurant.

They all looked at the menus, although they knew more or less what they were going to order before they all arrived. It would be the same as they had ordered the last time and probably the time before that. Certainly the drunken prawns were a favourite with all of them. These were prawns that were marinated in wine while still alive, before they were cooked, and the flavour was superb. The other favourite of the group were the black peppered and chilli crabs, which were huge Sri Lankan crabs and simply the best available.

Michelle and Linda were still talking about the maid situation, while Daniel and Luke were discussing the shares of a Malaysian company for which they had been advised to buy stocks. Needless to say the shares had dropped the moment they had written the cheque out, but they were both convinced that they would bounce back in the near future. They certainly needed to, because both of them could do with the money as soon as possible, particularly if they were going to invest in the new products, with all the marketing that was going to need.

The Chinese tea was poured and the black peppered crab was on the table. They all started to tuck in. They were all listening avidly to a particularly good-humoured story from Michelle with fingers full of crab when Daniel's mobile started to ring from the depths of his trouser pocket.

"Oh, goodness that's probably Salvia" Linda said, a slight trace of alarm in her voice. They all fell silent as Daniel wiped his hands on the complimentary scented towel and dug into his pocket for the phone. He looked at the screen, but no identity showed up. He flicked open the front and put it to his ear.

"Hello?"

"Hi, Daniel?"

"Yes."

"This is Louise, i'm sorry to disturb you at this hour, but I am afraid I have some bad news."

"Bad news, what do you mean?"

The others had all stopped eating now and focused on Daniel.

"There is no easy way to tell you this, but I'm afraid that Gordon was found dead in his car this morning. He was found in a car park on a hill with a hose plugged in to the back of the car and an empty bottle of scotch in his lap."

"Oh my god. Suicide?"

"Yes, the police say it was a fairly typical suicide and that he had been drinking heavily last night at the Hatch. The barman reckons he was pretty low and had his whole life history. He apparently left the pub in a right state, and got in his car and drove off. He apparently told the barman he had just been sacked."

"Do the police think that was the reason?"

"They didn't say as much, but he was apparently waiting at the pub for someone who didn't show."

Daniel turned back to the table and mouthed the word "Gordon" to Luke. He drew a finger across his throat. All at the table looked at Daniel in disbelief.

"OK Louise, thank you, I'll call you tomorrow" Daniel said quietly. He flipped the phone closed and looked at Luke and then the others. They all sat in silence for what seemed like an eternity. Linda was the first to speak.

"Well, what has happened?"

"Gordon has gassed himself in his car, apparently paralytic. I somehow feel desperately guilty, he was apparently very low. I'm sure sacking him... it must have pushed him over the edge."

"Don't talk such rot" Luke interjected. "He was no good, and he had to go. We can't be everyone's guardian angels, and we certainly couldn't have foreseen the consequences of what was a proper business decision. Any company worth its salt would have made the same decision. There are probably many reasons in his life for doing what he did."

"Sure, I hear what you're saying, but what do you think others are going to say? Sacked one day, dead the next. I can't help but feel the two are related, particularly as I said to you before, he took the sacking so badly."

"Well don't let it get to you, either of you. You most certainly had nothing to do with it and any thinking along those lines will be totally counter productive" Michelle chipped in. "Where did all this happen anyway?"

"No, you're right. It happened on one of the hills near Dorking."

"Who found him and when?" asked Linda.

"I don't know honey, I was a little too shocked to ask anything further."

There was a further silence for a few minutes and then they all started examining the little they each knew of Gordon's life, with Daniel and Luke tempering and correcting the girls exaggerations on the gossip that they had heard about him from the staff in the UK and their husbands. Daniel and Luke said little. They were both lost in thought.

They all left almost as soon as the last course had been devoured. Daniel and Linda drove home in silence and shared a brandy on the couch. Salvia had not heard from Salim that evening. She disappeared to her room.

Daniel tossed and turned in bed that night, unable to sleep. Although he had not particularly liked Gordon, he still felt awful about what had happened and visions of Gordon gassing himself in his car haunted him all that night. Daniel and Luke were both shocked and surprised about what had happened, as they had both thought Gordon was too selfish and too much of a coward to have taken his own life.

CHAPTER THIRTEEN

A whole week had now elapsed since Xu's meeting with Daniel, a week in which Xu had spent the time putting together attractive specifications for the models of boat Daniel was interested in. He had consulted Han every day and in the end had decided upon the exact models to offer Daniel and Luke. The specification sheets were currently at the printers in Holland Village and Xu was due to pick them up the next day, but he would phone Daniel today to arrange a meeting. Han and Xu were now desperate to get this business moving.

It was the following Wednesday morning in the office when Lim made contact again. Vera took the call and put it through to Daniel.

"Hi, Daniel, Edward here, I am sorry to take so long to come back with your details but I have been very busy."

"Not a problem Edward, there's no breakneck hurry for it."

"I have the details, can we meet to discuss them?"

"Yes, when did you have in mind?"

"How about tomorrow evening?"

"Er… well, I think we're out to dinner tomorrow evening. How about tonight, or during the day?"

"Unfortunately tomorrow evening is the only time I have before my trip back to Europe. What a shame. I really wanted to speak to you about it personally before I left."

"Well I tell you what" Daniel said slowly as if thinking out loud, "perhaps you and your other half could join my wife and me for dinner tomorrow night?"

"Oh, I don't want to put you out, but if that's the only time then let's make a social occasion of it. It would be a nice excuse to meet your wife as well."

"OK, I have a table booked at the Elizabethan Grill at Raffles for eight, so how about we all meet at the Long Bar at say, seven?"

"That sounds very nice, see you then."

Daniel replaced the receiver and thought for a while before he picked up the phone to Linda to try and explain to her that others would be joining them for their dinner at Raffles. Both Daniel and Linda loved Raffles very much and ate there at least once a month, usually eating in the open air of the Palm Court listening to the string quartet playing from the gallery. It was a very special place for them. The following evening they had arranged to meet their friends Pierre and Betty there at 7.30 pm, so Daniel thought that half an hour would be adequate to take the spec sheets from Lim and get the business chat out of the way before the others arrived.

Linda was not impressed when Daniel told her that two complete strangers would be joining them for dinner, but after a short while she understood the reasoning. No doubt they would be very pleasant people.

The following evening Daniel and Linda decided to ask one of their neighbour's daughters if she would mind babysitting Sam. They were not convinced that they had seen the last of Salim, and certainly were not going to take any risks. Isabelle was a 17-year-old student studying at the United World College, and she was always up for a earning a few dollars as and when she could.

Linda drove them that evening, and as they arrived at the main entrance of the Raffles one of the valets recognised them instantly and came towards them with a beaming smile even before they had stopped the car. He opened the driver's door and Linda got out, leaving the keys in the ignition, at which point the valet got in and the car was whisked away to be parked in the underground car park.

The Raffles Hotel was an imposing, elegant and indeed magnificent building which had been completely refurbished, or more precisely, practically rebuilt, only a few years earlier. Daniel remembered vividly the 'old' Raffles in which they had stayed all those years previously. The old hotel had had a certain charm and character about it, albeit having a very well used and casual appearance. The new, although sharing the same façade, was very different and very, very smart. In order to compete with the best hotels, something Raffles was certainly worthy of, it had needed its re-vamp to bring it into the 21st century with mod cons such as central air conditioning and mini bars which travellers paying top dollar were now demanding.

They walked through the main foyer and around the Palm Court to the opposite corner of the hotel, where the long bar was now situated, upstairs on two floors. It had originally been a bar of immense presence and character just off the main foyer.

They went up to the first floor and entered the bar; the hum of the crowd could be heard some distance from the doors. Daniel had a quick scout round the first floor but did not see Edward Lim, so they walked up the spiral central staircase to the second floor, which was a little quieter. Here Lim was waiting for them at the bar with a very attractive lady. Daniel made the introduction to Linda.

"The pleasure is all mine, Linda, how very nice to meet you" Lim offered a hand.

"Good evening Edward, it is good to meet you too."

"May I introduce you to my better half, Doris?"

Daniel and Linda laughed politely. "Well at least he recognises the better half" said Daniel as he and Linda shook hands with Doris while Lim asked what he could get them for drinks.

"Gin and tonic please" replied Linda.

"Make that two" Daniel added.

They picked up their drinks and wandered to a table near the top of the spiral staircase, crunching empty pistachio husks underfoot as they went. It was the done thing at the Long Bar to throw the shells of the nuts on the floor and the ground was, even at this time of the evening, covered in them.

As they sat down, Lim opened his case beside him and extracted the details of the boats to show Daniel. As he did so he offered his apologies to Linda for having to conduct some business that evening.

"Please don't worry" Linda replied and turned to Doris. "Whereabouts on the island do you live?" she inquired.

"I sorry, but not speak Inglis." .

"OK don't worry" Linda said with a smile, and in a louder than normal tone, as if the volume would enable Doris to understand.

That's a good start, Linda thought to herself. What an evening this is going to be! She turned towards Daniel, who caught her look; nothing needed to be said. Linda then turned her attention back to the discussion between the men.

Xu had known Doris for some years now, having used her services as a high-class prostitute in his native China. Knowing that she spoke no English, he knew his secret was safe and that she would pass as his other half without problem or question. He had briefed her as to the nature of the evening and she was happy to play along - for a fee.

Xu had been down to the shop earlier that day to collect the printed specification sheets for Daniel, who was studying the figures. As he did so, Lim was sitting quietly watching him for any sign of dissatisfaction, or otherwise.

"What type of buoyancy foam is used, is it open or closed cell?" asked Daniel.

"I am sorry Daniel I really do not know, you will have to talk to Han about the details."

"OK. The specs look good on the face of it. The next thing will be to talk to Han about the import logistics and the fine details of the construction and CE certification."

"Well Han is here the week after next, so maybe you can meet then?"

"We're pretty tied up with the other side of the business and we're going to be with our factories in Hong Kong and China for the next three weeks or so, but there is no real panic at the moment. Luke and I have some serious number crunching to do and comparisons with the American boats we are looking at. Unfortunately we can't afford at this moment in time to take on both franchises."

"But you are interested?" said Lim, almost, thought Daniel, letting some frustration show through.

"Yes, very much so, but we would be looking at doing something after the London Boat show after Christmas and we would obviously need to see the product before committing."

" Oh I see, I see... you want to see the boats."

"Well yes of course, we would never buy anything, even from a company that is as big in boat building as yours, without seeing the product first. No offence, but brochures can be deceiving."

The frown disappeared from Lim's face and he started to smile.

"OK, I tell you what. We can send two boats to you in London for when you arrive at Christmas for you to see, completely free of charge."

"That's very kind of you Edward, but we could not possibly do that at this stage. I need to do some serious talking with Han before that. What I would suggest is that if Han could come and meet us in London during the show we can talk about the whole situation then. After all, it would be only a few weeks after I return from my trip to China."

"I'll arrange it with Han then and you can talk to him."

Lim had suddenly taken on a more sullen tone, after Daniel's dismissal of his kind offer to send two boats in free.

At that moment Pierre and Betty appeared at the top of the spiral staircase. Linda started waving and they wandered over. Everyone stood and Daniel made the introductions. Betty made a beeline for Daniel and gave him big kiss. Lim began to look more uncomfortable at the appearance of Betty, who was Singaporean Chinese and would obviously be able to communicate fluently with Doris.

Daniel caught the eye of a waiter and ordered another round of drinks.

Doris was now sandwiched between Linda and Pierre, with Betty sitting the other side of Linda.

Linda explained to Betty that Doris spoke no English, so Betty immediately switched into Mandarin to address Doris in an effort not to let her feel left out.

Linda started to talk to Pierre, and as there was some cross chat going on, Linda suggested swapping places with Doris so that she could communicate with Betty.

At that point Lim realised that things were going to get awkward. He stood and announced that the time had gone so quickly, and that he and Doris would have to go for their dinner appointment.

"I thought you were joining us?" Daniel said with some surprise.

"Only for the drink, I thought? And we do not want to gatecrash the meal with your friends." With that, he spoke to Doris, who picked up her handbag and stood up, downing the rest of her champagne as she did so.

"If they have other arrangements, honey, don't make them feel bad about leaving" Linda said to Daniel, with a look that said more than the words.

"Well Edward, thank you for coming down to bring the spec sheets, I am sorry you can't stay longer."

"Next time for sure" said Lim. He bid goodbye to Pierre and Betty, took Doris' arm and left.

"What did I say wrong?" said Pierre, looking puzzled.

"I have no idea" said Daniel. "I thought it was arranged that they would eat with us this evening. Maybe I got the wrong end of the stick somewhere down the line."

"Well look on the bright side, It'll be a much more pleasant evening without them" said Linda. "Doris did not speak a word of English, and we couldn't have put that strain on Betty all night."

Daniel proceeded to tell Pierre and Betty the history behind meeting Lim and his other half while they sipped their drinks in the relaxed atmosphere of the Long Bar.

"Seems very odd that an international businessman has a wife or partner who doesn't speak English, particularly in Singapore" noted Pierre.

"From my brief discussion with her I would say she was from mainland China, not Singapore" said Betty.

"Perhaps he was embarrassed to admit that his wife was from China for some reason. Anyway, wherever she was from, he at least brought the information I needed, which was kind of him. I'm sure the double booking dinner was just a misunderstanding."

"You say you met him at the club?" Pierre asked.

"Yes, that's right."

"It's funny, while I don't claim to know even a fraction of the people at the club one does tend to recognise people. I have to say I have never seen Edward Lim before."

With that they finished their drinks, and headed to the other side of the hotel for their dinner.

Lim and Doris were soon forgotten and they all proceeded to have a wonderful evening, laughing, joking and putting the world to rights in general.

They all had too much to drink and ended up leaving the cars at the hotel and getting taxis home, not for the first time.

CHAPTER FOURTEEN

It was a couple of days later, on the Saturday morning while they were relaxing at home, that they next heard from Lim. He phoned the house, explaining that he had got the number from directory inquiries as he had wanted to apologise for the misunderstanding on the Thursday evening, and that it was all an embarrassing mistake on his part. He explained that he had also forgotten to give Daniel one of the sheets pertaining to the build lay up on the boats and offered to run it round to the house for him that afternoon. Daniel agreed and gave him the address and directions.

Linda answered the door to Lim, who had left his car parked in the mouth of the drive outside the gates. As she asked him through to the veranda, before she had closed the front door she noticed the white Mercedes in the drive and thought for a moment that she had seen the car before, but she dismissed it from her mind and closed the door. She showed Lim through to the veranda, where Daniel was working on his laptop and Sam was playing with a garage set he had had for his birthday.

"Do join us for a cup of tea" Linda offered.

"I would like that, thank you."

"Have a seat" Daniel offered, gesturing to one of the empty

rattan cane chairs. Lim took a seat and started to explain to Daniel again that he was sorry for his misunderstanding about the arrangements the other evening. He claimed to have had a roasting from his wife for getting it wrong. Linda came back with the tea, and Lim got the missing paperwork from his case and handed it to Daniel.

"The dates we are in London are as follows" Daniel told Lim. "If your colleague can see us during the show that would make good sense because either Luke or I have to go to the States straight after the Boat Show."

"Sure I'll pass those dates on to Han, he'll be in Singapore next week. Are you certain you won't have time to see him while he's here to answer the queries you have?"

"I'm sorry but I leave for China and Hong Kong on Tuesday and there really is not going to be time. London will be the best place, because there may be some valid points our manager may wish to raise that need addressing."

With that Lim turned his attention to little Sam and his garage set. Sam was impressed that someone was showing such an interest and started to show off.

"Cute kid you have" Lim said to Linda.

"Thank you very much Edward, he is our little treasure. He brings us an immense amount of joy, although he has his moments, don't you poppet?"

Sam smiled at his mother and brought yet another toy car over to Lim for his perusal. After about ten minutes, having finished his cup of tea, Lim suggested to Daniel that Han would ring him on the UK number shown on his business card to arrange the meeting in London. Daniel said that was fine and that he very much hoped they could do a lot of business together. He showed Lim to the door and walked with him to his car. They shook hands and Lim asked Daniel to contact him when he got back from China if he needed to discuss anything further.

As Daniel returned to the veranda, Linda commented "I am sure I have seen both Lim and his car before, you know."

"Honestly honey there must be thousands of white Mercs in Singapore, why does that one stand out?"

"I don't know, but it just does. Oh, never mind."

"Well you have probably noticed it subconsciously in the club car park, and perhaps you do recognise Lim from the club, after all you spend more time there than the rest of us."

"Perhaps you're right, but I'm not convinced. Still, it may come to me in time."

Linda poured them both another cup of tea and they sat and played with Sam, enjoying a lazy family afternoon at home.

Both Luke and Daniel spent a long day in the office on the Monday, speaking to customers and sorting out what they needed for their forthcoming trip. Strict instructions were left with Vera to contact them on their mobiles if there was anything that she could not handle, although they knew from past experience that this was unlikely and that in reality the office probably ran more efficiently when neither of them were about. Once the initial contracts had been set up and the product lines for the various customers were in production it was more or less an administrative operation, something that Vera was better at than any of them.

CHAPTER FIFTEEN

The trip to China was a success. Luke and Daniel sorted out new product production with the factories, and the meetings in Hong Kong had gone equally well. Once back in Singapore there was only four weeks to catch up on everything again before it was time to depart to London for the Christmas holidays. The last two weeks had been spent shopping for unusual presents for friends and relatives. Despite the upheaval they were quite excited at the prospect of Christmas with all their relatives in the UK, particularly as Sam was beginning to realise that Christmas was a special time, and his excitement was growing daily.

A few days before leaving for the UK, Lim phoned the office. Daniel was out, but Luke spoke to him. Lim wanted to confirm that Han would be meeting them at the Boat Show and that he had discussed with Han the supply of a couple of sample boats to them for evaluation free of charge if they wished. Luke thanked him for his call and said he would look forward to tying up the deal on their return.

Linda had let their Australian neighbours know they would be away, and that if they heard or saw anything untoward they would alert the police. They had Daniel and Linda's number in the UK if any problems should occur.

Two days before their departure, Skipper saw the suitcases appear and somehow sensed that this was not just Daniel alone going away on another trip. As the suitcases filled he realised that everyone was off and that he would not be going. He went into a sulk, lying in the kitchen and barely able to lift his head to acknowledge anyone. On the evening they finally left the house he went to the front door, where Linda gave him a big kiss on the cheek and told him that Salvia would be looking after him for a few weeks. As if he understood every word, but did not approve in the least, Skipper turned round, looking very forlorn, and slunk off back to the kitchen.

Daniel, Linda, Sam, Luke and Michelle were all flying together back to Heathrow, and they met up at Changi airport. Although Daniel and Luke did a lot of flying there was a sense of excitement and enjoyment about this trip, having the families there.

Flight SQ21 had been delayed for an hour and a half before take off, but apart from that the flight was faultless, except that Sam was over-excited about the whole venture and had worn himself out. He was now overtired, irritable and tearful, but still refused to sleep. In the end Luke, for whom Sam had an uncanny respect, had taken charge of him and crayoned a colouring book with him until he had eventually dozed off in Luke's lap with his thumb in his mouth, much to the relief of the whole party - and the surrounding passengers.

Unfortunately, as they travelled west with the darkness, it

was only about seven hours before Sam started to awaken, as his tummy told him it was approaching his breakfast time back at home. He woke Linda who was, as always, only catnapping; she never seemed to be able to sleep on an aircraft, no matter how tired she was. Linda switched on Sam's personal TV screen and hoped that the cartoons on the children's channel would capture his imagination, which luckily they did.

Coming in to land at Heathrow, they had to stack in a circular queuing system for half an hour before landing, but it was the beginning of a glorious day over London without a cloud in the sky. As the dawn broke the view below was spectacular, with the ground white with frost and the magnificent spectacle of Windsor Castle standing proudly below them.

They were all going to be spending the holiday at Daniel and Linda's house in Sussex and had rented a VW Sharan to get down there. They were keeping the rental car for the duration, because although Daniel and Linda had a car in the UK, Michelle and Luke did not, so they would use this for their independent transport.

It took them about a week to get over the jet lag, but the third day back Daniel and Luke spent the full day in the office and began working hard with the staff to get the Boat Show organised. They did not have much time, although having done the show for many years the staff were well clued up to what was needed. Daniel and Luke were told every detail of what had happened to Gordon, with many variations on the theme as to why he had done it. On their second day in the office Edward Lim called to confirm that Han would meet them on the Monday of the show.

The two girls and Sam appeared to spend the entire time Christmas shopping. The week before Christmas they joined Mary for a spree in Harrods, but managed to avoid spending too much. Daniel had spoken at great length to Linda about their current financial status and they both agreed to a very modest limit to Christmas spending. Being in the same situation Michelle and Luke had done the same, although they were all determined to have a thoroughly good time.

Christmas and New Year went as quickly as they had come, but all agreed that it had been one of the more memorable. They all, including Luke and Michelle, spent the break at Daniel's parents' home in Dorset, which was large enough to swallow them all with ease. It was the most delightful setting in which to spend Christmas, with the house's large inglenook fireplaces with blazing log fires and beamed ceilings adding to the atmosphere. They all delighted in roasting chestnuts over the fire in the evenings and became thoroughly relaxed.

Linda phoned Salvia on Boxing Day to ensure all was well and was assured that things were fine. She also called their neighbours, partly to wish them a Happy Christmas and partly to check out Salvia's story, which proved to be only partially true. Skipper was fine, everything was under control and there was nothing to worry about.

They spent New Year's Eve with Linda's parents, staying in a local guest house as their house was not large enough for them all, nor did they want to put her parents to too much trouble. They spent the evening at one of the local restaurants, which had gone to great lengths to put on a fine evening with an exceptional five-course menu and a good jazz band.

The office was shut down for the entire Christmas and New Year period and did not open again until the third of January. Luckily they had everything in place before Christmas so that they were ready to go and set up the London Boat Show stand on the fourth, fifth and sixth.

CHAPTER SIXTEEN

Earls Court, London

On the fourth of January Daniel and Luke were thrown back in at the deep end, because no matter how organised they thought they were, they were not. There were the usual last-minute panics for things that had been forgotten, and more frayed tempers the closer the opening date became. They were both still in the office long after the staff had slunk off home and were often still drilling and screwing things together when Earls Court had announced that the doors were now being locked and that all exhibitors and contractors should leave the building.

They finally had everything complete by nine o'clock on the evening of the sixth and drove back to Sussex exhausted. They had given strict instructions for Louise and the sales staff to be there by 8.30 on the opening day. Daniel and Luke would be in by about midday with families in tow.

The opening day was officially press and VIP day. They had all spent most of the morning finalising the stand, polishing bits of the boats, making sure the prices were with all the brochures and generally titivating things, so that when Daniel, Luke and families arrived, the stand looked superb and they congratulated everyone for their efforts, even though they both felt that most of the effort had come from themselves. Luke broke open the first bottle of Lanson on the stand and they all toasted to having a good show. The champagne flowed freely on that first day with every existing customer, press representative and potential customer offered a glass. It was a good kick off for the show.

While the staff were staying close to the exhibition centre in London, Daniel and Luke were commuting daily, making the most of the break from Singapore with their wives. Linda drove them all home that first evening, as she had been the nominated non-drinking driver.

The weekend at the show had been exactly as expected, with a complete deluge of the general public and their children, some of whom were extremely unruly and badly behaved. Everyone on the stand had had at least one run in with a parent who felt that their children had a given right to crawl all over the boats, scratching the decks with hard shoes and spilling Coke and ice cream over them. Luke had amused them all on the Sunday when a particularly obnoxious father, who could not string a sentence together without an expletive between each word, had argued about his filthy child not being allowed on a particular boat. Luke had reached the end of his tether and told him to piss off.

They were all looking forward to Monday when it was quieter but generally visited by a better percentage of serious buyers.

CHAPTER SEVENTEEN

Earls Court, London Boat Show

At about 11 am on the Monday morning, Daniel and one of the female staff were there alone on the stand. Luke had not come in that day as he and Michelle had gone to visit some of her relations in Bedford.

Han waited until the stand was free from customers before he made his approach. Daniel saw a tall man of Middle Eastern appearance approach, and wondered if it was Han, a fact that was soon confirmed as he came up and introduced himself. He was accompanied a few feet behind by a tall dark-haired woman who was dressed to the nines, but obviously not geared to boating, judging by the high-heeled shoes she was wearing. At first glance Daniel thought she was about to appear on stage at a night club and thought how thoroughly out of place she looked. Han did not introduce the woman but left her standing by one of the boats as he introduced himself.

"Good to meet you" Daniel remarked. "Mr Lim tells me you are the man with all the answers."

Han took a moment to remember that Lim was in fact the alias for Xu. Then he smiled and replied in strongly-accented

English. "Yes, I am in charge of the production and the European operations. Lim has very little to do with it really. I am very pleased to meet you."

"Lets go and have a seat" said Daniel as he ushered Han to the stand seating area. Xu had obviously informed Han of the models that were of interest to Daniel, and Han was armed with the relevant brochure as well as one for a range of larger sports boats. As they were seated opposite each other Daniel started to try and sum him up. He was very expensively dressed with a smart suit covered by a Mohair knee-length coat, had a gold Rolex on his wrist and was probably about 35 or 36 years old, with hair thinning on top but never the less fit and good-looking. Daniel thought he was probably quite a hit with the ladies, although judging by the one he had brought to the stand, not necessarily the right types.

As they started to talk the interruptions started, with questions from customers that only Daniel or Luke could have answered, and progress with Han was slow. After about 20 minutes and many apologies from Daniel for the interruptions, Daniel suggested that they meet after the show had closed that evening.

"Which hotel are you staying at?" Daniel asked.

"A little far from here" came the response.

"Well, do you want me to meet you at your hotel after the show?" Daniel had offered.

"Not necessary, we can meet around here. You suggest somewhere."

"Well OK, how about the Gloucester Hotel in the

Gloucester road, only round the corner, we can meet in the bar at about seven?"

"That will be all right, where is this hotel?"

Daniel spent the next couple of minutes drawing a map on the back of a flysheet brochure for Han. He handed it to him as yet another customer interrupted, requiring more information on any discount he might offer in lieu of a part exchange. Han handed Daniel a card, shook his hand and said he would see him later and wandered off. Daniel did not look at the card, but put it straight into his pocket and concentrated his attention on the customer in front of him.

The rest of the day seemed fairly hectic and certainly busier than he had remembered on the Mondays of previous years. He was pleased that Luke would be on hand to help again tomorrow.

At about 5.30 things were quietening down a bit and one of Daniel's friends wandered onto the stand. The three staff, who were now all on the stand, were easily going to be able to cope for 15 minutes, so Daniel and his friend Mike decided to go to the Guinness stand for a swift half before the close of the show. It was not until he started to tell Mike about his forthcoming meeting that he remembered Han's card and extracted it from his pocket. He looked at it and was slightly puzzled, because it showed an address in Israel, and there was no mention of the Singapore or Istanbul addresses. They both drew the conclusion that the card must have been for another venture Han was involved with and he had handed it out by mistake.

Daniel left at 6.40 and went down to the underground car

park to collect his car. His trusted BMW 635 had been in the family for many years and had become part of the furniture. It was getting on in age but still looked good. It was exceptionally comfortable, went faultlessly and was distinctive. It did not do many miles now and was ideal to keep locked in the garage for visits back to the UK.

The drive to the Gloucester took ten minutes, twice as long it would have taken to walk, but the traffic was appalling that particular evening. He drew up and was about to turn into the underground car park when the doorman ushered him into a place right outside the front doors of the hotel, where he duly parked and thanked the doorman. He entered the hotel and walked into the bar, immediately seeing Han sitting at a table in the corner.

Having sorted out some drinks, they made small talk. Han said he lived in Istanbul with his wife and three children and that before now he had not really been to London because they had not been doing business there.

After a few minutes Daniel got a sheet out of his briefcase with a list of questions he had prepared to ask for Han. He started to go through them one by one.

"Having looked at the specifications in depth with Luke, there are some fundamentals we need assurance of before we can take things any further" he said.

"Of course I understand" Han said sharply. "But let me tell you first about us. We make many type of boat for many people in all countries including Germany and Sweden and America, so we are very good at this job and you must not worry about specification, all our customers are very happy."

Daniel was annoyed at being told what he should and should not worry about, but let the comment go without showing his irritation. He replied in his normal soft manner, as diplomatically as he could. "Well, with all due respect we have never done business with your company before, and have never come across your products before, so I am afraid we do need assurance that everything meets the requirements for the UK and that the quality of finish meets our own standards. I'm sure you can appreciate that. If however you supply Germany, that does answer one of my questions, which was whether the boats all conform to the new CE regulations."

"Yes, yes, they meet all regulations. We can send two boats to you for you to see the quality."

Daniel did not particularly like Han's forceful manner and was determined to make sure he was happy with everything before committing himself. He was certainly not going to have two boats forced upon him in this way.

"I appreciate the offer, but to save you that trouble I have spoken with my partner who is going to the US in a couple of weeks' time" he said. "If it is OK, I will visit you in Turkey at the same time to see your factory and look at the product. If all is well we can finalize things then."

"But it is no trouble for us to send you the boats, you need not waste your time to come to Turkey."

"No, I really would like to. We would not entertain such a venture without visiting the factory."

Han looked slightly despondent at Daniel not accepting his offer and Daniel thought that perhaps that was the

Turkish way, and that he had somehow offended him, but he really did not care, he had to be sure.

"You will have to let me come back to you on that because I am not sure I am in Turkey then, and I may have to change arrangements" said Han.

"OK, well you let me know and we'll arrange dates shortly, but in the meantime, assuming that it all goes ahead, how about the payment structure and sole rights to the product? For example, on what terms do you normally do business? I assume you want telegraphic transfer of the funds before shipment? What guarantees can you give us to the UK rights for the products? I assume you have a dealer agreement I could look at?"

"No, we will supply the models you want and then we will split the profit when you sell them. Later on we will also want to set up a London showroom. We will pay for it."

Daniel looked at Han quizzically as he took a sip from his drink and sat quietly for a moment. It appeared that what they were really wanting was a joint venture company, which was not of the least interest to Daniel and Luke. As for a London showroom, Daniel was almost lost for words.

"A London showroom. That's an unusual way of thinking and would certainly not come cheap. I must say I'm not sure how effective it would be either, unless it was on the Thames, but it's very extravagant and the company would have to be making serious money to support such a luxury. I can't say we would necessarily want to be involved, if that's your future thinking."

Han realised he would have to back off a little. His idea

that this show of monetary power would impress him had backfired.

"Oh never mind, I am only thinking that it was a good idea but you must know better, we certainly want to work with you."

They continued chatting for about 15 minutes, but getting nowhere, with Han insisting that they would retain ownership of the boats until they were sold and that the profit would be split equally in two. This as far as Daniel was concerned was a very odd way to pursue a business venture; he had never come across such an idea from a manufacturer before. Most manufacturers were normally clambering to get the money even before the craft were built. There were numerous complications with operating the business in the way Han wanted, if indeed it was workable. Daniel needed to know exactly what the boats owed him.

Daniel thought about how they would cope with demonstration boats on which there would probably be an initial loss. Who pays the import duties and shipping? Who pays for the engines and trailers where applicable? Who suffers the loss from any over allowance on a part exchange? Whose half of the profit would foot the bill for all the show and marketing costs? The questions in Daniel's head were numerous. But it was clear that Han was simply not interested in the detail.

In the end Daniel decided that the best thing to do was to see the boats. If they were indeed as good as they promised to be, these points would be worth arguing about. He concluded that it was most likely just the Turkish way, and

Han was trying to be generous in helping with the set-up costs. However he could not dislodge an uneasy feeling in his gut about it.

Daniel asked Han for the second time that day where he was staying and if he could offer him a lift back.

"I am staying near Baker Street."

"I can give you a lift back if you like. I need to get on to the M40, so it's no trouble."

Han looked a little uneasy, but accepted the offer. Daniel got up, and said "I am just going to the toilet first, I'll be back in a minute."

With that Han got up. "I will come with you" he said.

"Er, OK" said Daniel. "We'd better take the coats and brief cases then, we can't leave them unattended."

Han followed Daniel to the toilets in the foyer, and much to Daniel's dismay stood at the next urinal shoulder to shoulder with him, although the rest of them were all free. Daniel hated people crowding him in the toilet, so he turned around and shut himself in one of the cubicles. When he came out Han was waiting for him by the basins. Daniel washed his hands and Han followed him through the foyer and out to the car.

When they got outside Daniel tipped the doorman and ushered Han to his BMW. Han's face lit into a smile and he immediately said "You have my car!"

Daniel looked at him. "What do you mean?"

"I mean I have this car at home. I love this car."

"Yes, I'm very happy with mine too."

They spent the 15-minute journey to Baker Street

discussing cars, and BMWs in particular. Han said he was having trouble getting hold of certain parts for his car back at home. Daniel was a little confused by this comment, as he knew that all the main dealers could locate parts for this model. He suggested that Han should give him a list. Provided they were not too big he would bring the parts out to him when he came out to Istanbul. Han was most grateful for this and said he would fax a list when he got back.

"Where is your hotel from here?" asked Daniel.

"I am staying at a friend's apartment, so please just drop me here."

"Don't worry, Ill take you to the door, it's a miserable evening."

"No, please drop me here. It is not easy to find, I can walk, it is very close."

Daniel found this most odd. For some reason Han clearly did not want Daniel to know where he was staying. Perhaps it was a little scruffy and he was embarrassed.

Before Han got out of the car he said to Daniel, "I would like to see your premises before I leave, when can I do this?"

This comment caught Daniel a little off guard as he had been so worried about things the other way round. It had not occurred to him that they would need to see his premises, to see if they were worthy of selling the Turkish boats.

"It is going to be difficult during the show this week, but how about next Monday?"

"That will be fine, where do I find you?"

"Give me your number in London and I'll phone you for your fax number and send a map through to you."

"I don't know my number, so I will contact you either here or in your office on Monday."

"Oh, OK" said Daniel. "We'll do it that way then."

Han smiled, they shook hands and Han got out and disappeared down the pavement as Daniel waited for a slot to pull out into the traffic.

Daniel spent the first ten minutes of the journey going over in his mind everything that had been said. Despite all the things that didn't seem to fit, and his gut instinct telling him to be careful, he told himself that if they viewed and liked the boats, they could make it work. After all there was good profit to be made, and from the brochures they appeared to be just the market fillers they were looking for. However, the Turks certainly had an unusual way of doing things.

Daniel stopped at a garage to collect a packet of crisps and a sandwich. He was very hungry and could not wait until he got home, so a snack was going to have to do for dinner tonight. He phoned home to let Linda and the others know that he was going to be too late to eat with them. As usual he spent as little time as possible on the mobile; he said what needed to be said and hung up. Linda was not offended by this. She knew how Daniel disliked cellphones and had his only as an absolute necessity. He had been telling her for some time now not to use hers for extended periods because of the radiation fears, and got quite upset with her when she gossiped on it for any length of time.

As he pulled off the M40 and onto the M25 southbound, he switched on the radio. It was tuned to Radio 2, something he missed in Singapore, although these days he was rarely alone to listen to it. *I Feel it in My Fingers, I Feel it in My Toes* broke the silence through the eight-speaker stereo system. He cranked up the volume and enjoyed one of his favourite tunes, one that conjured very happy memories for both him and Linda.

They were all in the sitting room in front of a log fire watching the end of the evening news when Daniel finally walked through the front door. He poured himself a whisky and sat down. After the news had finished they exchanged details of the day, and he brought them all up to date with his day's events and the meeting with Han, including his thoughts and misgivings. They all listened attentively.

CHAPTER EIGHTEEN

It was on the Thursday of the show that they next saw Han, or more accurately the lady who had been with him on the last occasion. Daniel noticed her as he came back from one of the café bars with a load of Coca Colas. She was standing beside one of the adjacent stands, and as Daniel walked back he approached her from behind. He recognised her only because of her unsuitable attire, although he had to admit she was better dressed than the last time.

She glanced at him as he walked by, but as he smiled at her she looked away, apparently embarrassed. He took the Cokes back to the stand almost at the run, about to drop the whole lot. He was going to go back and say hello, but when he turned round after placing the drinks on the table for everyone, she had gone.

About two hours later Han arrived on the stand, wanting to know when they could meet at Daniel and Luke's premises, and asking for directions. Daniel drew directions for him, suggesting that he come down on Monday and that they go out for lunch at the local pub. Daniel asked him if he had had any thoughts on dates for his trip to Turkey, but Han said it was yet to be confirmed. When Daniel said he had seen his female colleague at the show a couple of hours earlier,

Han said that was impossible and that Daniel was mistaken. Daniel knew that he had not been mistaken, but was not going to argue the point, particularly as he did not even know what the relationship between the two of them was.

Han handed Daniel another brochure and indicated that the prices marked were inclusive of shipping to the UK, with the freight being organised at the Istanbul end. This was something Daniel and Luke had wanted because they were sure that the freight rate from Istanbul would be cheaper. They were right, although Daniel was surprised at how much difference there was. Daniel could not help but think how casual it all was; no proper printed trade price lists detailing FOB prices, just prices jotted with biro on a brochure. Still, it was what the jottings said that mattered.

Han handed Daniel another business card, this time with a mobile number on it, and suggested he ring him on that number if he had any questions. It was a different card from the first one he had received and indeed carried an Istanbul address.

The stand was by this time busy. All of them were flat out, so Han did not stay long and was soon on his way.

Xu had arrived in London the previous morning, and that evening he and Han spent several hours trying to think of the best way to ensure that Daniel was given the right impression when he went to see the factory. It was no longer a case of if he might go to Istanbul but when, and the sooner the better now from their point of view so that they could get the business under way.

They had discussed the prices of the boats Daniel had requested and decided to subsidise the shipping cost considerably in order to make the deal tantalisingly attractive to Daniel and Luke, who despite the attractive pricing and all the assurances under the sun, were not going to simply bite, hook line and sinker - as they had hoped. Again they cursed the stupidity of Gordon and mentioned how much easier things could have been. After all, they only needed to get the first two samples to them and after that it would have been plain sailing.

Xu was on the midday flight the following day to Istanbul. He was going to get things sorted out with the factory. He would ring Han on Monday after the final meeting with Daniel.

The morning of the last Sunday of the show was always busy, but the quality of the customers tailed off after lunch as the bargain hunters came round looking for anything on sale 'cheap'. Daniel and Luke had never subscribed to the idea of selling off certain items of stock cheaply on the last day to a bunch of vultures who came specifically for that reason. They had always maintained that their goods were fairly priced from the word go. Why should someone on the last day pay anything less than people who came on the first day?

Before the show finished at 5 pm, they spent the last couple of hours looking through the order sheets to review how the show had gone. They had been keeping a rough tally as the days had drifted by, but now was crunch time. It had been a good show for them after all, and if all the orders taken went through to completion they could be very happy. The figures showed a one third increase on the previous year.

They packed up everything stealable that evening, leaving the bulk of the stand, and all the large boats, to be taken away during the next couple of days. However it was still after 9 pm before they made it out of the exhibition hall that night. They stopped for a Burger King on the North End Road on the way home. Linda and Michelle were not expecting them back before 10 pm anyhow and would not have cooked. They sat and had a post mortem about the show and how they had felt it had gone, how the staff had behaved and what they could do better for next year or the Southampton show in September.

They were in bed and asleep within half an hour of arriving home, both shattered from the week's events.

CHAPTER NINETEEN

The next morning the first person in the household to wake up was Sam, as usual. Luke was going to go back to Earls Court that day in the company van to oversee the dismantling of the stand, while Daniel was going into the office, primarily to meet Han and introduce him to everyone.

When Daniel arrived in the office at nine o'clock that morning he called Vera in Singapore to see if all was well. It was, indeed one of the large deals they had been working on for later that season had just come to fruition in the form of a confirmed order that had been faxed through. Daniel asked Vera to fax it to him at the UK office to see exactly what product they had finally decided upon. This cheered Daniel immeasurably, and he phoned Luke on the mobile to break the good news to him.

Han arrived at the office at 12.15 in a rented Ford Focus. He was accompanied by a different lady this time, a much smarter, extremely pleasant woman of about 36. Han introduced her as Maya, his wife. She was about 5'7" with shoulder length natural blond hair and beautiful pale blue eyes. Maya had a way about her that Daniel immediately liked and trusted. He could not help wondering what on earth Han had been doing with the other woman at the show.

Thinking of lunch and the presence of Maya, Daniel quickly phoned Linda to see if she could join them. She left Sam with Michelle and made the quick trip to the office in the rented Sharan. Louise made them both a coffee and Daniel started by introducing them to the office staff, those that were not at the exhibition centre helping Luke. They then moved out to the workshop and Daniel showed them round the warehouse.

Linda arrived just as they had finished the tour. They all hopped into the Sharan and went down to the Dog & Duck, a typical old English cottage pub with two roaring fires, for a hot pub lunch. Han got the first round of drinks while Linda fetched the menus.

It was at this point that Han announced that neither Maya nor he would be eating anything because of Ramadan, meaning they had to refrain from eating or drinking during daylight hours. Daniel shot a glance in the direction of Linda. "That's a shame, the food here is excellent" she said. "But I'm sure you don't mind if we order?"

"No, please carry on" said Maya. "Han should have let you know we could not eat at lunchtimes, I am sorry." Maya glared at her husband.

Linda also took to Maya immediately and they soon started chatting like long lost friends. She spoke word-perfect English with very little accent and was a senior nurse at one of the main hospitals in Istanbul. Daniel and Linda could see what a brilliant nurse she would make with her naturally calming way. Han on the other hand seemed quite agitated, and was almost trying to keep Maya from chatting, to the point of rudeness. He kept trying to drag the conversation back to what he wanted to talk about.

Daniel and Linda's food arrived and they started to tuck in as Han and Maya watched. Linda, sensing an atmosphere between the other two, managed to involve them both in light conversation, and soon the mood had lifted and they all ended up having a good time, with Han even telling some jokes.

Before they left the pub, Daniel asked Han if he had decided which parts he wanted for his car. Han said he wanted a driver's door window, because his had been smashed when his car had been robbed. Daniel said he could order one for him, but it would have to be sent out by courier because he would be unable to carry such a large object out with him.

"Thank you Daniel" said Han. "Please fax a price to my number in Istanbul, including the carriage, and I will let you know."

They all left the pub feeling comfortable in each other's company and returned to the office. Linda left straight away, telling Maya to keep in touch with her, while Maya and Han got into the Focus and Daniel waved them off.

Daniel spent what remained of the afternoon in the office. At about 5 pm he got into the BMW and headed home. Luke finally arrived back at the house at about 7.30 that night. He was pleased to be able to report that everything at the show was now clear and they would not have to go back the following day as they had done on previous years.

Michelle, Linda and Sam were due to fly back to Singapore the following evening, so Daniel and Luke got out of their hair, at their insistence, that morning. They arrived home at lunchtime to spend the afternoon with them before they departed.

Luke was due to go to the States the following Monday, initially to a trade fair, then on to the boat factory. Daniel, if all was confirmed, was going to Istanbul three days after that, on the Thursday. They would both head back to London and ultimately on to Singapore.

They headed up to the airport that evening in the two cars. They would drop the rented Sharan off on the way into the airport. Daniel and Luke took the rental back, having dropped off the girls to check in and put the BMW in the multi-storey. They then headed back to the terminal to meet them in the MacDonalds in the Terminal 3 departure area. For Luke and Daniel this would be their only meal this evening.

At passport control they all said their goodbyes. Daniel and Luke waved them off and headed back to the car and on home. They both collapsed in front of the late evening news and enjoyed the peace and quiet before Daniel retired for an early night, leaving Luke watching a late-night western.

CHAPTER TWENTY

They spent the next few days planning their requirements from the US boat company and what Luke needed to discuss with them, as well as exactly what Daniel needed to look for from a structural build point of view in Turkey. They both agreed that it all seemed much more straightforward with the US company (from whom they already had copies of the CE certification forms) than with the Turkish company. However they would not decide which company they would go with until they had both visited the respective companies to see in real terms what they had to offer. After all, the Turkish manufacturer was definitely better value for money, even if it was going to be more difficult to administer.

That Friday Han rung for Daniel to confirm that he could be in Istanbul for the end of the following week, and could Daniel let him know his confirmed dates and flights. Daniel had obtained details of the window glass for the BMW, but needed to know the chassis number. Han said he would look it up and fax it to Daniel.

They drove to Daniel's parents that weekend to unwind and headed back on the Sunday evening to give Luke a chance to pack. The following morning Daniel took Luke up to Heathrow early, to catch his 10 am Continental Airlines flight to Newark, New York. Daniel dropped Luke at eight and headed for the office, but it was not long before he was cussing at the amount of traffic he encountered on the M25. In fact the journey which had just taken half an hour in one direction now took just over two hours. Daniel had been through the frustration stage of getting up tight so he sat back, told himself to accept the traffic and thanked his lucky stars that he did not have to do this every day.

Daniel phoned Han that day and advised him that he would be arriving at Istanbul airport on the British Airways flight arriving at 2.10 Thursday afternoon. He would be staying until the Sunday, when he was flying back to London on the 1.30 pm flight.

Daniel had checked the prices of hotels in Istanbul and was advised that he could get a reasonable three-star hotel with en suite facilities for about £35-£45 per night. This was all important to Daniel because he knew he only had about £700 credit left on his Barclaycard. He did not want to appear a pauper, but equally he had to be very conservative with his spending; after all there was no necessity to spend too much. The simple fact was, he couldn't.

"With regard to the hotel Han, could you please book me into a three-star hotel not too far from the city centre?" he asked. "It doesn't need to be too grand, after all I only have to sleep there, so as long as it's clean and has an en suite bathroom that's all that matters."

"You do not worry about the hotel, I will sort it for you" Han responded.

"Thank you - I mean it though Han, nothing too

expensive. I know the Holiday Inn is good value so perhaps you could look at availability there first. Anyhow I will leave it to you."

"Yes, it will be done. I will see you on Thursday when I meet you at the airport."

"Thank you. By the way, I still haven't received the chassis number to order your car window."

"Yes I know, I'm sorry I have been busy."

"Don't apologise to me, it's not me who's having to drive round without a door window. It's up to you, if you get me what they need I am happy to order the part for you."

"OK. Thank you, I will see you Thursday."

Daniel put the phone down and thought this was the last time he would chase Han for the chassis number. If he could not be bothered to get it, it was his loss.

He spent the rest of the day in meetings with the sales manager, discussing how best to follow up all the leads from the show and where and when to offer sea trials and so on.

CHAPTER TWENTY ONE

Luke checked in for his economy class flight and by some quirk of fate got upgraded from steerage to business class, a fact that made his morning. The seven-hour flight from Heathrow to Newark seemed to take half that time, and before he knew it he was on a hotel bus heading for the Best Western in Manhattan. Luke and Daniel had both agreed to keep the costs to a minimum and Luke's wallet was suffering as much as Daniel's at that time.

Because of the time change, by one o'clock in the afternoon the same day, Luke was wrapped up against the bitter New York winter and making the 35-minute walk to the Javits Exhibition Centre, where he would spend the afternoon. He was there to look for new ideas, products and manufacturers for their leisure business. Luke was methodical and thorough, and Daniel knew that if there was something there worth looking at, he would find it.

Luke spent a couple of hours that afternoon at the show before returning to his hotel, via a Burger King, to have a shower and get a good night's sleep. He was going to spend the whole of Tuesday at the show before heading off on the Wednesday morning flight to Florida.

The show, as it happened, unearthed very little new or of

interest, but it was a good excuse for Luke to catch up with one or two of the companies they dealt with, as well as to get up to date with what the market was doing.

He was up early on the Wednesday morning and wandered to a breakfast bar he had seen on west 57th street for a big American breakfast which, even with Luke's enormous appetite, set him up well for the day. He left Newark later that morning and arrived at Jacksonville Airport late that afternoon, taking the short bus ride to the Alamo car rental centre, where he had a car booked. Fortunately they were out of compacts of the type Luke had booked, so they gave him a mid-size Pontiac Bonneville instead, at the same price. The car was brand new with only 12 miles on the clock. Luke was beginning to enjoy this trip.

Luke made the three-hour journey north west that evening up to the town of Waycross in Georgia, where he found a Days Inn, checked in and settled for the evening. He phoned the office back in the UK, which was 5 hours ahead, and gave the hotel number to Louise, who in turn got Daniel to phone him back for a catch-up. Unfortunately Luke's mobile phone, being on the European system, did not function in the US. Many years before Daniel and Luke had found using the hotel phone a little too convenient for quick conversations and had been bowled over by the size of the bills they had been presented with on checkout. Now they knew better. Daniel advised Luke that he would have his mobile with him and that he could be contacted at any time.

Luke ate out at a typical casual American steak house that evening. Its entire décor was in wood from floorboards to ceiling. When his ribeye arrived it was so large that even he could not finish it. He sat and watched the music video running on a TV screen hanging in one corner of the restaurant and generally relaxed and unwound.

The next morning he headed off for the half-hour journey west to see the US boat factory. He was greeted by Bob, their export manager, who gave him a detailed guided tour of the plant, which had boats at all stages of construction in different designated areas. The factory must have covered an acre of ground with a further two or three acres of storage area outside. There were dozens of people working in every section of the production line, all dressed in their white overalls and dust masks where necessary. It was an impressive place, as indeed it had to be to produce 4000 boats a year. Luke guessed that Daniel would find a similar picture in Turkey, as the quoted production from the two factories was similar, although he somehow doubted the working practice would be so tidy, organised and up to date.

Luke was then shown the new products which were due to be launched, and as if he were not impressed enough already, this tipped the balance. He began to think he could stop Daniel wasting his time going to Istanbul; they should be tying in with a company that was moving forward as aggressively as this one, and they could not have wished for nicer, more genuine and hospitable people to deal with. Both men liked the Americans' openness and warmth and had always felt at home there.

Heading back to the motel that afternoon, having been treated to a fabulous buffet lunch in the town by his hosts,

Luke thought hard about contacting Daniel and updating him, but he realised that Daniel would have already booked his tickets and hotel in Istanbul. Not to worry, he thought to himself, he could ring him on his mobile the next day to see how progress was and they could compare notes when they got back to London.

CHAPTER TWENTY TWO

Daniel was booked on the early-morning British Airways flight from Heathrow and had ordered a taxi to collect him from the house at 5 am. Before leaving he phoned home in Singapore and had a 20-minute chat with Linda; everything was fine. He said he would call her again on his return to London on Sunday.

As Daniel stood and looked at the screen to see his boarding time, a wave of uncertainty came over him, one he could not really justify. This was most unusual. It was dawning on him that he was heading out to Turkey, without knowing where he was staying or the location of the factory he was supposed to be visiting, and knowing very little about his hosts. He told himself it was a standard business trip, as he had done many times in the past, and dismissed the thoughts.

He moved to a place where there were a few vacant seats together and seated himself in the middle of them, putting his briefcase on the seat next to him. As he sat down he felt a sharp crack from the pocket of his overcoat and swiftly stood again to see what had made the noise. It was his Ericsson mobile phone. It looked OK at the first glance, but on closer inspection it had a large crack down one side and was now permanently off.

"Bloody typical" Daniel muttered, cross with himself for

his own carelessness. He sat down again and started to read the *Telegraph* he had bought at WH Smith's in the terminal.

He soon found himself looking at the page blankly as his mind wandered. Niggling doubts came over him as he remembered and recounted to himself the details of the meeting with Han at the Gloucester Hotel. He remembered how they had never really discussed the true course and operation of the business, and thought about how Han had wanted to control everything and have it all his way. He remembered how the monetary aspect of it had been so easily dismissed. He told himself again that this was obviously their way of doing business, but the more he thought about it, the more ill at ease he became.

Daniel noticed on the screen that his flight was boarding, so he got up and started to wander slowly towards the gate.

As soon as he got to his seat he pulled out the complimentary in-flight magazine, turn to the map in the centre and studied it to see exactly where Istanbul was. He had never studied that area in any great detail, and he had been slightly surprised when, during one of their conversations, Han had advised Daniel to bring some warm clothes, because it was in fact at that time of year colder than London.

During the flight the seat belt signs went off briefly once they had levelled out from take off, but they soon lit again and then stayed on for more or less the entire flight. It was one of the most turbulent flights Daniel had experienced in a long time.

He wondered how Luke had got on at the factory in the

US and looked at his watch to try to work out if he had finished there. He decided that with the time difference Luke was probably there at that very moment, and Daniel was itching to know how he had got on.

On touchdown he got off the aircraft and followed the flow of people through to immigration, where he joined one of the queues and shuffled forward patiently with everyone else. As he looked around he noticed that all the police or security officers were armed, and there were a lot of them. He was also aware how long it was taking to stamp every person through. When he finally got to the front of the queue he handed his passport over the chest height counter, from where it was smartly thrust back at him with the words "Visa, visa!" With that, the Immigration Officer started to usher the next person forward, but Daniel needed to know exactly what he meant. Nobody had mentioned needing a visa.

"What do you mean, visa?" Daniel asked.

"There visa." The officer pointed impatiently, so Daniel followed the direction of his finger and wandered round to a small kiosk alongside the main immigration desks. A sign 'Visa' was written above it, with a series of costs in different currencies below it. Here again was a long queue, which Daniel joined. "Great start" he mumbled, annoyed that he had spent all that time in the other queue without noticing this kiosk.

Once at the front of the queue he handed over his passport and a £20 note, the smallest denomination he had on him.

"No, ten pounds, see" the man pointed at a sign.

"Yes I know it is ten pounds, I am giving you twenty, you give me ten back."

"No, ten pounds only."

Daniel's irritation was beginning to show as he thrust the £20 note forward, only to have it pushed back at him again. The man in front had also come in from London and as he was about to walk off, seeing what was happening, he turned to Daniel and said. "I learned my lesson on this last time I came in, it's absurd. But to save any aggro, I have two tens for your £20 if you like."

"Thanks very much." Daniel took the two tens, handing one to the cashier and giving the gentleman back a twenty-pound note.

"Have a good trip" the other chap said as he headed to the queue for immigration. Daniel turned back and acknowledged with a wave. "Thanks again for your help."

They stamped Daniel's passport with the visa and gave it back to him without a hint of courtesy.

Daniel went back to the immigration desk and finally through to the luggage reclaim, where his case was one of the few still left on the carousel. Most of the other passengers had retrieved their cases and gone. Daniel gathered his and wheeled it through the customs hall, quite expecting to be stopped there as well, but to his surprise he went straight through and into the sea of people waiting to meet various flights.

He had a look around but did not see Han in the immediate vicinity, so he wandered around for a while looking for him. In the end, with no sight of Han at all, Daniel stood against one of the pillars close to the main exit point and kept a look out.

After about half an hour, he was becoming slightly anxious. He started to wonder whether Han had any intention of meeting him there. Maybe Daniel had missed a fax or something asking him to get a cab to a certain hotel. He realised that he could not phone Han, because the number was keyed into his broken mobile phone. The bad flight, the airport queues and visa drama were all adding up to make Daniel feel quite uneasy, and now with nobody to meet him he was beginning to feel bad tempered and fed up as well. He decided to give it another half hour before he made his own way to a hotel.

CHAPTER TWENTY THREE

Istanbul

It was with more than a small sense of relief that Daniel noticed Han walking through the main doors from outside and heading towards the meeting area. Daniel headed him off from where he was standing. As Han saw him he smiled. He had begun to apologise in his heavily-accented English before they were within 15 feet of each other.

"Have you waited a long time?" asked Han, to which Daniel responded in the British tradition, "No, no, not long at all."

"I was unavoidably delayed at the office, and of course I could not ring you to let you know."

"Don't worry, you're here now, that's the main thing."

"Let me take your case, my car is not far."

Daniel followed Han outside. The air was cold, but it was a beautifully sunny day. Daniel loved this type of weather, cold but clear and crisp.

"Was your flight from London good?" Han enquired as they made their way through the car park.

"I would like to say yes, but it was a little lumpy I'm afraid." Daniel was looking out for the BMW, but they came to a halt by the boot of a silver four-year-old Mercedes Benz 200. Han opened the boot and placed Daniel's case inside it.

"You've got a new car?" Daniel asked as Han shut the boot and went to the driver's side. Daniel got in to the passenger seat.

"No", replied Han. " I have had this car for many years, it is good for business." How odd he had not mentioned the Mercedes when they had been discussing cars back in London.

Daniel looked around the interior of the car. The windows were misted up on the inside and it felt damp, as if it had recently had all the upholstery washed. The dashboard had a sheen on it, as if someone had been let loose with a silicone spray. The car had an air freshener smell about it and the carpets had evidently just been wet vacuumed, as the lines were visible in the carpet. Daniel put his hand down to feel the edge of the carpet by the door, which was wet.

"Nice" Daniel said. "I hope you didn't go to the trouble of cleaning it all for my benefit."

"Thank you, and it was a good excuse because it needed a clean anyway."

There was definitely something strange about this car, apart from its recent clean. Then he realised what it was. There were no personal possessions in the car, not a packet of cigarettes, or sweets, or parking permits, or CDs, or loose change, or gloves, or window cleaning leathers; absolutely nothing. The boot, Daniel realised, had been the same, completely empty. He felt sure it was a rental car, but for some reason Han was claiming it to be his.

Daniel once again felt a little uneasy. He thought things through once again. He glanced across at the keys and saw that there was only one key on a nondescript ring. Most odd if it were privately owned, because most people had house and office keys and all sorts on the same ring. If the BMW was off the road because of its window, why would Han not admit to having rented this in the meantime? Very strange, but perhaps it would all make sense in time.

The Merc 200 was an automatic and incredibly sluggish, but that did not stop Han wringing every last drop of power out of it by keeping his foot welded to the floor and the engine revving near the red line most of the time, even from stone cold. Daniel noticed it had been on the gauge as they left the airport. As they swung straight into a main stream of traffic on a dual carriageway, causing others to brake, Han announced that he had once been a racing driver. It appeared he was determined to prove this to Daniel on the public roads in an automatic Mercedes E200. Daniel hoped that by engaging him in conversation he might slow him down a bit, because he had never before felt so uncomfortable as a passenger in a car. In fact he was plain frightened, and covering up his nerves the best he could.

"Of course the trouble is on the open road, it's not necessarily you but some of the other idiots you have to look out for" Han was saying. "I'm sure it's the same here as in England." Indeed there were idiot drivers, thought Daniel, and one of them was in the car with him.

When Han continued at the same furious pace, Daniel asked "Are we in a hurry?"

"Yes, we have to get to the restaurant for lunch before it closes. We were supposed to be there by now. It's my fault."

After about 20 minutes of their white-knuckle ride they arrived at a restaurant in a beautiful position set into the hill overlooking the Bosphorus.

The restaurant was virtually empty, with only a handful of diners finishing their lunch. Han and Daniel were ushered to a window seat, where Han ordered for both of them. He then began to explain their itinerary for the next couple of days.

"After lunch I will take you to your hotel, and then this evening we go to a very famous fish restaurant" he said. "Tomorrow we go to the boat factory. This will take all of the day."

"Where is the boat factory in relation to us?" Daniel inquired. He was now feeling a little more comfortable and having had a few slurps of Coca Cola was beginning to relax a little, hoping that the journey from now on would be slower, as there would surely be no breakneck hurry.

"It is about three hours to drive, but you will see it tomorrow. On Saturday I will take you for a ride on my boat. We see Istanbul from the water. It will give you another aspect of the city."

Daniel was already fascinated with Istanbul and was keen to learn as much as he could about it and its history while he was here. He hoped that Han would afford a few 'unorganised hours' for Daniel to do his own thing and see a little of the Ottoman Empire history.

They spent the rest of the meal discussing Istanbul, its politics, its building policies and everything that Han felt was wrong with those subjects. Nothing was said about boats. That could wait until the factory visit.

Daniel was not particularly hungry, having recently eaten on the aircraft, but made a good show of eating as much as possible of what was put in front of him. They eventually left the restaurant at about 4 pm. Han announced that he was going to drop Daniel at his hotel to freshen up before he collected him later that evening.

"Do you have much social life in Singapore?" he asked Daniel.

"Yes, my wife and I have a very enjoyable time, it's a sociable place."

"Istanbul is also sociable and I can assure you that while you are here you will not sleep."

Oh, great, thought Daniel sarcastically, that's just what I need. All he wanted to do was to see the factory and the products, see a little of historic Istanbul, and go back to his family. Han, it was beginning to materialise, had different ideas.

"That's very hospitable of you, but I'm not a great one for night life, I'm afraid, and I need all the sleep I can get after the last couple of months" explained Daniel. "A nice meal and bed will do me well."

"A few days without sleep will not harm you."

Again he's imposing his will on me, and I don't like it, Daniel thought quietly to himself, also now worrying about how to get out of it. He suddenly feared that this trip was not going to be what he thought it was.

The car had been more or less silent for some minutes when as they tore up one of the dual carriageways Han pointed, "There is your hotel." Daniel glanced in the general direction of Han's arm and could only see a magnificent modern skyscraper built from tinted reflective glass.

"Where?" said Daniel, sure that he had missed something.

"This one, you must be able to see."

"The big glass one?"

"Yes, this is your hotel for your stay."

Daniel looked again and felt a churning in his stomach and a feeling of dread. At the same time remembered he only had a little credit left on his Barclaycard.

"We have to do a U turn to get back to it," Han announced, "It is fantastic, yes?"

"Fantastic it may be, but it is not at all what I asked you to book for me Han, I really do not want to spend too much, it's... it' just unnecessary. I bet it's more than forty-five dollars a night."

"Of course, it is the best in Istanbul."

"Han, this really is not necessary at all. I have just had a very expensive Christmas and New Year and until I get back to Singapore to top up the finances I do not want to spend too much."

"You do not worry about it, you will enjoy it there!"

Daniel looked out of the passenger window, rolled his eyes, took a deep breath and let out a quiet sigh. He was not at all happy. It appeared that Han was not taking a blind bit of notice of his requests. Daniel thought back to how Han had imposed his will in London.

As they drew up under the canopy for the foyer, the doors of the car were opened. Daniel's cases were collected from the boot, and he was ushered to reception.

Han did all the talking. In seconds he had the key and was heading for the lifts. The hotel was very expensively appointed, with polished granite and marble adorning every surface. Han pushed the button for one of the upper floors, and the express lift had them there in a matter of seconds. They stepped out of the lift and within a few yards had reached Daniel's room. As he followed Han through the door, the porter followed.

Han watched for a reaction from Daniel as they entered the opulent suite. Daniel said nothing, desperately wondering how to get himself out of this pickle. Was Han paying for the room? He had told him not to worry, but he could not ask him. After all he was a businessman who wanted to buy products from this guy. He could not let on any more than he already had that cash flow was a serious problem at the moment.

In a resigned voice he said "Yes Han, it is a very nice room but not what I normally go for and certainly not what I really wanted."

"Look, you have a view from both sides of the hotel" said Han, ignoring him. He tipped the porter, who duly left.

Daniel wandered from the dining area to the main bedroom, to find the largest bed Daniel had ever seen. The view from the room was indeed magnificent, with views right down the Bosphorus and its large picturesque suspension bridges.

"The room is big!" announced Han with a smile. "But do not worry, you will not stay here alone."

Daniel thought for a moment, his mind racing with uncertainty as he suddenly had visions of women of the night being purchased for him, something he would not tolerate. Or had he misunderstood the heavily accented English?

"What do you mean exactly?"

"I will stay here with you."

Daniel's heart, for the umpteenth time that day sank into the pit of his stomach. He did not answer, but just tried to make some sense of what had just been said. Daniel looked around for any signs of a second bed or a sofa bed, but the sitting area was decked out in rattan and there was no sign of one.

"I will collect you at 7 pm," Han stated as he walked towards the door. "We will go for a meal and hit the town for an evening you will not forget." With that he closed the door and disappeared.

"Oh bloody hell." Daniel said out loud as the door slammed closed. He had already had a day he was not going to forget in a hurry, and now he truly dreaded what Han might have had in mind that evening. As for staying in the room with him, well that was simply going to be out of the question. However he was not at that moment sure how to get round it or what it all meant.

Daniel spent the next half hour pacing between the dining room and bedroom looking at the views, but taking none of it in. He tried to tell himself that he must have misheard Han's comments and that he was really beginning to make a mountain from a molehill, although his gut was telling him a different story. History dictated that Daniel should listen to his gut instinct more often, instead of always pretending that logic should override it.

He was tired after the travelling and decided he would feel better after a shower. He got undressed and wandered into the marbled bathroom, which was the size of most people's bedrooms and had a heated floor as well as a phone next to the toilet. "Very plush" Daniel muttered sourly. "How the hell am I going to pay for this if it's down to me?"

He turned on the shower and returned to the basin to brush his teeth. Looking at himself in the mirror, he said to himself, "The stupid fixes you manage to get yourself into! you should have listened to your doubts back in London. You're an idiot, Daniel"

He got into the shower and stood thinking as the piping hot water cascaded down his body. As he stood there, the words of Lucy, one of his close friends, back in the UK came to haunt him. When he had told her how Han had crowded him in the gents, she had said laughingly, "Oh he probably fancies you, you have to remember with some men it's women for procreation and men for fun." This had all been amusing enough at the time, but now that suggestion was becoming an increasing possibility. No, what a stupid thought, he told himself, but he couldn't stop it coming back to haunt him.

He finished in the shower, dried himself and with the towel wrapped round his waist went to lie on the bed to think things out logically. As he lay there with hands cupped behind his head his imagination started to run riot, and he became more and more frightened about the predicament he was in, despite the lack of a tangible reason.

The time was about right; mid evening in Singapore. He would phone Linda and discuss a few things with her, and no doubt she would throw some logic on the subject.

He then remembered that his mobile was broken and cursed himself once more for his stupidity for sitting on it. He would have to use the hotel phone and get Linda to call him back.

He dialled his home number in Singapore.

CHAPTER TWENTY FOUR

Medway Park, Singapore

Linda and Sam were still waking at all hours of the night, hungry and with their body clocks all over the place, but they were at last beginning to get back into their routine. The neighbours had mentioned their suspicion that Salim had been around several times while they had been away, but there had been no discernible trouble and when they had asked Salvia she had denied his presence.

Linda had been up at about five o'clock that morning when Sam had woken her, and they had gone downstairs and had a milky drink. Linda had noticed as she was making the drinks that Salvia's lights were still burning, thought Salvia would probably be as good as useless that day at work through being over-tired. She glanced out of the sitting-room window and was relieved that there was no sign of a car. She hoped Salim was not the cause of Salvia still being awake.

Sam finally went back to sleep again at about six, and she took him upstairs and laid him in his bed. Then she went back to bed, taking the opportunity to get about three more hours' sleep herself. She had not arranged to play tennis with her friends at the British Club until 11 that morning.

Linda woke before Sam and left him asleep as she had a shower and got dressed. When she went downstairs she was surprised to see that all the shutters and windows were still closed and Salvia had not opened up, or prepared breakfast. Initially her reaction was one of annoyance, and she concluded that Salvia had overslept through staying up late. She then heard shouting from the direction of her quarters and opened up the back door, calling Salvia's name. She turned back to get her flip flops to wander out there when there came a shrill scream from the direction of Salvia's quarters. With that Salvia came running out with only a towel to cover herself and flew towards the kitchen door shouting "Mem, Mem, help me, help me!" She was hotly pursued by Salim as she entered the kitchen at the run. He had slipped on the damp concrete but had recovered and was now only a few metres behind her. To Linda's horror, he was brandishing a kitchen knife. Salvia shot past Linda and out of terror grabbed her and tried to use her as a shield against Salim.

Salim's face was filled with rage as he entered the kitchen. He shouted at Linda as he brandished the knife, "Get out of the way or I kill you as well! I don't care Ma'am, I take you as well!"

Linda was petrified, but she responded as calmly as she could. "Salim, put the knife down! That is not going to do anyone any good" she said.

"It will do me good when it kill her!" He said trying to take a swipe at Salvia around the side of Linda. Linda raised her voice as she had never done before and surprised even herself at the note of authority. "Put that knife down now, Salim and get out of this house" she said. With that Salvia let go of Linda, pushing her in Salim's direction, and darted into the dining room and through into the hall, where she ran into the downstairs toilet and bolted the door. Salim pushed Linda out of the way and sprinted after Salvia, dizzy with rage.

Linda quickly decided that Sam was safe. Salvia was in the toilet and Salim outside it, so she dashed out of the back door to her neighbours Tara and John, who were having breakfast on the terrace. "Please help!" she screamed as she approached, bursting into tears as she got closer, hardly able to explain what was happening.

John jumped to his feet. As soon as he had realised what was going on, he was running towards Linda's house. "Call the police" he shouted back to Tara.

Linda followed, desperate to get to Sam. John ran through the kitchen and into the hall, where without a second thought he took a running tackle at Salim, who was shouting at Salvia and banging on the door and threatening to kick it in.

He was not expecting the attack from behind. John, a fit young six-foot-two Australian, swept into him, planting him half way up the stairs. The knife tumbling on to the tiled floor with a clatter. Salim screamed like a wounded animal as John pinned him down. "See what it's like to play with someone your own size, you pathetic bully," John said as he locked his arm round his neck and brought Salim to his knees.

Linda, who had been following closely behind, picked up the knife from the floor and took it to the kitchen, out of the way. John marched Salim out of the house and held on to him on the lawn. Salim would not have dreamed of retaliating against such a fit character.

Linda asked Salvia to unlock the toilet door, assuring her that Salim was under control. The maid came out reluctantly, sobbing and apologising. Linda went to pour them all a brandy.

The police were there within minutes and showed no mercy as they hauled Salim off to the police station, with the knife for fingerprinting, to be used as evidence. A second police car arrived and the long arduous task of giving evidence about what had happened started.

Tara rung Linda's tennis friends and explained that she would not be able to play that morning. Linda soon managed to recover her senses, but it was at least two and a half hours before the police had all the detail they needed from Linda, Salvia and John.

Linda asked John and Tara to come and join her for dinner that evening. They had asked her originally to dine with them, but she had not wanted to leave Sam unattended. She gave Salvia the rest of the day off and said they would discuss the situation the next morning.

John and Tara arrived at around eight o'clock. Linda was still visibly shaken by the experience earlier in the day.

At about 10 pm the phone rang, and Linda got up from the table and went to answer it.

"Hi, honey, it's me."

At the sound of Daniel's voice Linda burst into uncontrolled sobbing.

"Honey, what's happening? What's the matter, please tell me? Linda, what is going on? Is it Sam, is he OK? Are you OK?"

Seeing what was going on, John approached Linda, who muttered through the sobs, "Here's John" and gave the phone to him, as she was unable to speak coherently. Tara came in and gave Linda a big hug.

"Daniel, look mate it's John. Look all's OK now but there was a bit of a run in with Salim this morning which has frightened and shocked everyone, but nobody is hurt and the police have now taken him away."

"How is Sam?"

"He's sleeping like a baby mate, doesn't even know there's been any bother."

John gave Daniel a brief run down on the morning's events, and assured him that everything was now back to normal and they would look after Linda for him.

"Listen John, can you note down this number and get Linda to give me a ring when she is feeling a bit better?" asked Daniel.

"Sure mate, fire away."

John jotted the number down and promised he would get Linda to ring back.

CHAPTER TWENTY FIVE

Istanbul

Having heard Linda's distress on the other end of the phone, Daniel forgot his own self-sorrow and uncertainty. He put the phone down and lay back down on the bed, relieved that everything was OK but sorry he was not back at home to comfort his wife. It must have been some disturbance to have upset Linda like that, as he didn't remember ever having heard her so upset. Thank god John and Tara were around. He knew they would see everything was all right.

But he was soon thinking again about his own predicament. As he lay there his imagination started to go into overdrive. With nobody to whom he could sensibly discuss his worries, the situation in his mind started to escalate.

What was the rented car all about? Why did Han claim it was his? Was Maya really his wife? If so, who was the other lady in London? What was Han's true relationship with Edward Lim?

Was Han gay, and intending to spike a drink of mine and blackmail him with photos he would know nothing about? This seemed the most likely explanation. Although if that was the case, where did Lim fit into it all? After all he was a reputable member of the Tanglin club, wasn't he? The questions kept on coming, but could not be put to bed. There were quite simply no answers available. Was he being used as a pawn in some drugs game? Were they going to try and catch him in a compromising position to blackmail him? But surely not. Perhaps he had been watching too many films.

He decided once more that it was probably all in his mind and that tomorrow the boat factory would prove just what they needed, and all would be well. He had however made a decision not to go out that evening and to try and ensure that he had an early night while he had the room to himself.

He went over to his jacket and pulled his wallet from the inside pocket, from which he extracted Han's business card, which had his mobile number written on the back. He wandered back to the bed, glanced at his watch and decided that if he was going to try and get out of dinner that evening he had to do it now.

He picked up the receiver, pressed 9 for an outside line and dialled Han's mobile number. It was answered almost immediately.

"Hello?"

"Han, hi it's Daniel."

"Daniel, how are you, are you enjoying your suite?"

"Yes, well no, I mean yes, the room is lovely but I'm afraid that I personally am not feeling so well."

"What is the matter?" The response came in a flat, unsympathetic tone.

"I must have eaten something on the plane, because my

stomach is very upset and I really do not feel at all well. I hope you do not mind under the circumstances if I do not join you for your kind invitation to a meal this evening?"

"Yes, I do mind" came the answer "I have booked a table. I will collect you at seven o'clock."

With that the phone was hung up. Daniel looked aghast and stared at the handset for a second before slowly replacing it in the cradle.

"I guess that means not going out is not an option" He said out loud to himself. But he was damned if he was staying up all night, just a meal and back to the room. Although he couldn't eat much after telling Han he had an upset stomach.

Daniel went back into the bathroom. What if Han came up to the room to collect him? No, he'd make sure he was downstairs in the foyer in good time.

Daniel saw some Imodium tablets Linda had given him and decided that if he came up for some reason and saw that Daniel was indeed taking something for his ailment, it might tip the balance and add credibility to Daniel's story. He popped two of the tablets out of their foil sheet and threw them down the toilet, ensuring that the wrapping with the tablets missing was in full view should anyone venture in there. Then he wandered back into the bedroom and flicked on the TV, hoping there would be something on to take his mind off things. The only thing that was in English and of the remotest interest was CNN, so he left it on and slowly got dressed into smart casual clothing consisting of shirt, chinos, tie and a navy blazer.

At about 6 pm he decided to wander down to the hotel

bar for a drink before their evening out. He needed some Dutch courage and a change of surroundings, before he drove himself mad with worry.

Linda had not called back, but he realised that if it had been possible she would have done so. He decided to let reception know that he would be out for a few hours and if he had a call from his wife could they let her know that he was out to dinner and would be back within about three hours.

Daniel wandered into the bar, which was almost empty at that early hour of the evening, except for what sounded like a couple of French businessmen at one table and a big man sitting at one of the bar stools studying a screen in the corner playing MTV. Daniel nodded an acknowledgement to the man as he approached the bar and ordered a large gin and tonic. The man turned to face Daniel and introduced himself as Ged, a Canadian. Daniel was relieved to have someone to talk to. Ged was in the soft drinks business and worked for an American company, and apparently spent his time welded to an aircraft seat between the Americas and Europe.

They spent the next hour shooting the breeze. Daniel was keen to hear about Ged's experiences of the business world in Turkey and indeed the way they structured their whole business.

Daniel glanced at his watch, and seeing that it was nearing 7 pm he kept an eye open for Han entering the hotel. At about five past he saw the familiar figure enter the foyer, so he hastily said goodbye to Ged and made his way out to greet Han. His host was full of smiles and greeted Daniel like a lifelong friend. Daniel was less happy.

"How are you feeling , my friend?" Han inquired.

"Pretty lousy actually Han, and I really should be in bed, but I'll make the best of it."

"Good, good. Tonight we go to the best fish restaurant in Istanbul. It is in a beautiful position overlooking the Bosphorus."

"Sounds good."

Han led the way out, with Daniel a few steps behind him. As they left the hotel the Mercedes was parked under the canopy directly outside the doors, and the doormen almost bowed as Han walked out. Daniel had noticed this subservience at the restaurant they had eaten at that lunchtime as well, and had put it down to polite serving staff, but now he was not so sure because he noticed that other guests were not treated with the same amount of respect. Who *was* this guy?

As Daniel looked towards the car he noticed someone else in it, and to his delight and relief, realised it was Maya. He climbed in.

"I understand you are feeling unwell?" she said.

"Yes, unfortunately I must have had something that disagreed with me, it's a shame but I'm sure I'll live."

Maya laughed. It was reassuring to have her there, and he certainly felt more confident with her present.

Maya pointed out various places of interest along the route to the restaurant, but the journey only took about ten minutes. Daniel noticed that Han's driving was considerably more subdued when she was in the car.

"Will you be coming with us to the boat factory

tomorrow?" Daniel asked hopefully, realising that it would be a much more pleasant car journey if she was.

"No, unfortunately I have to work tomorrow."

"Oh, that's a shame." He meant it.

The restaurant was built into the side of a cliff face, in an unusual and spectacular position. The doorman took the keys from Han and disappeared with the Merc. Once again Han was greeted with an unusual amount of subservience and the restaurant manager was on hand to seat them all.

"Good evening Mr Cassidy, it is our pleasure to welcome you to our humble restaurant" he said.

"Well, thank you very much. It is my pleasure to be here."

"We have the best table in the house awaiting you. Please follow me."

"This treatment is one of the things that sets this restaurant apart from the others" Han explained.

Daniel could not help noticing that Maya was left until last with everything. He was beginning to see the signs of a male-dominated society.

The table was set in one of the bay windows, which by the look of it would have opened onto a small balcony during the summer. It was well laid with silver candelabras and fresh flower decorations.

Han ordered on behalf of them all, and when the crab starter arrived it looked magnificent and started to make Daniel's mouth water. He was now kicking himself for saying he was unwell. He announced that he was well enough to try some of the food, as it would be such a shame not to. In reality he was extremely hungry, but he did not want to claim that he had recovered from his ailments; there were still two more nights to contend with.

He could not help but think what an idiot he was being, but something inside told him that the sacrifice of the meal was worth holding out on. Despite his claim, he demolished at least half the starter and made a good dent in the main course. The ice cream for dessert, he told them, would do him good. He was able to devour all of that.

The conversation at the table consisted entirely of the culture and histories of their respective countries and families, nothing to do with boats or business at all. Daniel began to warm to Han slightly, but he thoroughly enjoyed Maya's company. She was intelligent, witty and, he sensed, warm-hearted.

As they were having their coffee, the talk turned to what they would do for the rest of the evening. Suddenly Daniel was on the defensive again. Han suggested a night club, but Daniel firmly said, "I'm afraid you really will have to leave me out, because I have to get to bed."

"No, you must come to the night club, it is a good place and you will forget that you are unwell."

"No, I'm sorry Han, it's very kind of you but I must insist on going to my room."

"Han" Maya interjected, "If Daniel wishes to go to his room, why do you not respect his request?"

"Yes, OK we take you back to your room" said Han, with a sense of resignation in his voice.

"Thank you, it's gone 11.30 anyway, and I'm sure we have a long day ahead of us tomorrow."

"Yes, the drive is about three or four hours, so I will collect you at about 9.30 in the morning."

Han summoned the waiter and asked to settle the bill. Daniel thanked them both profusely for their hospitality and a wonderful meal.

"Will you be around tomorrow evening?" Daniel tentatively enquired of Maya, with a lot more than she realised riding on the answer.

"No not tomorrow, but Saturday we have a family dinner for Han's mother at a local hotel as it is her birthday. We would love you to join us for that."

"That sounds splendid, and hopefully by then this wretched bug will be out of the system."

The doorman brought them their coats and they left the restaurant and drove straight back to the hotel. Daniel waved goodbye to them and then, extremely relieved, went straight into the bar for a double whisky and topped up his appetite with as many snacks as he could get hold of.

Daniel paid for his little midnight feast with his Barclaycard. He did not want his midnight feast to show on the room bill. He sat at the bar and re-ran in his mind every little detail of what had been said that evening, analysing every comment and every word, trying to make sense of the whole situation. It did not seem Maya had anything to hide, but he still thought that was far from the case with Han. Tomorrow would tell.

At about 12.30 am Daniel headed back up to his room, stopping at reception on the way through. Linda had indeed rung, just after he had gone out. He undressed, brushed his teeth and sat on the bed. He would give her a ring in the morning. It was the early hours of the morning in Singapore now and she would surely be asleep. Much as he longed to hear her voice, she would not thank him for a call.

Despite being exhausted from nervous energy Daniel had a fitful sleep that night, spending hours just lying there thinking over the various scenarios that could face him over the next few days. Everything seeming ten times worse in the dead of the night.

CHAPTER TWENTY SIX

Daniel finally woke from his less than adequate night's sleep at 7.30 and hit the button for the electric curtains. They slid silently open, allowing a panoramic view from his bed. He flicked on CNN and got up to make a cup of tea in the kitchenette area. Then he took the tea and a couple of biscuits back to bed and sat there looking at his surroundings, wishing that he could enjoy them.

He took a sip of his tea, and as he always did in hotels abroad, grimaced at the fact that he had to have it with UHT long life milk, which simply did not taste the same. He picked up the phone to ring home but got no reply. Linda was obviously out at one of her many social events. He felt sure that she was OK. He showered and dressed and made his way down to the dining area for breakfast, determined to have a good wholesome meal before the forthcoming day's events.

The choice of food on offer was comprehensive and Daniel did not even think twice about a second helping of a full cooked breakfast consisting of egg, bacon, mushrooms, grilled tomatoes, sausages and sliced fried potatoes.

With a much greater air of confidence, he strode out into the lobby to wait for Han. Somehow this morning everything seemed a little better, and he told himself that everything would be just fine. His main fear was the thought of the treacherous car journey with Han at the wheel, and he was seriously concerned for his own safety.

After about five minutes Daniel saw the Mercedes pull up outside the doors. He walked out to meet Han, who once again met him with a beaming smile and a hand shake. The doorman opened the car door for Daniel. It closed with a solid Germanic clunk and Daniel thought to himself that if he was going to have a prang he would rather be in nothing else, although the speeds with which Han drove would probably even test the strength of a Mercedes.

They took off from the hotel under full throttle as expected, with the automatic transmission only changing up a notch when the engine was reaching its rev limiter. It occurred to Daniel that if he engaged Han in conversation the pace might relax a little. He began to demonstrate an interest in every landmark and everything unusual he saw, but the distraction had the opposite effect on Han's driving; while the speeds remained the same, Han now spent more time looking sideways at Daniel as he explained something, keeping only one hand on the wheel. It was going to be a long three hours.

It was another clear and crisp day as they set off over one of the bridges over the Bosphorus and Han explained that they were going to the Asian side of Turkey and would have to take a ferry for a short while. He still did not tell Daniel of their final destination, despite being asked on more than one occasion. Why the big secret, Daniel asked himself. Oh well, he'd soon find out first hand.

Daniel was amazed by the number of half-built blocks of flats in the hills. While the top halves were open to the elements with no roofs or windows, the bottom levels were apparently inhabited. Daniel asked about this, and discovered that it was a subject Han was particularly passionate about because of the way, in his view, the lack of proper planning consent had ruined the natural beauty of the countryside.

They passed through a number of tolls on the route. As they queued to go through, children of no more than nine or ten years of age would knock on the window of the car and offer for sale a selection of old audio cassettes. This happened at every toll. Han instructed Daniel to ignore them.

As they motored in the fast lane of a congested motorway Han suddenly swung the car straight across the inner two lanes and straight off at the exit, all without dropping below about 90 mph. The cars in the other lanes had to take serious evasive action to avoid a collision, and showed their indignation with horns. This made Han smile. Sensing Daniel's unease, he said, "Do not worry they expect this driving in Turkey, everyone is the same."

Daniel did not comment, but he had not seen anyone else make a manoeuvre like that, and a collision had been avoided by luck rather than judgement.

As they descended a steep slope, the view that opened up in front of them was stunning. The sun reflected off the smooth waters of the sea and the white-capped mountain ranges on the far shore made a superb backdrop. From Daniel's sketchy knowledge he assumed they must have been crossing Izmit Bay, an extension of the Marmara Sea.

"It's beautiful," remarked Daniel. His anxiety was beginning to return as he realised that not a soul in the world, not even he, knew exactly where he was, or where he was going.

"Which stretch of water is this, is it the Marmara?" he asked.

"Here is the ferry we take to the other side" said Han, failing to answer the question. "It is beautiful over there, you agree?"

"Yes, well it certainly looks very impressive from here. Are we going over those mountains?"

"No, only along the bottom."

As they descended the slope Daniel glanced down toward the ferry and casually thought how ancient it looked, as indeed it was.

"Do you have a map Han, so I can see where we are going?" he asked. "I mean it's a shame to go on this trip and not know where I am, it would be interesting to see."

"No, I have no map. You can see maybe when you return to your hotel."

Well I guess that answers that, thought Daniel, already thinking about how to memorise where he was going, as he had seen no place names he recognised, and most were unpronounceable anyway.

They drove onto the ferry, which was of a roll on, roll off design. They were one of the first cars on and consequently were parked up near the front.

"Would you like some fresh air? It will take about half an hour to cross" said Han.

"Fine by me," said Daniel, who thought at the time how deceptive distance over water was, because it looked as if they should have been across in about ten minutes maximum. They got out of the car and Han lit a cigarette as they approached the side rail.

"You will not be disappointed with our factory" he said. "I think you will be happy to do business with us."

"I certainly hope so, or else we have all wasted a lot of time and effort."

This was the first time since arriving that Han had mentioned the business in hand and it somehow reassured Daniel a little, although he was still far from happy, which must have been obvious. He decided to continue to play the upset stomach card, which gave him an excuse to be a little uncommunicative.

The temperature on the deck could only be described as bracing, and it was not long before Daniel decided to go back and sit in the car. Han finished a second cigarette and had a couple of animated conversations on his mobile phone before he joined him.

As he got back in, Daniel asked, "Have you heard from Edward recently?"

"Oh yes, I spoke to him just yesterday and he will join us tomorrow for a ride on my boat."

"Oh, is he here in Istanbul already?"

"No, he arrives tonight."

"Which model of your boats do you have?" asked Daniel, genuinely interested.

"You will see tomorrow."

"I will look forward to it. Is it one with a cabin or a sports boat?"

"You will see tomorrow" came the response again.

They sat in silence as the ferry approached the far shore and within minutes they were on their way, although for some reason the driving had slowed down considerably.

The phone rang again and Han spoke in Turkish, but from the tone Daniel could tell that he was not happy; the phone was shut off and slung into the door pocket. Nothing further was said for a while, but Daniel noticed the roads were now considerably narrower than before, with a single carriageway in each direction. He looked at the signposts, trying to make sense of where they were going. The only name that consistently appeared was that of Bursa, which was, he guessed a city of reasonable size.

They turned off the main road onto a smaller road and continued for another 20 minutes or so. Daniel glanced at his watch and noted that they had been travelling now for over three hours. Surely they were not far away now.

"It can't be far now," commented Daniel.

"Still half an hour" replied Han.

They turned off the main road on to a smaller single tarmac road and accelerated on. There were no signs now that Daniel could make any sense of at all. After a further fifteen minutes they took another turning onto an unmade dirt road and drove through a small village with mangey dogs and dirty undernourished children in the middle of the road. Daniel was now seriously concerned as to where he was going to end up.

"This is very remote for a boat factory," he commented.

"Well actually you realise that I am kidnapping you," came the matter-of-fact answer. There was no trace of a smile or humour in Han's voice.

Daniel's mind raced in a number of directions at once. His heart sank and he was overcome with a wave of nausea, but he responded in the best humour he could muster with a laugh and then said in a similar tone, as if it was all a joke, "Well I can tell you now you won't get very much for me, I'm not worth much."

Han laughed, but did not comment further. Was this his idea of a sick joke? His earlier misgivings and his current surroundings made the comment all too plausible. His feelings of unease grew as he realised he had no way of contacting anyone, and absolutely no idea where he was.

As the minutes of silence ticked by and the road became more and more bumpy, Daniel started to sweat, though he was trying not to show it. He began trying to memorize the road since getting off the ferry, and which turnings they had taken.

Then, out of the blue, completely incongruously located in the middle of nowhere, on the side of this bumpy track, appeared a brand new boat showroom with bold writing on the fascia: 'United European Marine Ltd'. Daniel did not know whether to laugh or cry with the relief of seeing the building, or his own stupidity at his thoughts. Either way, he was mighty relieved as they pulled up at the gates and a guard opened them and let them pull in. Daniel tried to hide any signs of relief, but he was acutely aware of how much more chatty he had just become. He got out of the car with his briefcase and stood and took stock of these strange surroundings.

CHAPTER TWENTY SEVEN

Asian Turkey

As they got out of the car Daniel noticed a crowd of shabbily dressed men standing in silence towards the back of the building, watching them. There were about fifteen of them. Daniel looked around him. The showroom they had just driven past was very much a new façade, as the buildings behind were a mix of different-sized old buildings all built around a central courtyard. Some of them could be classed as garages and some were more barns than anything else.

Han walked round the car and ushered Daniel into the building through a side door that entered straight into the showroom, where four sports boats sat on their trailers.

A gentleman of about fifty who spoke Turkish was introduced to Daniel just inside the door. He was introduced as Han's partner and the Managing Director. Daniel could not believe that Han had yet more partners in this business, but couldn't be bothered wasting the breath inquiring further as to the set up. The MD, whose name Daniel couldn't have begun to pronounce, was cleanly dressed, but did not look prosperous and showed all the features of hard graft. Daniel noticed the years of grime in the creases in his hands and his down-at-heel shoes which had clearly been polished for the occasion, probably the first polish they had seen in years. His shirt had worn through on the collar but had been heavily starched and ironed, and the tie would have been in fashion several decades earlier. His face was heavily tanned, but equally heavily creased and wrinkled from many years of exposure to the sun.

There were several staff in the showroom, but they were workmen, not salesmen. As Daniel got his bearings and took a grip of the situation he realised that they were in fact builders and decorators who were still painting the final parts of the walls, while another was nailing down the carpet in one corner. Daniel then realised that the familiar smell was nothing to do with the boats; it was the newly laid carpet. It was obvious that the whole showroom had just been built.

"Is this all new?" he inquired of Han.

"No, just a small refurbishment."

Looking at the power points and places where new wiring was showing, the ceiling, the lighting, and the newly undercoated woodwork, Daniel somehow doubted that it was very old at all, but who was he to doubt? Maybe this was why Han had slowed down, because they were not ready for their visitor, Daniel thought sarcastically, realising that the tense phone call was possibly to get it finished, or at least respectable in time for their arrival. Anyhow it was not the state of décor that interested him - it was the boats.

Turning his attention to the boats in the showroom, he made a beeline for the nearest boat on show. Although it bore no resemblance to any he recognised from the brochure, it would give an idea of the quality.

He looked around, studying the finish and the seating, the woodwork and general fittings. Then he got down on his hands and knees and looked at the fibreglass finish on the hull. He was not impressed. He made no comments for at least five minutes. Han and the MD stood watching with interest and commenting quietly to themselves, but not interfering.

Daniel then stood at the back of the boat, looked at them and said "May I?" In response to Han's nod he climbed aboard for a closer inspection from the inside. He opened the stern lockers on either side of the transom and had a look at the thickness of the transom and at the general lay up. It looked flimsy and agricultural, and certainly did not consist of any of the modern high-tech woven mattings which were now being used in their own latest craft, but he kept reminding himself that they were being built to a budget.

Daniel finished inside without saying anything to the other two, and climbed out. As he did so Han translated something the MD had said.

"He says this is not a new boat but an earlier model, and when you look at the other ones you will be impressed."

"I didn't say whether I was impressed or not."

"No, but what you do not say tells him a lot."

Daniel smiled and walked over to the next boat, which looked a lot more modern. He followed the same routine round this boat before moving back to a smaller one sitting in the middle of the showroom. It was more of a small tender than anything else.

"Could you give me a hand to turn it over please?" he said

to Han, who quickly obliged and they both came over to help flip the boat onto its back. To Daniel's surprise, it took all the strength of the three of them.

Daniel then invited Han to come over to where he was standing and look at the hull, pointing out the ripples in the finish of the fibreglass. "This would not be acceptable in the UK" he said. The MD did not come any closer. He appeared to know what Daniel was going to point out. He lit a cigarette and muttered something in Turkish, and Han gave a knowing nod and appeared to respond by explaining what Daniel was pointing out to him. The MD nodded with a slight smile and turned to look out of the window.

Daniel explained to Han that it would appear from the ripples in the hull that the moulds were not of particularly good quality. Daniel was quietly thinking to himself that the boats he was seeing looked as if they had been made from a cheap mould made from another boat and not from an original mould plug.

Han agreed that the moulds were not to a very high standard, but said these were old moulds and that new ones were under construction at his other factory. Han turned to Daniel and said "The MD think that you're not impressed."

"I have to say that if they were all like this then sadly we would not be interested. However, if the boats are to be produced from new moulds, then let's look at the general construction beyond just the finish of the hull. Then let's look at the new moulds."

Daniel wandered over to one of the other boats in the showroom, the largest and best looking boat of the bunch.

He looked at the hull for any signs of specification plates, designating the hull's performance ratings, but could see nothing on the transom at all.

"Where do you locate the hull plate on your boats?" asked Daniel.

"This boat is too new and it has not been fitted yet. Normally it would go just there" Han said as he pointed to the transom.

The boat Daniel was looking at was indeed a good-looking boat, and somehow it smacked of familiarity. While the inside finish was indeed very acceptable, the finish on the hull did not come anywhere near expectations.

The MD wandered over and Daniel asked Han if he could ask him what the lay up of the hull was, and what criteria and regulations it had been built and certified to.

"I assume all these boats meet the current CE regulations and that the factory has all of the relevant paperwork to support this?" he said. "As part of the European Union it is illegal for us to sell any type of boat that does not meet the CE regulations in full." Han repeated all this in Turkish for the benefit of the MD. The MD said something to Han and gestured towards the door which led from the back of the showroom.

"He say, please come and see the manufacturing and then we go to my office for a talk afterwards."

The MD led the way towards the back end of the showroom and held the door open for Han and Daniel to exit into the courtyard. The MD led them towards the far end of the courtyard to one of the larger barns.

As they stepped in the courtyard, Daniel realised how very quiet it was. All the workmen who had been standing watching them get out of the car had now disappeared. Han could hear chatting and the faint sound of rubbing down coming from one of the sheds on the left hand side, so he presumed they had gone back to continue their work, but there was a lack of buzz about the place. Even in much smaller-volume factories there were usually people running around with paperwork and pots of resin, deliveries and despatches, but here there was nothing.

Walking a couple of paces behind the others, he had a good look round, thinking how eerily quiet it was for a factory that was supposed to produce 4000 boats a year. From what Daniel had seen so far, they would be lucky to produce four boats a year. Maybe the other factory Han had spoken about was where the bulk of production was carried out. This place simply did not have the infrastructure to do it. If that was the case, Daniel wondered why they were showing him this ghost town.

As they walked across the courtyard Daniel asked "How far away is the other factory you have Han?"

"Oh, it is many miles away."

"Is most of your production done here or at the other factory?"

"Both places really."

"Are we going to see the other factory?"

"No, we won't have time to do that."

They entered one of the larger barns towards the end of the courtyard, where a number of different models of boats were lined up down the right hand side, with the left-hand side and the centre of the barn filled with a number of moulds. Daniel inspected the mould closest to him. While he was no expert, even he could see that it had not been used in a long time. Maybe they were trying to start again.

"This is the mould for the Phantom" Han announced proudly, this being one of the models Daniel was interested in. With that Han pointed to a Phantom sitting on a trailer down the right-hand side of the barn. They all wandered towards it.

"This mould looks fairly old, are you producing a new mould for the Phantom as well?" asked Daniel.

"Yes, yes, we have new moulds for all our models, but they are all being made at the other factory."

As they approached the Phantom sitting on its trailer, Daniel opened his briefcase and pulled the camera out. Han turned around and saw what he was doing. "Wait, no please wait a minute" he said. With that Han and the MD disappeared out of sight behind a neighbouring boat.

"You don't mind if I take couple of pictures do you, so that I have something I can show to Luke?" Daniel said with slight puzzlement. He continued to take several photographs of the boats, then put his camera away and clambered onto the Phantom to have a closer look at the internal finish. This time he was not disappointed. Again he looked for some form of registration plate, but could find none. Even if the boats were made to a higher standard from new moulds, he would have to tell his hosts that they would not entertain purchasing anything without the correct plating.

"Have you any boats that are actually in the production stage that I could have a look at?" Daniel asked. Han muttered something in Turkish to the MD before he responded.

"Apparently we show you those on the other side, we go there now."

They left the large shed and walked to the other side of the courtyard to the shed where the workmen were busying themselves. The low-roofed barn had a row of boats down one side, all in various stages of finish. Daniel started at one end with the other two following, and worked his way down the line, looking at the various stages of manufacture. He stopped occasionally to take photographs of relevant points. Daniel could not help but notice that whenever the camera was about Han and the MD both made themselves scarce.

"Why don't I take a picture of you by one of the boats?" Daniel suggested, already suspecting what the answer would be.

"No, I'm very shy of camera, I do not like it. Please excuse me" said Han.

Daniel asked what the workers were doing. They were all squatting in the middle of the floor rubbing down nondescript pieces of glass fibre. Daniel was told they were finishing a set of louvre panels for a large order.

They finished in the shed and Han suggested that they went up to the office for a coffee and a chat. Daniel had a last look round as he left the shed, not quite sure what to make of it, but relieved to know that the factory existed. He could now begin to relax a little.

They entered the showroom and Daniel followed them

upstairs to the offices above it. They looked as new as the showroom itself and had brand new carpet fitted everywhere and fresh paint on the walls. Brand new desks were scattered strategically around, no work was being done. Daniel's own office in Singapore, well run and tidy as it was, had full in-trays and papers scattered everywhere, as was the way with most businesses. This office was unlike any Daniel had seen before. Either they were exceptionally good at keeping the paperwork for 4000 boats filed away, or there was indeed very little going on. Daniel suspected the latter.

The MD went over to a large desk in the corner of the room and pulled up a couple of extra seats before taking up his place in the large black leather swivel chair behind the desk. The one secretary in the office was dispatched to go and make coffee for the three of them.

With Han as the interpreter, they sat and discussed the relevant CE documentation which was necessary for the importation of the boats to the UK. As the conversation got deeper, it was apparent to Daniel that they had little idea of exactly what manufacturing standards they were supposed to meet. Luckily he had copies of the relevant CE regulations, and he briefly ran through a few of the fundamental basics and suggested they photocopy them and ensure that everything conformed before taking things any further. He suggested that they should do this before spending any more money on new moulds, in case they needed changing.

The MD tried to assure Daniel that the boats met all the Turkish standards, which he thought were the same as the European ones, but said he would go through the regulations word for word to make sure. The MD listened carefully to everything that Daniel said and was making copious notes.

"Do not worry, we will not disappoint you," came the interpretation back through Han.

"He asks if you would like to go for lunch now, you must be very hungry?" added Han.

"That is very kind, but please explain that I'm not hungry due to my current illness. Under normal circumstances I would love to accept his offer."

Han immediately started laughing and said something to the MD, although by the length of the narrative Daniel felt Han had probably elaborated the point. This was shortly proven when the MD also started laughing.

Han then turned back to Daniel. "I tell him that you're not hungry because you are not so well, and that you are saving yourself for me!" Han was barely able to contain his mirth as he said it.

A shiver swept down Daniel's spine. He could not see one ounce of humour in what Han had just said, so he just played dumb. "I'm sorry, I don't understand" he said, shrugging the comment aside. He leaned forward and picked up one of the brochures to bring some focus back to the conversation.

There was more laughter from the other two men, and a lengthy exchange in Turkish which made Daniel feel extremely uncomfortable.

Daniel was in turmoil once again, realising he was in the middle of nowhere with somebody who not only thought it amusing to pretend he'd kidnapped him but who was now bragging about Daniel saving himself for him. Daniel just wanted to go. He would not now be happy until he reached the hotel.

After a further half hour of discussions, Daniel accepted another cup of coffee to quench his thirst. It was like black ditchwater, with very little in of the way of thirst-quenching properties, but it certainly kept him awake. He thanked the MD for his hospitality and they made their way back downstairs to the showroom where Daniel had one final look round and took some photographs of the boats. He shook hands with the MD and made his way to the door.

As he stepped outside and wandered over in the direction of the car, Daniel glanced into the courtyard to see no sign of life at all. He could only draw the conclusion that the factory, originally run by the MD, had been in financial difficulties, and possibly Han and Lim were putting money in to develop it into a successful business. On the other hand, if that were the case surely they would have shown Daniel the other factory, the one making the new moulds. Once again, things did not add up.

Han came back to the car and within seconds they were thundering off down the road. "So what do you think?" he asked proudly.

"It certainly gives me food for thought. It was very quiet though, I found it quite surprising."

"Yes, today was a day when many of the workers were off. If we had come on Monday you would have seen much more activity."

"Hmm." Daniel was absorbed in the passing landscape and his own thoughts.

"Do you want to work with us?" came the blunt question after a couple of miles.

"There may be possibilities there, but I would like to see better quality hull finishes before we could move much further" Daniel replied. "I also only saw three boats there that were similar to the models that we're interested in purchasing, and I have to say Luke would not be happy until we had seen all our chosen models from the new moulds."

"Do not worry, this can be arranged. We will send one boat of each model to London for you. I guarantee that the boats will be from the new moulds. You will be happy with them."

"We could not possibly expect you to ship any boats to us on that basis. It is not fair on either you or us."

"Do not worry about fair on us, we will do this, it is not a problem." This was said as a statement and not something that required an answer, so Daniel did not bother.

The next 15 minutes were spent in almost complete silence, apart from the odd comment about the landscape. Then Han's mobile phone rang, breaking the silence. He glanced at the screen and answered the phone in English. Judging by the conversation, Daniel assumed that it must have been Lim on the other end checking to see how the day had gone.

"Yes, very good, they like very much and we will ship the first boats shortly. I will telephone you later" said Han. That was all Daniel heard on his end, and Han did not elaborate on the caller's identity, so Daniel did not ask.

Han's driving seemed to be much more relaxed on the

return journey. Daniel was keeping a very close eye on the direction of their travel, but was relieved that they did indeed appear to be retracing their steps.

After another few miles the statement Daniel had been dreading all day finally arrived. "Tonight, I take you to a nightclub, you will never have a night like it before."

"Thank you very much for the offer, but please understand that I am still not feeling at all well" said Han. "I would please ask you just to take me back to the hotel. I know that this is very boring and I am sorry to turn down your kind hospitality, but I am afraid that this is the only thing I feel like doing. I also must phone my wife, because she had some trouble at home yesterday and I must check if she and my son are OK. I have not spoken to her since I arrived."

Han did not answer this, or even acknowledge that Daniel had spoken. They both sat in silence until they had almost reached the ferryport when Han asked," Do you want us to take the ferry back or we can take a different route round the coast?"

"I really do not mind Han, whichever route is the quickest would be the best by me."

"We will take the coast road which will give a different viewpoint for you."

"Thank you, that would be nice."

Han was now becoming more communicative, but Daniel was still not sure what he had in mind for him that evening. He decided to get a taxi back to the hotel if necessary.

They followed the coast road round and it did indeed make very pleasant viewing. As the journey progressed Han became more talkative, and by the time they reached the far side of the sea Han was in full flow with his life history, his political views and other small talk.

As they drove through one of the small seaside villages Han suddenly pulled the car off the road onto the dirt in front of a small parade of shops.

"Do you like chocolate?" he asked Daniel.

"Well yes, I don't have a very sweet tooth but sure, I like chocolate."

"You wait here. I get something typically Turkish for you."

Daniel sat and watched as Han walked round the front of the car, up the steps and into the small single-fronted shop. The car was parked directly in front of the shop, so Daniel had a good view of exactly what was happening inside. In the fading daylight, the lit interior of the shop was clear, and Daniel watched with interest as he saw Han having a laugh with the shopkeeper. Daniel saw Han sampling some of the sweets and pointing at various selections on the shelves. He then saw him heading out of the shop with a box. He walked up the to the passenger side of the car, opened Daniel's door and insisted that he try one of the sweets. Daniel duly obliged.

"Do you like?"

"Yes, it's certainly different."

"Good, I knew you would like."

With that Han disappeared back into the shop. The sweets were certainly unusual and Daniel wasn't quite sure whether he liked them or not. They were ultra-sweet squares with the texture of roof insulation. He watched as boxes of sweets were put into plastic bags and Han headed back towards the car.

He got in with two bags.

"These two boxes are for you and your wife, and these two are for you to take back for Luke and his family," he said as he placed the boxes on the back seat of the car.

"That is really very kind of you Han, thank you."

"It is my pleasure, you are my guest."

Daniel suddenly felt a pang of guilt for not accepting Han's hospitality more freely. Perhaps he had completely misread the situation, but then he made himself feel better again by telling himself to go with his gut instinct, because certainly things were not as straightforward as they should have been.

They pulled off back into the mainstream of traffic heading towards the city centre of Istanbul. Han was busy explaining the itinerary for the rest of his visit. Tomorrow he would pick Daniel up at about 9.30 when they would go to Han's office and meet with Lim. They would then go to Han's boat, where they would take a trip on the Bosphorus. In the afternoon Maya would take Daniel to the city centre to do some shopping in the White Shopping Centre and see a bit of the old city. After this Maya would take Daniel directly to Han's mother's home, from where they would go out for a celebratory meal.

Daniel was relieved to hear that Maya would play a large part in the following day's proceedings, and as they approached Istanbul city he was once again beginning to relax. He had suddenly become quite tired, although his hunger pangs had now long gone. He closed his eyes to save further conversation as they approached the outskirts of the city.

Within a short time they had drawn up at the hotel, where Han made one final vain attempt to entice Daniel out for the evening. Daniel very firmly told Han that this was not an option. The doorman opened the passenger door of the car. Daniel got out, thanked Han for the day and wandered into the lobby.

CHAPTER TWENTY EIGHT

The evening was young, but Daniel made straight for the bar and ordered a double whisky. He then made his way to one of the empty tables and sat down, exhausted. Not having eaten, the whisky soon had more than the desired effect, so Daniel thought he had better go into the dining room for dinner before consuming any more. He left the bar, wandered into the lobby and approached the reception desk on his way to the restaurant.

"Do you have any messages for me please?"

"Yes, Mr Cassidy. Your wife telephoned. The message was to stress that she is fine, but please call her if you're back before midnight Singapore time."

"Thank you."

Daniel would go and have a quick meal in the restaurant, then retire to his room and telephone Linda; he would be in good time. He wandered in to the restaurant and ordered a large T-Bone steak and chips. He decided that he had had enough alcohol that evening, so he sipped a Coca Cola as he waited for his meal to arrive. It arrived within fifteen minutes and Daniel tucked into it as if he had not eaten for a month.

Once he had finished, he did not hang around downstairs but made his way straight back upstairs to his bedroom. He was undoing his tie as he walked down the corridor and once in his room he threw the tie to one side and went straight over to the phone.

"Hi honey it's me," Daniel said as Linda answered. It was great to hear her voice and it would be easy to sit and chat for the rest of the evening, but he knew he had to keep the conversation short. He would not worry Linda with his suspicions and problems, as from the sound of it she was going to need his support, and he did not want to add to her concerns.

"Darling, how are things going?" she said. "I'm sorry if the phone call the other night worried you. I realise that there was nothing you could have done from Istanbul. Everything's under control now anyway."

"How is Sam?"

"He is just fine, full of the joys."

"Honey just briefly, what happened?"

"Well, I'll tell you all about it when you get back in detail." Linda then proceeded to tell Daniel most of the story from the previous evening.

"Anyway, how is everything going out there?"

"Not too bad. Bit of a disappointment I guess. I'm not sure whether we will be able to do business with them or not, but it was certainly worth the visit. Have you heard from Luke at all?"

"Yes, he telephoned earlier today and was concerned because he couldn't get hold of you on your mobile. He's asked me to ring him if I hear from you."

"Yes, unfortunately I sat on my mobile and broke it. Do you know how he got on?"

"He did say that the factory was fantastic and that unless things in Turkey were the ultimate in perfection you would be wasting your time because the whole American deal gelled really well."

"Tell him I'll see him in England on Sunday, as arranged. If he could arrange the flight out for both of us, possibly on Monday evening, I'll be home on Tuesday."

"I can't wait, I miss you so much. By the way what is the hotel like, a bit of a flea pit?"

"On the contrary, the hotel is actually too grand, I'll tell all when home. I miss you too honey, and I can't wait to get back. I had better go now because of the cost, so a big kiss for Sam and I'll see you both Tuesday."

"I'll meet you at the airport darling, bye for now."

Daniel replaced the receiver in its cradle and felt uplifted having spoken to Linda. It was a great relief to know that all was OK at that end. He also felt easier in his mind about his situation, having seen that the boat factory did exist, albeit not up to scratch with what he would have liked to see.

Daniel went for a shower, telephoned reception to arrange a wake-up call for 7.30 the following morning, and drifted immediately into a long overdue, deep sleep.

CHAPTER TWENTY NINE

Xu had in fact been in Istanbul since well before Daniel's arrival, arranging with Han all the necessary details for Daniels visit, although he kept his contact with Han to a minimum. The news that Daniel had wanted to pay a visit to the factory, rather than just accepting the product for what it was, had put Xu and Han into a bit of a tail spin, once again leaving them cussing Gordon. Gordon would simply have accepted sample stock into the UK for appraisal. How easy it would have been if everything had gone according to plan.

The small glass-fibre factory which they had purchased from the liquidators had suddenly needed a major transformation to give any form of credibility. It had had to be done within the couple of weeks or so that had been open to them before Daniel was due to arrive. It was going to be a tall order to make a derelict factory look as if it produced 4000 boats a year. They had been quite happy with the results of the showroom and offices, but had paid less attention to the quality of the products they had available to show Daniel. This, they now realised, could be their downfall. They were trying to impress in every area except the one that mattered the most.

Han had dropped Daniel at the hotel and made the half

hour's journey to his office further along the coast. As he drove up he could see the lights burning, and knew that Xu was waiting for a complete update. He locked the car, let himself into the office and made his way up to the first floor, where Xu was standing looking out of one of the full depth, panoramic windows with a cup of coffee in his hand.

"Didn't sound convincing," Xu said, without turning round, as Han entered the room.

"What do you mean?"

"You did not sound convincing when I spoke to you on the telephone earlier."

"Things were a bit difficult, he was in the car with me."

"So how did it go then?"

"I think they will take the boats. He was unhappy with the quality of the boats we had on show but I think I have convinced him that the ones we send to England will be from new moulds. Unfortunately they were still finishing the showroom when we arrived, so I had to tell him that we were refurbishing. I am not sure whether he was convinced or not, as there was very little happening at the factory, completely contrary to our instructions. The few people they had available were working on a small number of fibre glass pieces, with not one person working on a boat mould or hull. I could have strangled them there and then. "

"I need to know whether he is going to play ball or not, because if not, and he's going to get in our way, we will have to put alternative plans in play tomorrow. It will be our only chance. You must tell me one way or the other whether we are doing business with them or not."

"I'm sure it will be OK in the end, I will ensure that we wrap up a deal. I do not know why you are worrying so much, after all he only knows you as Edward, and he hardly knew which country we were in when we went to the factory."

"I do not like it, and he is not stupid, that is why I am worried. He is so suspicious of everything. He could just jeopardize the entire future of our business. I have invested a large amount of money in this business now and I intend to see it succeed, so between us we must ensure that it does. I will leave you to think about it overnight, and I will do the same. Tomorrow we must make the decision to continue with Daniel's company or to eradicate this problem and find somebody new and less suspicious in England. We need that market place and it needs sorting, now!"

"Yes I agree with you. I am sure that after the first few boats arrive in England and they are OK and their dealers like them they will sell them and make a profit and all will be fine from then on. I think they are just cautious as a matter of principle because they have not dealt with us before. They would probably be the same with anybody. We are just reading more into it and into his questions than we need to."

"Well for your sake, I hope you're right. We will reach the final decision in the morning. What time do we meet?"

"We will be here at about 10.15. Anyhow, I must be on my way now, as I have to collect my wife. I will see you in the morning."

"Is Sunjin ready with the boat."

"Yes he is all ready, we will be out for a couple of hours or so."

With that Han left the office and went back to the car. He took out his frustration on the car during the journey home, revving the poor old 2 litre engine until it bounced off the red line at every opportunity. He was fed up with the negative attitude of Xu, but understood the caution necessary. He was just annoyed that things weren't going as smoothly as he would have liked.

CHAPTER THIRTY

It had the beginnings of another fabulous day over Istanbul, with temperatures hovering around freezing, a beautiful deep blue sky and no wind as Daniel's early morning alarm call went off. Daniel had slept as if he had been on tranquilizers, and it took him some time to master the courage to get up.

He finally threw himself out of bed, pushed the button to open the curtains and made himself a cup of tea. He then sat up in bed, pondering the coming day's events. He was actually looking forward to some time out on the water, and it would be interesting to see Istanbul from this viewpoint. He was unsure what type of boat Han owned, but he felt sure that it would have been one of the larger models they made, hopefully with a cabin for some protection from the cold. He was also looking forward to the afternoon with Maya and to seeing a little more of the city. Yes, he was a much happier person this morning, and although he had one more night to stay, he felt that his illness could probably have improved a little today. After all, that evening's events were already planned, and he now felt more secure.

He whistled to himself as he had a shower, something he had not done since arriving. Once again he took full advantage of the superb breakfast on offer, after which he waited in the lobby for Han to arrive. He had already decided that if there was a problem with the hotel bill he would have to get Vera to telegraph some money into the hotel's bank account. While he was not happy about this he could see no other option. He had looked on the back of the hotel door to see if the tariff and room rate were published, but they were not. He was quite convinced that the rate would have been in the region of $1000 dollars per night, and while he was extremely upset the thought of spending this money, in reality he was just happy to get out. If that's what it took then that's what he would do. He would cross that bridge when he came to it.

Daniel had been waiting for at least half an hour when he saw the familiar Mercedes pull up to the front door of the hotel. He did not wait for Han to get out of the car but walked straight out and got into the passenger side. Han was full of smiles and immediately asked after Daniel's health.

"I feel a little better today thank you very much" he replied. "I'm sure that the fresh air out on the boat will help."

"Good, we will go to the office first and collect Edward. He has arrived and that is why I am a little bit late, I'm sorry."

Because they were running late, Han had obviously decided to stretch his racing skills to the limit, and within half a kilometre Daniel wished he was not in the car. He had to close his eyes at almost every turn of the wheel. They soon reached some single carriageway roads which were densely populated with traffic, much to Daniel's relief, and they followed the coast road round the edge of a large harbour. Daniel looked at the various shapes and sizes of boats moored on swinging moorings in the middle of the harbour. A little further on, the pontoons of a marina jutted out from the shore line. On the left-hand side of the road the shops were becoming smarter and the showrooms grander.

"Is your boat one of these in the marina? Daniel asked hopefully"

"No it is not one of these."

Daniel assumed that it must have been one of the smaller sports boats further out, bobbing about on their swinging moorings. He thought he recognised a couple of boats similar to those he had seen at the factory.

As they proceeded down the road the shops became more expensive and the boats on the other side got larger. It reminded Daniel of the south of France or Marbella.

Daniel was busy studying some of the shops on the left when Han pulled the car up abruptly on the right. He opened the window on Daniel's side of the car and leaned across. There were a number of extremely large motor yachts moored in a 'stern to' fashion against the wide pavement. The yacht opposite had its passerelle down, and a man of about 50 was standing on its fly bridge. The boat was extremely grand, but very sleek. Han shouted at the gentleman on the fly bridge and a few words went backwards and forwards in Turkish. After a minute or so Han indicated left, closed the window and they pulled back into the stream of traffic.

"Friend of yours?"

"Yes, actually he is my captain."

"Your captain?" Daniel said incredulously. "You mean, that is your boat!"

"Yes, you like it?"

"Do I like it - it looks superb! What is it?"

"She is an Italian Ferretti, 82 feet long. I have just had her built last year at a cost of $2.5 million." He announced this almost arrogantly, without a trace of humility.

"I very much look forward to seeing her more closely."

"Yes, first we go to my office and collect Edward. He is looking forward to seeing you again."

As the heavy flow of traffic crept forward slowly, Daniel doubled round to have another look at the yacht, which he had to admit was totally beyond anything he had imagined. However, this brought with it further doubts, and he wondered how Han could afford a yacht like that from a small boat building business. Either the other factory was as busy as Han described, in which case he should have been shown it, or his host had fingers in other pies, possibly not legitimate.

Again, the thought of drugs went through Daniel's mind and a new sense of unease crept over him. In what way was he being used, and for what? Again he told himself not to be stupid. It was probably just family money, and he should enjoy the experience. However, much as he told himself not to, his mind could not help reverting to the thought that he was involved with something far greater than just boat building, and that he could be in some sort of danger.

Approximately four miles on, they pulled up again on the side of the road. Han switched off the ignition and announced that they were at the office. Daniel glanced at the shoreside buildings and got out of the car. He followed him across the road and into one of the many doorways that led up some stairs and opened out into a hallway. They were met at the top of the stairs by a secretary who took their coats and offered Daniel a coffee, which he accepted with thanks. Han showed Daniel into one of the offices and asked him to have a seat. Han then disappeared from the room and went into one of the other offices, where Xu was waiting.

"What are your thoughts?" asked Xu.

"I think he will be fine. We should just carry on as normal."

"Well I hope you're right, but I don't trust him and I'm sure he's cottoned on to us. If anything comes to light this morning that makes us think he will jeopardise things we must be ready. Is everything on board?"

"Yes, but we must remember that if anything happens to him we will have the best of the police forces from Singapore to Scotland Yard asking around, and surely that is the last thing we need. We are better just letting things quietly drop."

"You may be right. Anyhow, let me come and greet our friend."

Daniel had not yet sat down. He stood at the full-length window, marvelling at the panoramic view which looked right out over the harbour and on down the Bosphorus. Suddenly he heard the door open behind him and turned to see Lim walking towards him with an outstretched hand and a smile. Daniel smiled and walked forward to shake his hand.

"Edward, it's very nice to see you again. How was Singapore?"

"Daniel," Lim said with a slight bow "Likewise. Singapore is very wet at the moment, it is good to enjoy the climate here."

"Yes I'm sure, when did you arrive?"

"Only last night, so I am suffering a little with jet lag. I hope Han has been looking after you during your stay?"

"Yes, he's been looking after me very well, thank you."

"Good. Well, tell me Daniel, what did you think of our small factory?"

"Well I have to say Edward, if I am honest with you, it was a little quieter than I expected and the quality of the hulls was not as good as I would have liked to see. However Han assures me that there are new moulds being built, and if this is the case then maybe there is something we can do with this. I have made it clear to Han and the MD of the factory that we would be unable to do anything until the all CE ratings were surpassed and certificated. Please don't think we are trying to be awkward, this would be the same with any importer in any European country now. All we are trying to do is to make sure we all do the job properly. After all, the last thing any of us want is the boats stuck at customs due to the wrong documentation."

"OK, OK, I see, so when the new moulds are done you will have no problem?"

"Yes, it is obviously something I have to discuss with my partners in the business, and I have to say we are looking at other manufacturers at the same time, but as with all these things we will have to throw price and quality into the melting pot and make sure that the package we come up with is the one we're happy with."

"I understand. Han and I are quite convinced that we will be doing many years of profitable business with you."

"That would be very nice, let's hope so."

"When you have finished your coffee we can make our way back to the boat."

Daniel finished what he had left of his coffee, which had not been particularly warm anyway, and they headed out of the office. He followed Han across to where the Mercedes was parked, while Lim headed off in a different direction to collect his own car. As Han turned the Mercedes round in the side road, a brand new Jaguar XK headed down the road towards them.

"Ah, here's Edward now," announced Han, pointing at the Jaguar.

"Does he keep that in Istanbul just for the short periods that he spends here?"

"Yes. He says he has more opportunity to drive it here than in Singapore."

"Well I can believe that, but he has more opportunity to write it off here as well!"

Han laughed at this comment and they drove off. They followed Lim the few miles back to the boat and parked behind him, opposite the stern of the yacht. The Captain was standing on the aft deck waiting to greet them.

As Daniel walked aboard he was trying to take in every detail. He was dumbstruck at the beauty of the vessel. It was truly magnificent in every respect. Even the after-deck floor was beautifully-laid teak and the fixtures and fittings were better than any Daniel had seen on a boat before.

Han had a quick discussion with the captain and then led Daniel and Lim into the main saloon, where once again Daniel was almost at a loss for words. The seating was all finished in a fine soft cream Italian leather. The latches and fasteners were all finished in gold, contrasting with the deep polished walnut. The cream carpet in the main saloon was so thick that Daniel thought if he fell off it he would sprain his ankle.

One of the cupboards along the side of the saloon was open and Daniel could see inside it a top-of-the-range Bang & Olufsen hi-fi system, which Han was quick to point out was plumbed to wherever required throughout the boat, including the engine room, at the flick of a few switches. Han then pushed the button on a remote control unit and another walnut fascia slid aside, exposing a 40 inch LCD wide screen television set. This could also be played through six speakers in the saloon. Within a few minutes Han had inserted the DVD into the player in another unit next to the television and was demonstrating the superb sound quality of the system. Daniel had to admit that it was the best he had seen and in truth he could have played with that alone for hours on end.

They then moved on to the galley area, which was all finished in limed oak with the surfaces and backdrop in what looked like solid marble. It was naturally very well appointed, with everything one could need, including a full height fridge freezer and microwave oven. Opposite the galley area was a large dining table with seating for twelve.

The next stop was the helm area, which had seating for eight people, all forward facing. The dashboard area alone was approximately two metres wide and loaded with instruments, dials and gadgets of all shapes and sizes and equipped with the very latest in satellite navigation aids. They then made their way down the forward staircase, where every step was under-lit and even the continuous handrail was lit with fibre optics down to the cabins, which were now all much as Daniel had come to expect. Every wall was lined with polished walnut, and every cabin had an en suite heads with plenty of room.

They made their way back and through a door into the engine room, where two huge Caterpillar diesel engines of 1300HP sat, one on either side. Again Daniel could have spent hours just looking and playing with machinery in the engine room.

As Daniel looked around he muttered "It really is a fantastic." Han overheard and responded "You too can have one of these my friend if your business goes well. Perhaps we sell many boats next year!"

Daniel laughed. "I like your optimism Han. Unfortunately I am a realist, but it's good to see it anyway."

They left the engine room through a door at the other end and entered another section of the boat with three more cabins. Although these were slightly less glamorous than the others, they were still better than those found on the average boat. These, Han informed him, were the crew's quarters. They left via an aft staircase and found themselves back up on the aft deck.

"That was quite a tour, thank you Han."

"I am very pleased you like it. Now we can show you how she performs."

With that Han went forward and issued some instructions

to the captain, who immediately fired up the two huge engines. After a few minutes of warming up, they cast off the lines and headed off down the Bosphorus. They helmed the boat from below in the warmth of the central heating in the cabin; none of them ventured up to the fly bridge as it was simply too cold. They had pootled out at a leisurely 10 or 12 knots until the harbour was but a speck in the distance before the captain felt it prudent to open up the two Caterpillars. Daniel could feel the immense power coming into play as it hurled this enormous piece of machinery up and onto the plane.

It was then that Daniel decided to wander outside. It was only as he opened the rear sliding doors that he realised how well insulated they all were inside. The noise outside was by comparison enormous, but the deep roar of those two thumping great engines was far from unpleasant. The temperature, on the other hand, was, and Daniel soon retreated back inside.

Their captain, who appeared to be the only member of staff on board, had left Han in control of the boat while he made a hot drink for everybody. Daniel gratefully accepted the cup of tea, as much as anything to warm his hands on. He went forward and sat up on one of the helm seats as the Ferretti ploughed forward at approximately 35 knots. Daniel now needed to use the toilet, and out of courtesy advised Han of his intentions before heading below.

"Wait, wait I come with you and show you."

"No, it is not necessary, I have used many sea toilets in the past. I honestly will be OK."

"OK, you go, you know where to go?"

"Yes, I remember, thank you."

With that Daniel made his way down the forward staircase, into the master cabin and through into the heads. While he stood at the bowl he looked at all the gadgetry and the fittings attached to the marble basin and shower units. He was impressed. When he had finished he looked for the toilet flush, but could not make sense of anything. The larger motor boats or yachts he had been used to had had a very obvious plunger-type handle next to the bowl, which when manually pumped, sucked raw sea water into the bowl and flushed it. He finally saw a small button down the side of the bowl itself, he assumed this must have been flush facility. Although he thought it was in an odd place, he bent down, and gingerly at first, pushed the button. He heard a motor whirr into life. He quickly took his finger off the button, and as he did so the motor stopped. He pushed the button again, but this time kept it depressed. He heard the motor start again, and within milliseconds a huge gush of high pressure water shot upwards from a small hole in the back of the bowl. It caught Daniel square in the face, completely drenching him.

He let go of the button in shock and jumped backwards as if he had just been shot. He grabbed a towel from the rail and quickly dried the worst of it off. Daniel looked in the mirror, covered with confusion and embarrassment. He did not dare push any more buttons, so after about five minutes he made his way back up the stairs with the damp still all over his clothing. Luckily, when he got back into the main saloon, Lim and Han were deep in conversation, so he quietly made his way to the other helm seat and sat down to take in the view.

Han started pointing at some of the historical buildings along the waterfront, while Daniel lapped up the information. Lim disappeared back to the main saloon with complete disinterest, and it was apparent that they had had an argument of some sort while Daniel had been below. The atmosphere was tense.

Han turned to Daniel. "Maya will be waiting for you in about one hour, so we have to turn round now" he said. With that he gently turned the Ferretti in a wide arc and they headed back on the other side of the waterway. The only chatter during the last hour of the trip was Daniel's questions about various monuments, palaces, or other interesting buildings which they saw en route.

The captain re-emerged approximately ten minutes from the mooring and took over the helm from that point. As they neared the bank Daniel could see Maya standing on the pavement, waiting to see them in. As the captain went astern into the mooring, Daniel jumped off to throw the lines aboard. For some reason he was pleased the trip was over. He went over to greet Maya, and they stood and talked while the others gathered their possessions and made ready to leave.

CHAPTER THIRTY ONE

Lim followed Han off the boat and they walked up to where Daniel and Maya were talking. Lim approached Daniel and offered a hand. He did not look Daniel in the eye but simply said " I must go now. I will see you back in Singapore." With that he turned his back on Daniel and Maya, muttered something to Han and then made his way back to his car and drove off.

Han, obviously feeling guilty for Lim's lack of communication, apologised and explained that Lim needed to go to an urgent meeting and that he had a lot on his mind at the moment. Daniel sensed that there was probably a lot more to it than Han was suggesting, but did not pry further.

The captain was busy tidying the ropes on the boat, so Daniel went back on board and thanked him for his hospitality before making his way back to the pavement, where Maya and Han stood by Maya's car.

"Maya will now look after you for the rest of the day. Maybe you can keep an eye on her for me to ensure she does not spend too much money!" Han said in jest, raising his eyebrows at Maya as he did so. "I too have a meeting now, so I will see you this evening for the dinner with my mother, you will enjoy this evening."

"I look forward to it Han, and thank you for the trip on your magnificent boat. I have to admit that I have learned a lot." Daniel got into the passenger side of Maya's car, and as he did so Han wandered back up to the Mercedes.

Daniel felt much more comfortable with Maya's driving than he did with Han's, and during the course of the journey, when Daniel was on the subject of cars, Maya made a comment that did not come as a surprise to Daniel.

"I did not like Mercedes before, but now Han has rented this one, and I have driven it a couple of times, it is really a very nice car."

"What has happened to his BMW?" Daniel asked.

"Oh, it is so old it keeps on breaking down and now something else has gone wrong. That is why he rents the Mercedes for your visit."

Daniel was relieved to hear that the BMW did in fact exist and thought Han's comments about owning the Mercedes must be nothing but bravado. He could not help but wonder why somebody who owned a $2.5 million yacht had to rent a car because his own was so old and unreliable. It simply did not make sense, but it would not be fair to push Maya for answers.

Within twenty minutes they had arrived at the White Centre and parked in the multi-storey car park. They could have been in the car park of any shopping centre in the world, but Daniel was looking forward to seeing the different shops, and the products they had to offer.

Daniel was impressed by the general quality of the goods on display and within the hour had made several purchases, mostly of clothing. Maya, he noted, had refrained from spending money, but was able to give Daniel good advice when it came to his indecision about what to buy for Linda. They left the White Centre on foot and wandered around some of the local streets, which turned out to be a less pleasurable experience. They were hampered by begging children at every corner, tugging at their clothes and asking for money. It was all very different from Singapore.

Later that afternoon, when they had been walking for several hours, Maya suggested they went for a coffee at a little coffee shop she could recommend. It was a very old building, heavily beamed inside, and decidedly cosy on this cold afternoon. They both sat and sipped at cappucinos while Maya gave a general insight into life in Istanbul, telling of her own upbringing. It was apparent that she knew very little of Han's business.

Daniel wanted to stop at one of the many carpet shops he'd seen that afternoon, just to get an idea of the prices. There were vast quantities of superb rugs on offer, many of which he and Linda would have loved, but he knew the practicalities of getting them home were not so straightforward. So with an idea of the price in his head, he left the shop before getting involved in any bargaining with the very persistent shopkeeper. They left the shop laughing at his hard-sell attitude, and slowly wandered back towards the White centre and to the car. The afternoon had been the most relaxed since Daniel had arrived in Turkey, and he wished the whole stay had been as pleasurable.

Time was marching on as they left the car park. Maya

announced that it was only a fifteen-minute drive to Han's mother's apartment. "We should arrive at the perfect time, exactly when Han arrives" she said.

As they waited in the traffic on the way out of the city centre, Daniel decided to probe a little into Han's family background.

"Does Han's mother have an occupation, or does she lead a life of leisure now?" he asked.

"No, Eila does not have to work. When her husband died he left her very well provided for and she now spends most of her time travelling the world. In fact she has only just returned from Australia, and she's leaving for America in three weeks' time for a cruise. She is very much the lady of leisure, and I think you will like her very much."

"Very nice too! From that one assumes that her husband was a very wealthy man?"

"No not particularly, but he had a good job and they have led a comfortable life. They were able to give Han a good upbringing, but when her husband died he had a good insurance policy running and there is no doubt that she will never want for anything again."

Daniel thought once again about the boat and the two and a half million to buy it, as it was now apparent that it had obviously not come from that direction. Once again his suspicions were aroused.

As they approached the outskirts of the city the traffic began to thin and it was apparent to Daniel that they were entering a better neighbourhood, certainly a far cry from the half-built apartment blocks on the other side of the city. As they descended a hill on one of the quiet suburban roads, Daniel could see the Mercedes parked near the bottom.

"He has beaten us here. We will park behind Han," Maya announced a she pulled the Volvo into the kerb. They got out of the car and walked down the hill to Eila's house. As they approached the front door, it opened and Han greeted them. The house was built into the side of a hill, set back from road, but only accessible via a small footpath. It was no architectural masterpiece from the outside, but nor were any of the houses. They were shown through into the sitting room, where Han's mother greeted them.

Eila was tall, younger looking than Daniel had expected, and expensively but tastefully dressed. The moment she greeted him he realised that he was indeed going to get on well with her. Han opened a bottle of champagne which they had put on ice, and they toasted Eila's birthday, which Daniel guessed was probably about her 60th. As they started to talk it was obvious that Eila was indeed very well-travelled, and they were soon lost in chatter about various parts of the globe.

After about an hour it was time for them to depart to the restaurant Han had booked in one of the hotels. They all made the ten-minute journey in the Mercedes, with both Han and Eila pointing out various aspects of this part of the city.

As the evening progressed Daniel was beginning to see a more human side of Han and he could see that Eila was very fond of her son, and that the feeling was mutual. Despite his confused state of mind, Daniel's confidence was beginning to grow, and he even started to risk a bit of banter and humour, some of which was at Han's expense, as he gradually tested the water. Han took it well. Daniel was definitely beginning to feel better now and even announced that he was in a fit state to enjoy a full meal that evening.

With tomorrow's departure now imminent the only main worry Daniel had was the hotel bill. While he knew he would be able to sort it out, it was the embarrassment and the time it would take to do so that was worrying him. He tried not think about it and to try to enjoy at least one of his evenings in Istanbul.

They left the car in one of the side roads, and as time was on their side, they spent half an hour wandering around the waterfront streets, which were waking up for the evening and already busy. The restaurant Han had booked for the birthday celebration was, it turned out, extremely large and took up a good percentage of the ground floor of one of the larger hotels. They were all shown to their table. No sooner had they sat down when Han's mobile rang, and he spent the next fifteen minutes away from the table talking to the caller. By the time he came back the rest of the group had already decided what to order. He sat down for five minutes and had just made his choice from the menu when his phone rang again, and as before he disappeared from the table for a further fifteen minutes. When he returned the second time, Maya decided she had had enough of this, and instructed him to turn his phone off. The request did not appear to go down well.

Halfway through the starter it was apparent that Han had not observed Maya's request. The phone rang again and Han, leaving his plate half full, disappeared to a corner of the restaurant for a third time. When he returned Eila had a go at him and Han apologised to Daniel for the interruptions. He explained that he had a big business deal which was not going as smoothly as he would have liked, and he needed to sort it out.

The rest of the meal was relatively uneventful until the dessert arrived, when Han excused himself and said he would be back in five minutes. Daniel did not mind this, as he found the company of the two ladies far more stimulating and interesting, particularly that evening, as Han appeared to be in a very vacant and distant mood.

When Daniel had finished his dessert he decided he needed the toilet and so he excused himself and wandered in the direction of the main foyer. On the other side of the foyer, he noticed Han with two similarly-aged, swarthy-looking Turkish men. The three of them appeared to be involved in a heated discussion. Daniel kept well out of their way and made his way to the gents and then back to the table. He had no idea that they were talking about him.

They were all on coffee and mints when Han finally returned to the table, apologising for his absence. It was immediately noticeable that the apology was not acceptable to either Maya or Eila, but in order to avoid spoiling the evening they continued to chat and enjoy themselves. There was no immediate necessity to leave, so they sat and talked for a good hour after they had finished the meal and during this time Han visibly began to relax. Daniel had to admit to feeling slightly sorry for him, because if his problems were bad enough to disturb an evening such as this, then he was obviously a fairly worried man.

Daniel was feeling weary by the time they left the restaurant, and back at Eila's house he declined the offer of a nightcap. Maya offered to drive him back to his hotel. They were due to collect him at nine the following morning for a visit to the Topkapi Palace of the old Ottoman Empire, something Daniel was looking forward to immensely. From there they were to go straight to the airport for Daniel's return flight.

He said goodbye to Maya and made his way straight up to his bedroom, where he enjoyed a long hot shower before collapsing into bed. He knew London was behind the local time zone, so he thought he would make a quick call to see if he could get hold of Luke and find out how he had got on.

"Welcome to the Orange answerphone" was the first response he got, with no reply coming from the house, which suggested that he had gone out for a meal. Daniel rolled over, and with the knowledge that there was nothing further to worry about that night, he swiftly fell into a deep, dreamy sleep.

CHAPTER THIRTY TWO

Daniel's blissful dream was interrupted by the sound of knocking. He somehow managed to build the knocking into the story that was going on in his head. It stopped and his dream continued, but then the knocking started again. He was finally thrown into the realms of semi-consciousness and realised that the knocking was in fact reality. He sat bolt upright in bed, sitting absolutely still, listening. It was dark, and for a few moments he was on the verge of panic as his brain raced to try and work out where he was, and when it was. He flicked on his bedside light and glanced at his watch; 12:30 am. He slowly realised that he had been in bed for only three quarters of an hour, and felt awful at being awoken from such a deep sleep.

The knocking started again, making Daniel jump. He leapt out of bed and made his way through the dining area into the main hall of the suite. He could see a glow of light coming through the peephole in the door and approached it gingerly. Perhaps there was an emergency, and staff were trying to inform him that he needed to leave his room, but as he looked through the spy hole reality set in once again. Han was standing there with two heavily made-up women.

He quickly withdrew his head and stood absolutely still,

his heart pounding. He continued to stand rooted to the spot as once again the knocking started, this time with more fervour.

He wondered how on earth to get out of this predicament. As he stood there the knocking started yet again, so he made his way back almost on tiptoe to the bedroom, where he sat on the end of the bed. He sat in silence with his mind racing, but drawing no sensible conclusion. He knew that if he let them in he would not be able to get rid of them, and the consequences did not bear thinking about.

The knocking had now stopped and Daniel started to make his way towards the door once again when suddenly a shrill ring from the phone broke the silence. He stared at the phone. There was no way he was going to answer it. As it continued to ring, he checked the spy hole in the door. He was horrified to see that the two women were still there.

Daniel was now panicking, wondering what would happen next. As he stood by the door his mind was piecing together the evening. He realised that as Maya was bringing him back to the hotel, Han had gone off to collect these women of disrepute. He was kicking himself for having admitted to feeling better, and again wondered what this was all in aid of. Perhaps blackmail was somehow on the agenda? But in any case he was married, and wanted none of it.

As he stood there he heard chattering outside the door and took another look to see Han appearing from the other end of the corridor with one of the hotel bellboys in tow. As they approached Daniel could see the bellboy laughing at whatever Han was telling him, and Daniel saw that he had a swipe card key in his hand. He was going to have to confront the situation, and it would be better done while there was a member of the hotel staff there. The bellboy knocked on the door, and almost before he had withdrawn his hand Daniel threw the door open, rubbing his eyes as if he had just been woken. He decided attack was the best form of defence.

"What the hell's going on?" he bellowed as he opened the door, "it's one o'clock in the bloody morning, and I was fast asleep, what on earth do you want?" He looked up, and, as if surprised to see Han standing behind the bellboy, said "Oh it's you Han, what is the meaning of this?" As he said this he looked disdainfully at the two ghastly women, leaving them with no illusions as to what he thought of them. Han muttered something in Turkish to the bellboy, who laughed and started to retreat. "Whatever it is you want Han it will have to wait till the morning" said Daniel. "I'm in no mood for games and I'm going back to bed." He slammed the door behind him. Daniel could tell Han was trying to get the bellboy to open the door, but he refused and continued on his way, much to Daniel's relief. Han started knocking again. Daniel put the security chain on the door and opened the door against it.

"Look Han, I don't know what you're playing at, but please just leave me in peace" he said. "I wish to get some sleep."

"No please just think, the girls... it will be fun, I get them specially."

"I don't care how specially you got them, I am not interested. Now please go away! I will see you in the morning."

"OK, but you will regret" Han said threateningly, with a look so cold it could have turned the Mediterranean to ice.

Daniel closed the door and a shiver ran down his spine. He was now wide awake. After he had unplugged the phone from its socket, he sat on the bed watching CNN, his mind churning over his situation. He was now so worried that he thought seriously about doing a midnight dash to the airport and getting on the first aircraft out of Turkey, but it was late, he was too tired, and while it seemed a good option right now he was sure he would be able to look at it more objectively in the morning.

He turned the TV and lights off and rolled over to try and get some sleep. But sleep now seemed far away. His imagination once again ran riot, particularly at Han's last comment.

CHAPTER THIRTY THREE

Luke made the journey from Waycross down to Orlando that same Thursday evening. He had been told about an exhibition at the Orange County Exhibition Centre in Orlando which finished on Saturday. It was midnight by the time he checked in to the Howard Johnson Motel near the West Gate of Disney World, and once in his room he spent a further hour updating the notes on his computer before retiring to sleep.

The next morning he did not wake until 11 o'clock, and the first thing he did was change his reservation with Continental Airlines to leave on the Saturday morning flight from Jacksonville rather than the Friday evening. Luke guessed that there must have been about a seven hour time difference between the United States and Turkey, so he tried to ring Daniel on his mobile and was surprised to get an English voice stating that the mobile was turned off. He assumed Daniel must have forgotten to take his mobile with him, and was curious to know how he was getting on.

Luke made the most of a huge fry-up breakfast at one of the many restaurants not far from the motel before heading to the convention centre. He spent the rest of the day once again looking for new ideas and new products. He left at about six o'clock and started on the five-hour drive from Orlando up to Jacksonville, stopping en route only for a Burger King. The exhibition had revealed nothing new, but it had certainly been worthwhile visiting.

He finally checked in to the Days Inn Motel at about 11 pm and organised a 5.30 alarm call. He had booked on the early flight from Jacksonville to Newark, where he would have a two-hour wait for the connecting flight to London. He would be back early Sunday.

CHAPTER THIRTY FOUR

Although only dozing in semi-consciousness, Daniel was woken by the alarm on his watch that Saturday morning and had a cup of tea in bed before starting to pack for the return journey. He was looking forward to going home, and as he looked round the room he hoped he would be able to afford a room like this with Linda and Sam at some stage in the future, when he would actually be able to enjoy it. He packed the bulk of his clothes, then went and showered before doing the final pack. Because of the bulk of the boxes of sweets, he put two boxes in his suitcase and the other two in his hand luggage.

As Daniel packed he was now seriously wondering whether Han would turn up that morning and pay the hotel bill? Would he be taken to the airport? Or did Han and Lim have something else in store, like an accidental drowning in the Bosphorus? The questions were endless, and Daniel was quite convinced now that boats were not what this was all about. He would not be happy until he was on the British Airways flight home.

He left his belongings in the room and wandered down to breakfast. Unfortunately his stomach was in such a knot that he did not eat much that morning, although he managed to force down some cereal and a little fruit. After breakfast he went back up to the room, collected the belongings he had put together on the bed and started to make his way back down to the foyer.

As he stepped out of the lift he could see Han at the reception desk. He took a deep breath and headed towards him. It appeared he was settling the account, but he was not sure.

When he was halfway across the grand marble foyer, Han turned round and saw Daniel walking towards him. He gave a big smile, but immediately dropped his gaze and would not look him in the eye. As he reached Daniel he held his right hand out to shake hands. Daniel dropped his cases and held his hand out, but could not bring himself to return the smile.

"Daniel, how are you? I am sorry for last night, I got carried away, please will you forgive me. Maya is in the car, do not say anything. She thinks I was at my mother's for longer. Please can you do this for me?"

"Yes Han, I will not say anything to Maya of course, but I have to say that your actions last night were wholly unsuitable, and while it is none of my business, I will speak my mind and say that I think you have a super wife, who quite honestly deserves better. With that, as far as I'm concerned, it is a closed chapter."

"Thank you, and once again I am sorry, but if we can put it to history then let's go and enjoy the morning."

"OK, let's go, but first I have to go and pay my bill."

"No need, it is already settled."

"That's good of you, thank you." Daniel managed a faint smile, more of relief than anything else.

Han had left the Mercedes outside the hotel with the engine idling. Daniel could see Maya sitting in the passenger seat looking in their direction. He put his case in the boot and got into the back of the car. As he did so Maya greeted him with a smile and said "Good to see you Daniel, how was your night? You must have slept well."

Han glanced at Daniel in the rear-view mirror as Daniel replied "Fine, thank you Maya, I must also say how much I enjoyed last evening. It was a wonderful end to a day with a relaxing meal and splendid company. How could one fail to sleep well after an evening like that?"

Daniel thought he saw Han almost physically relax at his comments, and smiled to himself. They took off in a remarkably relaxed manner, considering Han was at the wheel, and headed towards the Topkapi Palace, where they were due to spend the morning before going on to the airport. Maya pointed out her hospital and indeed did most of the talking in the car that morning. Han was unusually quiet, probably his conscience, Daniel thought.

They parked a short distance from the Palace and enjoyed the cold, bracing fresh air as they walked up the hill towards it. Daniel was fascinated by history, and as they entered the outer walls of the Palace he was determined to forget about the previous evening's events and enjoy the morning, making the most of the short time he had left there.

They wandered slowly through all the rooms full of memorabilia, slowly making their way to the inner chambers of the Palace from which, in the days of Constantinople, the Sultan had ruled the Ottoman Empire. It was truly fascinating, and as they wandered through the rooms of the harem and the eunuchs' quarters and on to the Sultan's quarters, it appeared as if the last Sultan could have walked out only days earlier with everything in place just as he had left it. They made their way to one of the Palace coffee shops and the three of them sat down for refreshment. Daniel noted that Han would not look him in the eye when he spoke or was spoken to, but Maya chatted away happily, enjoying the morning as much as Daniel was.

They passed down the other side of the Palace on the way out, viewing all the ancient horse-drawn coaches that had once transported some of the most powerful people in the world. The overall sense of historical magnificence left the imagination wondering in awe.

Much too quickly for Daniel's liking, it was time to head for the airport. They walked fairly briskly back to the car and within a short time were drawing up at the airport departures drop-off. Maya had been insistent that they should park and see Daniel into the airport and maybe have a drink with him before he left, but Daniel had been equally insistent that this was not necessary and that he would go through immigration and sit and read. They all stood outside the car, where Maya kissed Daniel goodbye and Han shook his hand. "It has been good to see you, thank you for visiting, and we look forward to supplying the boats" he said.

"Well, thank you very much for your hospitality, it has certainly been, er... a different experience. As for the boats, well, just let me know when you have the new moulds ready and I will see what we can do."

"Yes, you do not worry, we will sort it out for you and you will be very happy with what arrives, it is my guarantee!"

Daniel ignored the last comment, knowing perfectly well that he'd made it very clear that there was a lot more work to be done on the boats before they would accept them as a product line into the UK.

Daniel picked up his bags, said goodbye to them both once again and turned and headed into the airport terminal building. He stood just inside the doors fishing his passport and tickets from the inside pocket of his blazer and watched as Han and Maya drove off. As he saw the Mercedes disappear from view an overwhelming sense of relief overcame him, and his mood lifted as his brain began to work normally again.

He glanced up at the departures board and headed in a leisurely manner to check-in. He then wandered through to the departure lounge, where he browsed through the various duty-free items available. These included variations of the special Turkish sweets Daniel had been given by Han, and he decided to buy a further box for his parents. They were, after all, a bit different.

He sat down and opened his book. There was another forty-five minutes to go before boarding, but as he started to read the first page he was flooded with an overwhelming sense of tiredness, so he went to one of the bars and ordered a coffee. He sat and watched the world go by until the flight was called.

Daniel's British Airways flight to London was eventually called, so he made his way to the relevant gate, where a pretty

British Airways hostess was greeting people. As Daniel walked past she smiled at him and said. "Good afternoon sir, welcome to British Airways. Can I ask you if you are carrying anything for anybody else?"

"Good afternoon. No, I am not" Daniel said with a smile. As he was stepping into the elephant's trunk leading to the aircraft, he realised what an odd question this was to be asked at this stage of boarding. In all the many hundreds of flights he Daniel had done in his lifetime he did not ever recall being asked such a question by one of the airline flight crew upon boarding. He missed a step as an unpleasant thought occurred to him, immediately followed by a wave of nausea.

What was in the sweets? Han had looked as if he had known the person he had bought them from. Was this all a big set-up? Was he being used as a fall guy to provide a diversion from something else, something bigger that was going on? Once again Daniel's imagination let rip, and by the time he reached his seat on the aircraft he was perspiring with worry. His mind leapt back to a book he had once read called *Midnight Express*, in which somebody caught trafficking drugs had been put in a Turkish jail. If this was some big set up, Daniel decided he would rather get arrested in England, where there was more likelihood of people understanding the truth of what had happened.

Daniel thought through things again and tried to pull his brain into order. He remembered that it was a standard sweet shop they had stopped at, and everything had been wrapped and sealed. No, he was once again being daft. He tried to force the issue from his mind by thinking about Linda and Sam.

The tug began to push the aircraft back and within ten minutes they were airborne. As time proceeded Daniel once again began to relax, admittedly with the aid of a whisky and American dry ginger ale, going against his normal policy on drinking, but he decided he deserved it and it was after all a relatively short flight. He was too tired to read and soon fell asleep with his head on a pillow wedged between the seat and the window pillar.

The flight became increasingly bumpy as they approached Heathrow and it was no surprise to hear that the weather was wet, windy, and only four degrees Celsius. In the heavy crosswinds the landing was particularly heavy, leaving Daniel marvelling at how the tyres withstood such punishment.

As they taxied towards their gate for disembarkation, the stewardess gave the normal routine speech of how far the airport was from the centre of the city and the various options of how to get there, as well as where to go for onward reservations. The aircraft came to a halt, and even before the doors had been opened everybody was clambering to stand in the small aisles and retrieve their goods from the overhead lockers. They waited for a further five minutes before the stewardess announced over the tannoy, "Ladies and gentlemen, Her Majesty's Customs and Excise are waiting outside the aircraft doors, would you please all ensure that you have your passport readily available for inspection as you exit the aircraft. Thank you."

This was another new one on Daniel, and his heart began to beat so heavily he could almost see his shirt moving. If he had wanted confirmation of his suspicions then this was surely it. What the bloody hell should I do now, he thought to himself. The only thing he could do was to be perfectly honest. He was, after all, completely innocent.

The column of people on the far side of the aircraft started to move first, but within minutes his aisle was shuffling forwards towards the door. It was taking time, because every passport was being inspected. When Daniel finally approached the door a female officer in the smart dark customs uniform was standing just outside the door checking the passport of everybody that stepped off the aircraft. Daniel handed her his passport. She glanced at it and quickly handed it back to Daniel. "Please continue, Mr Cassidy" she said.

Daniel was in such a confused state of mind that the fact that the officer had used his name sent further panic through his body, but he soon realised that she had simply read it on his passport. He continued up the elephant trunk to the main walkway, where to his surprise there was a further queue. Two more customs officers were standing at the top of the gangway, accompanied by a Weimaraner sniffer dog. Daniel was once again plunged into a state of complete panic and on the verge of fainting, but he wandered on, not knowing whether to say anything voluntarily or not. The dog had a good sniff around Daniel's hand luggage but he was allowed to continue, which gave him a moment's relief until he realised that if they were going to pick him up they would anyhow wait until he had his main luggage from the aircraft hold.

He did not romp on down the moving walkway, as he would normally have done, but just stood there slowly making his way towards the baggage reclaim, not really knowing what was in store for him.

CHAPTER THIRTY FIVE

Grant Woodward had worked for HM Customs for the last 15 years and was now head of the Drugs Squad based in central London. He was 42 years old, six feet tall, fit, blonde-haired and of a burly build. During his time with Customs he had seen multitudes of imaginative ways that criminals had utilised to try and profit from their filthy trade. He had also heard all the excuses, and seen the damage that their greed caused to life. He was a seasoned officer of impeccable integrity, deeply respected by all those around him. Nobody questioned his judgment and authority.

Gill Bordeman was one of the drugs squad team leaders. She had been with Customs for eight years and was equally well-respected by those below and above her. She was set for greater things, and all the clever money was on her to take over from Grant when the time came.

Gill was monitoring a developing situation that had been brought to her attention by Turkish intelligence. There had apparently been a tip-off to the authorities in Turkey of a possible large drugs deal where the suspected target country was Great Britain. The Turkish authorities had been monitoring the situation for approximately three weeks and had recently had the suspected ringleader under surveillance.

Daniel's arrival in Istanbul had heightened speculation that London was the final destination for the goods, and they had not let Daniel or Han out of their sight since Daniel's arrival in Turkey, except when they had lost them when they had failed to get onto the ferry across the Marmara Sea. They had re-established contact when Han had gone back to his house on the Saturday evening.

Gill had recently received a telex advising that Daniel was on the British Airways flight to Heathrow. She and some of her colleagues would be there when he arrived. Grant had asked to be kept abreast of all the latest developments.

At this stage they only had suspicions to go on as a result of a tip-off from a Turk who claimed to know what was going on. As in many cases, the tip-off could be from somebody trying to cause trouble because of a grudge or jealousy that he or she was bearing, but all leads had to be followed up. In this particular instance the Turkish authorities seemed fairly certain that there was a foundation to the case, so both they and the British authorities were allocating a reasonable amount of time to the inquiry.

When Daniel had been collected at the airport by Han in Istanbul the Turkish authorities had set to work straight away to find out who he was and where he came from. The details had been passed to Gill in London and her team were doing the rest of the research. They now knew most of Daniel's movements for the previous few weeks and indeed had the Singapore authorities doing some homework over there. Daniel Cassidy did not even have so much as a parking ticket to his name and certainly did not frequent the company of any known villains. It was at this stage a mystery to the team as to what his involvement was with Han. It could in their opinion, only have been money-motivated if he was indeed part of a plot.

Gill and two other members of her team sat and watched the video monitors as the British Airways flight from Istanbul disembarked. The call came through from the customs official standing outside the aircraft doors advising them what Daniel was wearing. They would keep track of him on video from now on.

They caught sight of Daniel standing on a moving walkway and watched as he passed through immigration. They had specifically requested that BAA use the carousel for luggage closest to the customs post for this flight, baggage reclaim number five. Daniel's luggage had been tagged in Istanbul and would be inspected before it ever reached the carousel.

Gill gave instructions to the uniformed staff on the ground, and they waited.

The Customs team watched the different monitors as Daniel progressed through the airport and came into view on different cameras. Gill remarked on how uncomfortable he looked "A man with something on his mind, if ever I saw one." she remarked.

Daniel followed the path for EU passport holders and stood patiently in the queue, which was progressing quite quickly. When he reached the desk he was convinced that they were taking a far longer look at his passport than any of the others that had preceded him, but then the officer handed back to him with a smile and without saying anything looked at the next person in the queue. Daniel moved on and put his hand luggage down for a moment in order to put his passport and paperwork in his inside pocket. He then looked at the television monitor advising him which carousel would carry the luggage from his flight. Seeing it was belt number five, he made his way down the escalators to the baggage reclaim hall.

When Daniel reached reclaim number five he was one of the last to arrive, but he soon found a gap in the waiting crowd, where he stood patiently and watched for his suitcase. After a couple of minutes the carousel started to rotate and after a couple of minutes more the first cases started to appear. About fifteen minutes had now passed and still there was no sign of his case. Daniel was beginning to get worried as there were now only about four cases doing a continual loop round the conveyor and all but a few people had now retrieved their luggage and gone on their way. He stood with his hand luggage between his feet and looked around him, noticing that the green 'nothing to declare' channel was right opposite the carousel.

The tall, grey-haired customs officer stood at the entrance of the nothing to declare zone. His hands were clasped behind his back as he rocked on his heels and looked straight ahead to where Daniel was standing. Daniel averted his gaze and looked back at the carousel, again telling himself not be so daft and wishing to himself that he did not have such a fertile imagination. Daniel stood for another five minutes, during which time a few more bags had appeared. He was totally alone and on the verge of going to lost property when he saw his case come through the rubber curtain at the beginning of the belt. Daniel sighed with relief and took a couple of steps closer to the belt ready to pull the case off.

Daniel picked up his hand luggage, pulled the handle out on his wheeled case, and made his way towards the 'nothing to declare' zone. The customs officer did not look at Daniel as he passed. Daniel entered the section with white tables down either side and there were no other customs officers in sight. Daniel's mood immediately lifted, but this was short lived. The officer who had been standing outside the zone turned round behind Daniel and followed him.

The next thing Daniel knew was an authoritative voice behind him at close quarters saying, "Excuse me sir, would you mind stepping over here for a minute." It was an order, not a question.

Daniel turned round with a start, and must have looked as if he had just seen a ghost, as all the colour drained from him. He just stood there and stared at the customs officer for a moment that seemed like an eternity.

"Over here, please sir," the officer said, gesturing toward one of the tables.

Daniel said nothing and almost as if in a trance wandered over to one of the tables on one side of the hall.

"Where have you just travelled from sir?"

Daniel simply looked at the officer blankly while his mind tried to make sense of the situation. He thought to himself what a bloody stupid question that was, because he had seen Daniel standing at the Istanbul carousel for the last half an hour.

"Where have you just come from sir?" the officer repeated, with noticeably less empathy.

Daniel was so worried about the situation in hand that his voice box and jaws just simply would not work.

"You do speak English don't you sir?"

Daniel, realising how stupid he looked, finally managed at to utter "Istanbul" although it sounded as if it has been spoken by somebody who had lost their voice.

"I'm sorry sir, I did not catch that, what did you say?"

"Istanbul" Daniel managed to say with a little more gusto.

"Would you mind putting your cases up on the table please sir?"

Daniel put his hand luggage on the table and then heaved his suitcase up as well.

"Did you pack your suitcase yourself sir?"

"Er... yes, yes I did."

"Was it at any time out of your sight between you packing the case and checking it in at the airport?"

"Well, it was locked in the boot of the car while I did some sightseeing this morning but apart from that not at all."

"Are you carrying anything for anybody other than yourself?"

"Yes, well sort of, the only things I have are some sweets that were given to me by my hosts in Turkey."

"And just what was the purpose of your visit to Istanbul?"

"Well, I am in the marine industry and we were looking at a factory in Turkey that may possibly be able to make some products for us, so the idea was to inspect the factories and the products to see if they were suitable."

"I see sir."

Daniel was now beginning to feel a little easier, having offloaded the reason for his visit and the fact that he was indeed carrying some sweets which he had not personally purchased.

"I trust it was a successful trip sir?"

"I hope so, but time will tell on that one."

To Daniel's surprise, the customs officer did not ask him to open his case, but simply said "Have a good onward journey sir, and I'm sorry for the inconvenience."

Daniel collected his luggage from the table without saying a further word, and continued through the customs hall and out to where the throngs of people waited. He walked through them completely oblivious to everybody and everything. He was dizzy with relief, and it was almost as much as he could do to stay upright without his legs collapsing from underneath him. He made his way on the underground walkway to the bus terminal, where he would get the airport link bus to Gatwick airport and a taxi home from there. He thought he had truly been through the worst few days of his life and was once again overcome with tiredness. He could not wait to get home to his own house and his own bed. He felt he could sleep for a week.

As Gill Bordeman stared at the monitor, thinking it to herself that it could not be this easy, the phone on the desk in front of her rang. She picked it up before it had a chance to ring a second time. It was Bill, the customs officer on the air side who had made the inspection of Daniel's case.

"Gill, it's completely clean, only a couple of packets of confectionery which are all in order."

"Thank you Bill, we'll take it from here." She replaced the receiver.

"He's clean," she turned and repeated to the others sitting around her, "Let's use standard monitoring, but I don't think there's any need for surveillance. He's fairly predictable and got a family to look after. Just get the guys down there to ask him what the nature of his business was over in Turkey and let's see what story comes back, he's probably completely legitimate."

Gill went over to another desk, picked up the phone to Grant and updated him on the situation.

Daniel's journey seemed to have gone on forever, but he was now on the final leg back to his house with a taxi driver who would not stop talking. He was tempted to say something to the driver, but decided to grin and bear the incessant chatter about what the weather had been doing over the past few days and his views on other political hot potatoes such as the price of fuel.

He arrived home not long before midnight to see the house welcomingly lit up. Luke was obviously home, and Daniel started to wake up at the thought of all the information the two of them had to share. He was dying to know how things had gone in the US. He almost laughed out loud at his own stupid suspicions that had made his life a misery over the last few days. He knew only too well what Luke's view on it all would be.

Daniel's keys were in his case, so he rang the front doorbell, stood and waited. Luke eventually appeared, looking groggy-eyed and dishevelled. He had been asleep on the sofa waiting for Daniel's return. He put two more logs on the fire, which had almost gone out, as Daniel poured them both a whisky.

They collapsed into leather armchairs and Luke, unable to contain himself any longer, said, "So how did it go then, what were the boats like?"

Daniel paused for a while and then said. "In a nutshell, the boats were lousy and the whole trip was lousy, despite having money spent like water to impress me. To be honest I'm so pleased to be back. But it's a long story, so why don't you tell me how you got on first?"

Luke started to tell Daniel about his trip, with the bare minimum of relevant detail. Daniel had to ask question after question to build up a picture of the factory and its people and products. Luke then produced a brochure and a dealer manual with detailed product and accessory pricing, which they both pored over until the early hours. When they had both fallen half asleep, they decided that they would continue their conversation the next day.

As Daniel lay in bed waiting for sleep to overtake him, he knew that they would certainly be going with the American factory. There was no comparison. At that moment he did not care if he never heard the word Turkey again.

CHAPTER THIRTY SIX

The following morning Daniel was the first to wake, at about 10.30. There was no panic that morning, because Luke had asked Vera to book them both on the evening direct flight from Heathrow to Singapore. Daniel went downstairs to make a couple of cups of tea, then went and knocked on Luke's door. Luke was still dead to the world, but he opened an eye and made a grunting noise, which Daniel took to be a thank you as Daniel placed the cup of tea next to his bed.

About an hour later Daniel was preparing a cooked breakfast in the kitchen, made up of all the leftovers that needed using before their departure for Singapore. Luke appeared about ten minutes later, and they started to discuss over breakfast all that needed doing upon their return to Singapore. As they talked Luke made notes in his diary, between mouthfuls. Daniel made it clear to Luke that in his opinion the American factory option was the only one worth entertaining. He would tell Luke all about his trip on the plane or while they were waiting at the airport departure lounge, but he gave Luke a quick idea of what the quality of the boats were like. Luke replied "The last thing we need to do is get involved with that sort of shit"

They spent the early afternoon shutting the house down,

chucking out food from the fridge and packing, although it would only be three or four weeks before one of them was back again. At one o' clock they phoned their wives to let them know their ETA in Singapore, but as usual Vera had beaten them to it and Linda and Michelle already knew.

They left the house and headed into the office for a few hours to catch up and ensure that all was under control. However with email and fax there was very little they could not do from the Singapore office, simply by monitoring the daily reports they had agreed to send over in the absence of Gordon.

Daniel and Luke sat in their economy class seats by one of the fire exits, which they always specifically asked Vera to request because it allowed them a little more legroom. They both settled in with a glass of red wine while Daniel proceeded to tell Luke step by step what had happened during the trip to Istanbul. He left out nothing, and to Luke the whole saga seemed to be a source of amusement. Daniel's story took well over an hour to tell, and when he had finally finished, Luke was convinced that all Daniel's worries had been in his mind.

"I'd have told you not be so bloody stupid if you had phoned me" he said. "Yes, but Luke, there were so many things that did not make sense. It's not as if it was just one isolated incident, something kept on backing up my suspicions."

"Sounds to me like the onset of paranoia, if you ask me." Luke said.

"Well, I can assure you that if you had been there you'd

have probably felt very differently" Daniel said with a hint of annoyance in his voice, knowing full well from the outset that there would have been no sympathy from Luke.

They both sat and browsed the in-flight magazine, for the next half hour or so until dinner arrived. They started to discuss the next actions for the UK company and what needed to be addressed in the next visit. The subject of Istanbul did not come up again; they both knew that the option of building boats in Turkey had been consigned to history. They would now put all their efforts into moving forward with the American factory.

As Daniel and Luke walked down the steps to the baggage claim at Singapore's Changi airport they could see beyond customs, behind the glass, Michelle, Linda and Sam all waving at them furiously with beaming smiles on their faces. Daniel and Luke waved back and wandered towards the conveyor. Both their cases were among the first off the aircraft, and before long there were hugs and kisses all round as they were reunited with their families.

Linda, Michelle and Sam had all come up to the airport in one car, so they had to divert via Luke and Michelle's house to drop him and Michelle off on the way home. Luke and Daniel had very little to do in the way of talking, as Michelle and Linda tried to bring them both up to date with the gossip in Singapore. There would be plenty of time to tell their stories later.

Linda and Daniel, after having put Sam to bed at a slightly later time because Daddy was home, collapsed into the rattan chairs on the veranda with a large gin and tonic each, loaded with ice. Daniel inquired as to what had happened with Salvia, and Linda told him the whole story.

"She has taken her stuff and she's gone, thank goodness" she concluded. "We'll get an advert put in this week for another amah and put that chapter behind us."

Daniel then proceeded to tell Linda all about his trip to Istanbul, again, leaving out no detail. Linda, knowing Daniel's uncanny perception of people and situations, did not take the issue nearly as lightly as Luke had done, but genuinely felt that Han had probably been summing Daniel up for some sort of illegitimate business.

"I think it's a very good job you stuck to your guns and didn't go out each night gallivanting with him" she said. "Who knows where you could have ended up? It sounds to me as if it was a fairly close shave. But what I don't understand is the involvement of Lim, unless he just felt he could earn a buck or two because he knew Han built boats, and realised that you were in the boat business."

"Yes honey, you might be right, but there are still several things that don't make sense. Anyway, I guess we will never know now, as it is certainly nothing Luke or I intend to follow up on. I think we're best out of it."

"You most certainly are. I'd worry myself silly if I thought you were going back there again, knowing what I now know. In any case the American deal makes much more sense and maybe I'll now get my trip to Disneyland with Sam, what a great excuse that would be. Perhaps when you and Luke go out to sign the contract with them we could all go, including

Michelle, and make a couple of weeks of it."

"Steady honey, perhaps a week at the most. But that's not a bad idea actually."

Within an hour they were in bed, but despite their tiredness, sleep was on neither of their minds. There was some serious catching up to do, and tension to relieve.

Daniel arrived in the office before seven o'clock the following morning and to his surprise found that Luke was there already. They both spent the next couple of hours going through the mounds of post Vera had left on their desks. She had looked after all the urgent mail that had come in and all the queries and new inquiries that had been made during their absence. She really was an angel of efficiency, and both Luke and Daniel knew that she was worth every cent they paid her.

They decided to fax the factory in Georgia and confirm their interest in becoming the sole agents for their products in the UK. They drafted a letter to give to Vera when she came in. They also copied all relevant information to the UK office and asked for any thoughts they may have on the subject before taking it further. They would shoot a fax off to Han stating that they were unfortunately not interested in the product they had to offer and thanking them for their hospitality. This letter would be copied to Lim at the Singapore office.

Vera arrived in the office at bang on nine o'clock, as always. Luke presented her with a box of Scottish Highland shortbread and some Russell and Bromley soaps that Linda and Michelle had bought during their trip to London. Every time either of them went away they always tried to buy a little something for Vera to show her that she was appreciated.

At about 9.30 Linda rang to remind Daniel to place the advert for the amah. She had not seen Daniel that morning, as he had been up and out of the house well before she had woken.

"Vera, did you hear about the frightening time Linda had during my absence?" he said.

"Yes, Linda spoke to me about it, it was most unfortunate and very frightening for her, but she handled it impeccably. Since that happened I have been asking around and I know a very good amah. She is working for some Chinese friends of mine, but she is looking for new employment when my friends go to work in Hong Kong next month."

"What is she like?" Daniel enquired.

"I think she might be a bit too strict for you Daniel, she is an old black-and-white Chinese amah, but very, very good, very clean and a good cook."

"Have you mentioned this to Linda?"

"No, I thought I would wait until you got back and discuss it with you before interfering."

"Well, I have no hesitation in asking if could you arrange a meeting for us, in fact I will ring Linda right now."

The meeting was arranged for the following morning, and the new amah was everything and more that Daniel and Linda were looking for. Her current employers had written a glowing reference for her and stated that they would not hesitate to recommend her to any future employer. She would start as soon as her other employers left Singapore, in about four weeks' time.

For the next few weeks their lives returned to a relatively mundane but settling routine, into the office at nine, home at five. Daniel and Linda got back into the social swing of things and thanks to Linda booking things up while Daniel was away, they were out three nights a week. During this period, in the absence of an amah, they had to utilise their new found babysitter, who was grateful for the money.

They had no response from the faxes to Han or Lim, so they assumed the Turks had let the whole lot drop. Curiously enough neither Luke nor Daniel had met Lim again in the Tanglin club, despite having been there a great number of times during those few weeks. They simply assumed he was out of town.

It was four weeks later, as they were planning the next trip to London and on to the United States with the families, that the phone rang in the office one morning. To the surprise of both of them, Vera announced that it was Lim on the phone.

Luke looked at Daniel quizzically.

"OK, I'll take it," said Daniel.

"Edward, Hi. Luke and I were just saying that we have not heard from you. How's it going?"

"Fine thank you Daniel. How are things with you?"

"Not too bad Edward, but very busy. Still I suppose I should not complain about that. Anyhow to what do we owe this pleasure Edward?"

"I am just phoning to let you know that I have just received word from Han that the first four boats are on the water on the way to your company in England, and he has asked me to assure you that they are all from the new moulds. You will be very pleased with them, they arrive in two weeks."

Daniel sat speechless for several moments before responding.

"But Edward, you must have received a fax? We specifically said that we were not interested. Following the trip to Turkey and the unsatisfactory state of the boats and, well, really the whole set up, we have signed up with another factory. I'm sorry Edward but your product cannot fit in with our modus operandi."

"What fax are you talking about?"

"We faxed you shortly after arriving back in Singapore. We also faxed Han with the same information."

"Well we never received the faxes and the boats are on their way to you, so you can take them in. We can discuss terms later."

"Edward, I'm sorry to be abrupt but there are no terms to discuss, we simply are unable to do business with you."

"This is very bad news, very, very bad news" he said gravely. "Well if you just look after the boats for a while, then we will arrange to take them away."

"Edward, are you in your office at the moment?"

"Yes."

"Let me have a talk to Luke about the situation and I'll ring you back this afternoon, but I have a funny feeling his reaction will be similar to mine. We have made a decision, and we do not have room to store excess stock. Anyhow leave it with me and I will come back to you later in the day." Daniel needed time to think.

"OK, I will talk with you later."

Daniel replaced the receiver and stared at Luke in disbelief.

"What's up?" asked Luke.

"They have only got four bloody boats on the way to us. They say they didn't get our faxes. I simply don't believe it."

"They can't do that!"

"I agree with you, but they just have, and they want us to take them in until they sell them on or remove them."

Vera, Daniel and Luke sat in silence for a few minutes. Daniel was the first to speak.

"I'll phone him back right now and inform him that under no circumstances can we take any responsibility for the boats and that they'll either have to find someone else in the UK or turn them round on the docks and ship them back. Vera, could you also do a letter to the same tune and fax it as well as posting it, with copies to Han in Istanbul?"

"Sure." She turned round and started tapping away on her computer keyboard. Daniel picked up the phone and dialled Lim's office. Lim answered the phone himself. "Hello?"

"Edward, it's Daniel. I have spoken to Luke and we agree you will have to find someone else to take the boats in. I'm sorry but we cannot help on this one."

"Well they are on the way, and all the documentation is filled out as coming to you, so can you just let them come to you before we arrange to collect?"

"No, I'm sorry we cannot Edward, we have a reputable business and we are not prepared to import boats that are not to our standards and more importantly ones that have no CE ratings or certificates. We could get into all sorts of trouble just importing them and that is something we are not prepared to do."

"We will pay you well for your inconvenience."

"Edward it's not about money, I can assure you, I am truly sorry but we are going to be unable to help."

"OK I will talk with Han." With that Lim simply hung up. Daniel was left just looking at the receiver.

"I think he's pissed off" Daniel announced to the other two as he replaced the handset in its cradle.

"Who gives a damn" Luke responded, without looking up from his computer screen.

"I had better go down and see him later in the week. After all he is a Tanglin club member and we're bound to bump into him sooner or later. It's better not to fall out with these people."

"Sure, but business is business" Luke responded. "So who cares?"

Daniel let the last comment drop. Vera handed the completed letter to him for his approval and signature.

He left the office that night and wandered out onto Beach Road, where the heat and humidity hit him as if he'd just walked into a steam room. As he walked towards the car park, he could not help but feel that they had not heard the last of Edward Lim. His thoughts again wandered back to Istanbul.

CHAPTER THIRTY SEVEN

After leaving the boat in Istanbul, Lim made his way back to the office on the harbourside to see Han before flying back out to Singapore via his home town of Kuala Lumpur. He entered the office by the side entrance. He was always careful about how he contacted Han and where he was seen with him, and used the alias of Edward Lim, the name shown on his false passport, in Istanbul as well. About two minutes later, Han arrived.

"In case there is a problem with them?" Lim said, laughing sarcastically. "I don't think there could be more of a problem! You have certainly picked the wrong partners for this one. You told me they would not be very thorough, but they want to know the ins and outs of everything. You told me the factory was ready and that you had answers to all his questions. All I can say is that you had better have the back-up in place mighty quick, because the boats have got to be in London in eight weeks. We are running out of time. This is the most important and critical part of the new business. It was left to you to organize it, and it is now becoming a fucking cock-up. You had better get things straight from here on in, or else! Do I make myself clear?"

"Yes perfectly. It will all run smoothly, believe me."

"I wish I could believe you. Unfortunately I am going to have to. You know the consequences if you fuck it up further."

Lim turned from the window and walked to the door. Just before he walked out he stopped. "I leave tonight for Singapore and by the time I get there I expect to hear some good news from you" he said. "In the meantime I will have another word with Daniel and Luke, and see if this is still a route for us."

With that Lim left the room. The next thing Han heard was the side door banging as Lim slammed it.

Lim drove straight from the office to the airport, where he returned the rented XK and got on the courtesy bus to the terminal. Within a couple of hours he would be airborne and heading for Kuala Lumpur.

Han wandered over to the drinks cabinet, poured himself a large whisky and went back to his desk. He took a large slurp and began to think of the best way to co-ordinate things. He still hoped in the back of his mind that Daniel's company would agree to be the consignee, but with this far from guaranteed, he now needed a reliable back up. The consequences otherwise did not bear thinking about.

The boats would not be ready to leave for another four weeks or so at the earliest, but he would see if Eugene, his colleague in London, had any ideas. He would talk to him in the morning when he would be less stressed, and put option two together. Plan one was still the preference, as it would look far more conventional and raise no questions.

Eugene was of Turkish origin, but naturalised British. He

was a short swarthy character with a friendly face and a good sense of humour. He had known Han for many years, and owned a small second-hand car yard in north-west London. It was not an ideal place to store boats, but it would have to be a back-up in the event of plan one failing. It was certainly less than ideal importing boats to a non marine-based company, and to get round this they would have no option but to consign them to Eugene himself as personal imports. Eugene was in any case going to help with the dispatch and general logistics once boats started to come into the country. He had actually been at the Boat Show in London with Han and had seen both Daniel and Luke, although he had stayed well out of sight. Han was to have introduced him as the buyer for the boats when they arrived.

Han had only spoken three or four times with Lim since the trip out on the Ferretti, and that was to advise him of progress. He could only ever ring him on his mobile, Lim's only point of contact. The mobile was in the name of Edward Lim, which would serve the purpose well should it ever be traced.

The boats were now in build, and would be ready for shipping on schedule. Approximately four weeks had now passed and Han sat in his office waiting for word from Lim, once he had spoken with Daniel or Luke. He now needed to know urgently whether they were on or off, as he had to start progressing the shipment. They had of course both received the fax from Daniel stating that they were not interested, but they had decided to bulldoze on and see if they could at least get the first two boats into the UK by the British company.

The phone on Han's desk rang and prompted him out of his daydream.

"Han, it's Edward. They are definitely not going to play ball. If we send the boats in consigned to them, they will end up sitting on the docks and we will be unable to move them. You will have to talk to Eugene and use plan two."

"OK, I will get everything moving and make the plans to collect the boats and get on to London."

"Let me know the schedule when you have it. I'll meet you in London, and by the way I'm pulling out of Singapore tomorrow, there is no further need to stay."

Han replaced the receiver and immediately picked it up again to phone Eugene.

"As I expected," said Eugene. "I have already started making some room in my yard. It's OK, they will be out of sight from the road and behind the yard gates. I have set up a company called Marinetrade Ltd. I know it has no history and is not known, but it might give some credibility when importing, rather than two boats coming to an individual."

"Good, please send me all the details for the shipping documents" said Han. "I will arrive in about three weeks and we can make the final preparations. Do you still have your Landcruiser?"

"Yes of course."

"Good, we will need that, and one more vehicle to tow the boats from the docks. Can you arrange that?"

"Leave it with me. Just let me know when you arrive and I will collect you at Heathrow."

"OK Eugene, I'll ring you."

CHAPTER THIRTY EIGHT

Daniel found Linda spring-cleaning the amah's quarters, which Salvia had left in a mess. She was dripping in perspiration and filthy, and had as much paint in her hair as she had managed to get on the walls, but she had done a fine job.

"I've only got another ten minutes or so, why don't you go and change?" she said. "By the time you're done I will be in to have a shower."

"OK honey. How was Sam today?"

"He's been asking about Disneyland again."

"Well it's all arranged honey, we will be going in three weeks' time. I'll spare you the details until you've got a drink in your hand."

He made his way back into the house and went upstairs to shower and change into some shorts and a T-shirt before coming back downstairs and pouring them both a gin and tonic. "A picture of contentment" said Linda as she joined him on the veranda.

"Unfortunately, the picture is deceptive" Daniel answered as his wife sank down next to him.

"Why do you say that?"

"Edward Lim was on the phone again today, and I can't help feeling we have not heard the last of him."

He told her about the conversation with Lim. Linda listened carefully, as she always did, before she passed comment. The sun had now slipped away behind the trees and darkness was falling, although the temperature did not change. Linda got up to switch the veranda lights on.

"So long as you have told him you will not accept any responsibility for the boats if they arrive in the UK, I'm sure he will heed that" she said. "After all it will cost him money if they sit at the dockside with delays, or are returned to him. Just make sure you have copies of the fax that was sent to him with the time and date of transmission in case there are any queries, but I don't see how there could be really."

Daniel pulled her closer and gave her a kiss on the forehead. "I'm sure you're right honey, I'll try and forget about it."

"Tell me what you have arranged for the States."

"Well, we're off, not next Friday, but the one afterwards. We fly to Jacksonville, then go straight to Georgia for two nights, where we are also meeting Bob Johnson from the UK office at the boat factory. He then flies back to the UK and the five of us are off to Orlando for a week. We'll then go back to the UK for two weeks although Luke and I might have to stay a little longer than that. Then home. What do you think?"

"I don't know how Sam will contain himself, but then come to that I don't think I can either, It'll be a wonderful trip. I can't wait!" She turned and gave him a big hug, almost spilling both their drinks.

"Steady honey, steady. You really are worse than Sam!"

"I'll go and put the pizzas in. Thank goodness Sue Lee starts in the morning."

"Yes, it will be a godsend. What time are we expecting her?"

"I told her to come at around elevenish."

The following morning, Daniel decided to stay at home to greet Sue Lee with Linda, which would also give him a chance to spend the morning with Sam. He had had too little time with him in the past few months and was missing him growing through this wonderful period of his life.

When Sam came in and woke them at eight o'clock, Daniel got up and went to make them both a cup of tea. They all went for a swim before breakfast and while Daniel washed up, Linda tidied the house, making sure it was in a presentable state, and one in which they expected it to be kept.

Sue Lee arrived at eleven sharp and Daniel carried her luggage from the taxi to her quarters for her, much to her embarrassment. They then all sat down to discuss timetables for meals, the dog's food and Sam's needs. It was clear that Sue Lee was going to run a tight ship.

Two days before they were due to leave for the US, Daniel was on his way home from the office when he decided to see if Lim was still in town. He got the lift up to the 12th floor, stepped out into the landing and made his way towards the offices of United European Marine Ltd. The door was closed as expected, so Daniel rang the intercom. There was no answer, so he tried once more. As he rang the second time a door opposite banged shut and there was the rustling of keys as a secretary locked up for the evening. When she turned round and saw Daniel she said. "Nobody there any more."

"I'm sorry" said Daniel "What do you mean?"

"They close up about a week ago, move out. Gone. My boss say he very naughty, he not pay any rent since he arrive."

"Oh, well thank you, I guess that's that then."

Daniel wandered back towards the lifts with a puzzled look on his face as the secretary made off in the opposite direction. He turned to ask her if there had been a forwarding address, but then realised that would have been a stupid question if he owed rent.

Daniel made his way down to the car park, trying to add this latest piece of information to the jigsaw in his mind. He would try calling Lim's office to see if there was an answering machine message. If nothing else, it would satisfy his own curiosity.

CHAPTER THIRTY NINE

Two days later they were all aboard a Singapore Airlines 747 400 jet eastbound for California via Hong Kong. They would spend one night in Bel Air to break the journey, particularly for Sam, before catching an onward flight to Jacksonville the following day.

The hotel in Bel Air was one Daniel had visited many years before with his parents. While not being the most expensive hotel around, it was delightful, with a fine pool and a good restaurant all set in pleasant gardens and surroundings.

They all arrived there late afternoon, all very tired. Sam was the only one who did not appear to be suffering too much, partly through having slept on the aircraft but more due to the prospect of Disney World. As they were checking in, the question came for the umpteenth time "Is this where Pooh Bear lives?" Once they had checked in, they all agreed that after they had taken their bags to the rooms a quick swim was in order, followed by a drink at the pool bar before changing for a quick meal and an early night.

The sun was beginning to set in the deep blue, clear sky over Los Angeles and the landscaped gardens were bathed in sunshine.

"I wish we were spending the entire break here" said Michelle. "It's paradise and Disney Land is only round the corner."

"You have to remember it's not all play" said Luke. "We've got work to do on the East Coast in Georgia, which is the whole excuse for the trip."

"How silly of me to forget!" Michelle responded sarcastically, without looking at him, but catching Linda's eye. Daniel noticed this but decided not to ask.

By the time they had finished dinner they were all ready for bed. Sam was the first to disturb the peace after only four and a half hours, when he decided he was hungry. Daniel took a while to wake up, initially not quite sure whether it was day or night, so he went to the window and drew back the curtain to see if it was daylight. It was not. He gave Sam some Weetabix they had brought with them, using the milk supplied in the fridge. Daniel decided to join Sam, and within minutes so did Linda. They switched on the television and ended up watching a re-run of 'I Love Lucy'. They were all back to sleep within the hour and woke up with the alarm call later that morning.

By the time they arrived at Jacksonville they had spent yet another entire day travelling and still had the journey to make up to Waycross, but they were all exhausted and decided they would wait and meet Bob Johnson in Jacksonville. He would be arriving the following morning and could join them all for the journey to Waycross the following day. They picked up their rental Chrysler Voyager people carrier and drove to the nearest motel. Here they checked in to the local Days Inn, then drove around and found a local Wal-Mart, where they stocked up on biscuits, milk, cereal, fruit juice and the other goodies they would require for the journey and the motel rooms over the next week.

They had supper at a local Pizza Hut before retiring for the evening.

Bob Johnson was as surprised as anyone when he saw the entourage waiting for him at Jacksonville airport the following morning, but he looked relieved, as he was not a well-travelled man. The mere thought of going to the States and having to find his way around had given him sleepless nights. He was relieved at the thought that he could now just tag along.

Daniel sat in the back with Sam, who had suddenly become very coy at the appearance of a new face. Luke, who had made the journey before, drove the few hours north to the factory. Linda and Michelle nattered to each other while Bob kept a barrage of questions coming at Luke.

They checked into the hotel in Waycross, which they had booked specifically because it had a pool, and left the women with Sam while Daniel, Luke and Bob headed off to the factory about fifteen minutes away to start discussing the finer points of the deal and the logistics of the operation.

Both Bob and Daniel were overawed by the immense scale of the production and efficiency of the plant, and delighted with the new products on display for them. The more Daniel saw, the more he realised what a contrast there was with Turkey. They had definitely made the right choice.

The heat was extreme, and after walking round the factory

for some thirty minutes they all welcomed the idea of returning to the air-conditioned meeting room for an ice-cold Coca Cola and to resume the talks. Daniel was immensely reassured by the whole business ethic of the US company; this was a normal way to do business. They wanted paying for the product before it left their shores. Parts inventories were discussed, and marketing budgets and support. There were certainly no oddities or suspicions here.

They spent the rest of that day at the factory, asking relevant questions and gleaning advice for the forthcoming partnership between their businesses. Bob, being at the sharp end of the business in the UK, was particularly happy to be part of the meetings and had much to input.

They had a working lunch at the premises and finally headed back to the motel at about 6 pm. After a swim with the girls, they headed off to the steakhouse that Luke had found on his last visit for dinner. Sam fell asleep during the supper, but by 9 pm they were back at the motel and all sound asleep. They were all tired and had an early start the next morning.

They drove back to Jacksonville early the following morning, dropping Bob at the airport for his flight back to the UK. Then they headed down the A1A towards Daytona Beach. While Sam enjoyed the sand, the others chatted and sunbathed. They left at about 4 pm and were checked in to the Howard Johnson by seven, where they would now stay until they returned to Jacksonville for the return flight at the end of that week. The girls were happy to be able to unpack clothes and hang them up, knowing they were staying for a while.

The hotel ran a shuttle bus to the main gate of Disneyworld, and they were all on board the first one to leave the next morning. It wasn't just Sam who enjoyed the day, and they were thoroughly relaxed by the time they sat around the pool that evening discussing the day' events. The following day they were due to go to the Epcot centre, then Universal studios. Daniel and Luke were particularly keen to go to the Kennedy Space Centre, which they planned for the last day while the girls went shopping to Florida Mall. Before it was finally time to fly back to London, they all agreed that they needed three times as long to enjoy Florida properly.

CHAPTER FORTY

Daniel and Luke spent all the following week at the office preparing the staff for the new products that were due to arrive, as well as trying to smooth things over with one of the Singapore company customers who was not happy when a forty foot container had arrived with everything damaged. It had taken all Daniel's diplomatic skills to calm the customer down, as the damaged goods could not be sold and they would lose a number of weeks' sales before replacements could be manufactured and brought in. On further investigation it transpired that the shipping line had actually dropped the container from a crane on the docks, when it had been incorrectly hooked up, so they would pick up the tab.

They were all heading to Dorset that weekend to stay with Daniel's parents before flying back to Singapore on the Monday. The original intention had been for Linda, Michelle and Sam to head back to Singapore, but they had decided that there was no real urgency, so they would wait until the boys went back and make more of a break of it.

They travelled to Dorset on the Friday night and were up early the next morning for breakfast. Daniel's mother asked if they had seen the news that morning.

"No, why do you ask?"

"Just that there was quite a bit about boats."

"Oh really," said Linda, "tell us more."

CHAPTER FORTY ONE

Grant, Gill and the team at HM Customs had over the past few weeks realised that there had been no contact between Daniel Cassidy and the Turk. Having monitored his movements and tapped into the office and home phone lines, they were now fairly sure that Daniel Cassidy did indeed have nothing to do with Han.

The Singapore authorities had advised Gill that there had been one or two faxes to Turkey initially, but these had been intercepted and read. The relationship was clearly an honest one, at least from one side. Of more concern to the authorities in Singapore was the identity of a Mr Edward Lim, a person with whom Daniel had had some contact in the same connection, but for whom they could find no background information. They had kept an eye on his office after the phone calls to Daniel, but found no movement. It was not until a week later, when they had let themselves in and found the office deserted, that their suspicions were even more aroused.

Daniel Cassidy was out of town, but they wanted to talk to him when he returned to see if he could help solve this mystery, although they knew from the nature of his fax that he was innocent of any involvement with him.

The British authorities were convinced that Han was up to no good, although no proof had yet been forthcoming and it had all been very quiet for a while. They were beginning to lose interest. Then one day they had a message from the Turkish authorities advising them that two boats had arrived at the docks and that one of Han's companies was the consignor, with a company called Marinetrade Ltd being the consignee in London. The boats would be inspected before leaving Turkey. The boats were due to be shipped on the vessel the *Pan Ultima* in two days' time.

Han had been extremely good at covering his tracks in Turkey, and indeed had spent a lot of time in Israel while things at the factory had been put together. He had only made contact with the managing director of the factory by phone since the visit with Daniel, and always from public phones, never any phone which could be traceable to him. This was on the advice of Xu, advice he had adhered to closely. He had not visited the factory again, and would not now see the boats until they were delivered to the new owners in the UK.

The boats had been towed to the docks on their own trailers by two separate vehicles, both with false plates and driven by two of Han's acquaintances, who had owed him a favour or two. The paperwork was sealed in envelopes and all they had to do was drop the boats off at the docks and leave.

It was while the paperwork was being processed that the warning bells had rung in the shipping company's office. They had a list from customs, and if any name on it appeared on any paperwork, they were to be informed immediately. Customs hauled the boats to one of their sheds and had a good look round them. They also put the dogs through the boats but touched nothing. Their observations were forwarded to London.

The two boats were cleared from the Turkish side and duly loaded into the belly of the *Pan Ultima*, which was sitting at the dockside, the next day. The sailing would take just over a week.

Gill and Grant would have a team standing by to do a closer inspection when the boats arrived at Southampton.

A week before the arrival of the *Pan Ultima*, Grant's phone rang.

"Grant, it's Gill – listen, there's an interesting scenario developing."

"How do you mean?"

"Guess who has just arrived on a flight from the US into Heathrow?"

"Han, I would think, but that would be no great surprise."

"No, think again, our friend Daniel Cassidy."

There was a moment's silence.

"Well, that is a coincidence – what timing!"

"Exactly. Maybe our hunch was wrong and Daniel has been cleverer than we think in all this. He's got his whole family in tow and he's here with his business partner and his wife as well."

"We'd better see what he and his partner are up to, make sure we know where they are at all times. By the way, what's the word on Han?"

"He was last seen taking a flight to Israel from Istanbul, but we're monitoring all likely entry points. He's bound to show if he has two craft arriving, I'll keep you informed."

"I have asked the boys at Southampton to tow the boats to one of our sheds immediately they are off loaded from the *Pan Ultima*. We'll head down first thing Friday morning, if you're happy with that?"

"Sounds good to me."

Three and a half hours later Gill rang Grant again.

"Grant, he's here, just flown in on a flight from Geneva to Luton. He seems to be heading to London, possibly to see his friend Eugene of Marinetrade Ltd."

"Well that would make sense. Two arrivals in one day, it's certainly all happening. Who's on that surveillance?"

"Mike and Helen are on that one at the moment."

"Good, allocate all the resources you need, I'll catch up with you later."

Gill rang off and started to make the necessary arrangements for the arrival of the boats, which they were quite sure contained some sort of illegitimate substance. They had already informed the Metropolitan Police of the possibility of it arriving on their patch, and that assistance would probably be needed if it did. They would wait and determine the substance and volume before causing a lot of upheaval for a few grams of dope.

Mike and Helen had followed Han in his rented Nissan to exactly where they thought he was heading, Eugene's car yard, the home of Marinetrade Ltd. They had logged onto his mobile frequency and were privy to everything that was said and it was all taped. They mused over the fact that nothing untoward was said and that most of the phone calls to him appeared to be from various women he was in different stages of relationships with. He seemed to have as many as eight women on the go, from those who were fresh into a relationship with him to those he was trying to get rid of. Nothing was said about the boats.

Han had booked into a local hotel within walking distance of Eugene's in an attempt to separate himself from Eugene and the storage place for the boats. He had told him not to talk to him by phone about the boats and only to discuss things when they were out in the open, and thought Eugene understood. Eugene, however, was not quite as careful about his conversations. While he may not have discussed things with Han over the phone, he was not so cautious with others. It was soon apparent that the boats were due to be towed back that Friday, with the money changing hands that same evening.

Grant and Gill, with the new information that was now forthcoming, gave the operation their undivided attention. That Friday morning, as they headed down the M3 from London to Southampton, they were quite chatty as the adrenaline started to flow with the anticipation of what they had in store that day. They now had ten undercover operatives on the case as well as the Met standing by for the anticipated bust later.

The *Pan Ultima* had docked the previous evening and had already started discharging. The boats were at that moment being taken into the customs clearance shed. Grant looked at the clock on the dashboard and pressed the accelerator a bit harder.

The news was that Daniel and Luke had done nothing of interest at all that week except work, and nothing unusual had occurred. Paul, who had been assigned to keep tabs on them, was becoming bored and felt he was missing out on the action. He smiled to himself as he remembered how the job had been described to him once by a colleague with whom he had been doing a stake out – 'hours of boredom, punctuated by moments of panic, followed by months of paperwork.' How very true, he thought, but he would not change his job for the world.

He knew from the telephone conversations he had been monitoring that they were all heading down to Daniel's parents that weekend, so Gill decided to call him off and told him to get himself to London to assist that evening. Paul had the engine running and the car rolling almost before Gill had finished giving the instruction.

Grant and Gill arrived at the docks at 11 am and had just walked into the office when one of the customs officers put the phone on hold and said to his boss, "I've got the shipping agents on the phone – want to know if the two boats have been cleared yet. They've got the customer on the line wanting to know when he can collect them."

Grant immediately intervened. "Tell them they will be cleared and ready for collection by 3 pm."

He looked across at the local division chief, who nodded and replied, "Yes, that should give us enough time."

"Make sure the shipping line stress that there is no problem and that they are going through the fast track clearance" said Grant. This message was relayed back to the shipping agents and ultimately on to Han and Eugene, who were standing by with two 4x4s ready to head down to Southampton to collect the boats. Based on this latest information they would make plans to leave London at 12.30.

Grant, Gill, the local divisional boss and three other officers headed down to the shed, where two springer spaniels and their handlers were waiting patiently for them.

"The Turkish authorities reckon there is something in the bow area of both boats, but they have not been in to investigate what" said Grant.

"I should say there is" said one of the handlers, "Poppy here is going mad and she's not been within ten feet of it yet."

"OK then" said Grant. "Let's get on with it."

With that they sent the first dog, Poppy, into the cockpit of the boat and gradually worked her forwards, ensuring that she investigated every locker and compartment. As she approached the bow area she started to whine and whimper, her tail wagging like mad. They removed the seat cushions on the forward V berth in the area of interest, but there were no lockers or compartments. She scrabbled at the surface of the fibreglass frantically.

"OK, cut it open, but in a way that we can patch it back up again, for his collection this afternoon. I don't want him to know we've been in here."

One of the officers came in with a small jigsaw and started to cut the hull open in an area that followed a natural ridge, one that could be patched up and not show to badly. The others waited outside while the glass fibre was being cut.

They heard the saw stop and then a shout.

"Fucking hell – You lot won't believe this!"

Grant was the first to scrabble back up onto the boat, hotly pursued by Gill. He peered into the small hole that had been cut.

"Jesus Christ, this is unreal!"

Stuffed inside the hull were what appeared to be a number of plastic bags. He made a small slit in one of them and brought a small amount of the substance out on the end of the knife.

"Well chaps and chapesses, we've got ourselves a whole lot of top grade heroin by the looks of it" he said. "The next step is to see where it's going. Patch this back up, and we'd better make bloody sure we don't lose sight of this lot. Are we equipped if the boats go in different directions?"

"Yes, it's all covered" replied Gill. "I don't think there are any eventualities I've missed."

"Good, get on to the Met and tell them we definitely will be needing their assistance tonight, and tell them to give it top priority. I don't want any of their usual excuses about manpower."

"Will do. If both these contain the same, there must be upward of thirty million pounds' worth here."

Everyone stood silently for a few moments. This was much, much bigger than any of them had dared imagine. It was going to be one of the largest drugs hauls ever.

They all wandered up to the offices. They would wait to celebrate after they had captured the people responsible. They were more than excited by what they had achieved, but knew it was far from over yet.

Grant was straight on to the Turkish authorities, who had wanted to be kept up to date with the situation. They were keen to get to the source of it, but still had no idea where the boats had originated from.

The hole was patched up so that it would only be noticeable on close inspection and by removing some carpet. It was allowed to dry for half an hour before the seats were put back in. The boats were then towed back to the shipping company's storage yard to await collection by Han or an accomplice.

Paul's phone rang as he was on his way towards London.

"Paul, it's Grant. Listen, I want you to get straight up to Eugene's yard, as we're fairly sure that is where they are going to be heading. I want you to find any vantage points that overlook the yard, set up the video - you know the form. I also want you to liaise with the Met. This is far bigger than any of us expected. There must be upward of thirty million quids' worth of heroin here."

"Bloody hell! That would be one of the biggest hauls in history."

"How right you are. That's why I don't want any screw-ups."

Paul had a renewed sense of urgency and put his foot down, taking his Omega up to 95 miles an hour. He kept an eye open for the traffic police. He couldn't be bothered with the agro of being stopped right now. It would only delay him.

As Paul approached, he met up with Mike and Helen a couple of streets away from Eugene's yard. They had been keeping an eye on the movements of Han and Eugene, and updated Paul with the geography of the yard and the offices. Another team had taken on the shadowing of Eugene and Han as they had left London in the Shogun and a rented Discovery.

They were all surprised that Han was personally getting so involved. This was unusual, as they normally would have sent disposable people until it was completely safe. He obviously thought he was invincible and had got away completely undetected.

Helen and Mike had witnessed new gates being put up in the entrance to Eugene's yard a couple of days previously. They were solid gates rather than barred gates as had been there before – they obviously did not want anyone to be able to peer in. There was a bathroom-type window overlooking the yard in one of the adjoining houses which would afford them the best view. Paul left the others and went to speak to the owner, while Mike was going to let himself into the yard and then into the offices to wire the place.

A young mother answered the door, with a baby in her arms and the sound of a toddler crying out from the kitchen at the back of the house. Paul explained that they were carrying out some routine surveillance and that they would like to use the room with the east facing window. After satisfying herself that he was indeed who he said he was, she reluctantly agreed. It had taken all Paul's charm to swing it. He had not wanted to get heavy with her.

The room in question was a small bathroom, with a toilet right under the window. The window was of a mottled glass with no proper visibility through it, and to Paul's disappointment the major part of the window would not open. The only part he could use was the small quarter window at the top. He clambered onto the toilet to see what view it afforded – it was perfect.

The next problem was how to set up the tripods for the video and the still cameras. It took him at least an hour to get the cameras into the right position, but when he'd finished, he had complete coverage of the yard. He could watch what was going on from the remote screen in the bathroom while the small quarter window only needed to be open a notch to allow full vision. Perfect.

There was no movement in the yard now, but it was not to be expected for a further three hours or so. He went to join Mike and Helen for a coffee at a local bar and to discuss with them what they needed to do from their side of things. They had just heard from Gill. Apparently the two vehicles had just arrived at the docks for the collection, and were with the shipping agents doing the paperwork at the moment. Han and Eugene would probably be back in London within a couple of hours. They needed to get back to their places round the yard in case anyone arrived early ready to collect the goods. They cut the coffee break short. Things were hotting up.

Gill and Grant were to follow the shipment, supported initially by some plain-clothes officers from the Hampshire constabulary. This duty would then be handed over to the Metropolitan Police, who would take up the operation from the Fleet motorway services London bound. Once the boats had been hooked up, Gill and Grant moved to a service station outside the docks; they would pick them up from there. They would be on the customs surveillance cameras until that point, so if there was an unexpected change of route, Gill and Grant would be informed by the officers watching the cameras.

Eugene followed Han and they exited the docks in exactly the anticipated direction. Before long they were on the M27 and heading north on the M3. Grant and Gill followed at a safe distance while two other Hampshire cars tailed them, one in front that would turn off at a junction and then reappear behind while the other moved up – they had the situation covered. Grant was happy for the moment. He phoned Paul to update him on the situation.

Immediately after putting the phone down to Paul, Grant's mobile rang again. It was head office in London. They had been monitoring all conversations on both Eugene's and Han's mobiles. Han seemed to think he was home and dry, because he had made a call in connection with the boats. It was to a Singapore mobile number but answered in London, not one they recognised as that of Daniel or Luke, but by a man calling himself Edward. The message was that everything was on schedule and that the goods would be collected on Saturday morning, as arranged.

"OK, thank you for that. Can you get on to the Singapore authorities and find out more on this number? Sounds like our friend Mr Lim has surfaced. By the way, with them returning this afternoon, I'm afraid it might be a late one, better warn the crew. Probably means we'll be out all night. But it'll be worth it."

Grant immediately phoned Paul, brought him up to date and asked him to brief the others in the field, as well as the police. None of them would be getting much sleep that night.

Han and Eugene trudged on up the M3 at a sedate 50 miles per hour; they were certainly not going to risk getting stopped for speeding, and blow it all during these last few hours before they made their millions. As they approached Fleet Services, they both pulled off. Alarm bells started ringing in the minds of the agents following. Could this be the actual drop point? Their fears were alleviated when Han and Eugene bought burgers, went back out and ate them in the car before continuing on their way.

The remainder of the journey was relatively uneventful, and the journey into London was not too congested, as all the commuter traffic was heading against them. It was not too difficult following a couple of large, white, slow-moving boats in any case.

As they arrived at the yard they blocked the traffic for a couple of minutes as Eugene got out to unlock the new gates. He swung them open and then pulled his vehicle in first. The yard was not enormous and the arrival of two large boats and their tow vehicles certainly dominated things, leaving only inches of room for Eugene to close the gates behind them.

Mike, Helen, Paul, Grant, Gill and three unmarked police cars, with three specially-trained officers in each, all took up positions. Paul was their eyes and ears inside, as the others for the time being could only monitor those arriving or leaving. None of them expected anyone to leave the confines of Eugene's place that evening. They would be too nervous about leaving such a valuable cargo unattended.

They all readied themselves for a long night, with one person at each vantage point staying awake to keep watch. Paul was joined by another colleague, Tim, at about 11 pm in the house, much to the disapproval of the owner, who by now wanted her bathroom back.

All was quiet until six minutes past eight the following morning, when Grant's mobile rang. It was a colleague from the office.

"Grant, listen, I'm phoning from home, it's all over the news this morning" he said.

"What on earth are you talking about, what's all over the news?"

"The BBC. The boats, the drugs. They even have pictures of the types of boats."

"Oh shit, you can't be serious! Get straight on to them, it's got to be blanked immediately or it will blow the whole thing apart, if it's not too late already. Also call ITN and anyone else you can. This must not go out again. Ring me back to confirm."

With that Grant hung up and rung Paul's number, briefly explaining things to Gill as he was dialling. Gill, who had been dozing in the back, was now wide awake and had listened to the conversation coming from the front of the car. She immediately rang the rest of the team.

"Paul, it's Grant. Is there any movement in there or is anything being said?"

"No, it would appear they are all asleep still, not a sound."

"Good, but I fear the contact may not show. It's been all over the news this morning."

"How can it have? Only we know!"

"Us and half the dockyard at Southampton by now. We're going to have to go in as soon as he tries to move the drugs or makes any attempt to leave. Keep me up to date, I'll warn the Met to be ready."

He closed his phone and swore as he chucked it into the floorwell. "People and their fucking big mouths, it's a bloody nightmare! Gill, can you brief the police?"

"Yes, sure." Gill contacted the officer in charge of the police operation as Grant sat in the driver's seat with his hands covering his face. They sat for a further hour, messages passing back and forth between them, their colleagues and the police. They were now all nervous, and it was beginning to show.

At about 9.30 Han appeared in the yard, followed closely by Eugene. Paul started to click away with the camera, simultaneously videoing every move. Han and Eugene had tools in their hands, which they then placed in the cockpit of one of the boats. They started to unhitch one boat and then move the tow vehicle into an L section of the yard, which had enough room for two or three cars, but not with trailers. They then did the same with the second boat, and then pushed the boats into the void left by the tow vehicles. Han then reversed the Discovery up to the back of the boats and opened the rear door.

"There is something going on, movement" Paul said into his radio. The others all just sat and listened, waiting, hardly daring to breathe in case they missed something. They knew it would not be much longer now. They were all quiet. They would not be happy until this was all over and everyone was safe.

"Han is entering the right hand boat with tools - it looks like a jigsaw" said Paul over the radio. "Eugene is laying an extension lead out to the boat. I can't see what's going on inside the cabin."

"Couple of minutes" Gill said quietly into her radio to all the teams waiting.

"Paul, when you have got video and still frame proof of preferably both of them with the substance, we'll move" Grant said.

"OK. I can hear the electrical appliance in operation, it won't be long now."

As Paul looked down he could see white dust start to appear from the cabin hatch. He stood on the toilet once again to look out of the small quarter window, which was clearer than looking at his small screen. It was the dust from the glass fibre and gel coat being cut by the jigsaw. Paul sat back down and watched his monitor once again, while Tim clicked away with the still camera every time anyone was in sight.

Eugene appeared at the hatch and got out of the boat, jumping to the ground. Han then appeared at the hatch and clambered out into the cockpit carrying two bags. He handed them to Eugene, who then turned round and placed them in the back of the Discovery. Han disappeared back into the boat and the procedure was repeated. Paul relayed to the teams all that was happening.

Grant and Gill had decided to wait until the men in the

yard had nearly finished offloading the second boat before they moved in. Before long they had moved on to the second boat and were removing its cargo in exactly the same manner. All of it was on film and still camera. There was now no doubt as to their intentions, and HM Customs had evidence that nobody could argue with.

"Knock knock knock!" Grant's words echoed through the radio system. Within seconds a sea of navy blue was surrounding the gate as the police opened it up by reversing a Range Rover into it. The gates gave little resistance and flew open from the centre as soon as the tow bar on the Range Rover touched them. The car pulled forward and the foot officers and Customs squads teamed into the small yard.

Han was standing in the cockpit of the second boat and Eugene had just placed another bag into the Discovery when the gates imploded with a crash, they both looked up, startled. Han could go nowhere, as he was immediately surrounded by armed police. Eugene thought he could run for it and bolted towards the road. The first policeman to try and stop him was sent sprawling, as Eugene hit him with enormous force, but after a small scuffle he was brought up short by the others at the gate, hopelessly outnumbered.

Han dropped the bag he was holding and looked around helplessly as he was told to put his hands on his head. They were both read their rights.

Grant's team spent the rest of the day taking down details and photographing the evidence and its places of concealment. Grant and Gill were annoyed at not having had the chance to catch the recipient of the consignment, but at least they had stopped an enormous amount of heroin hitting the streets. They would celebrate that evening.

One of Grant's first calls as he got back to the office that afternoon was to the Turkish authorities, without whom the raid might never have happened. He thanked them profusely, and they in turn said they would do everything possible to find out where the drugs and the boats had originated from, and to dam that flow.

CHAPTER FORTY TWO

Xu had been up early that morning. He was to do the money brokering with the customer who would pick up the merchandise, and it was all due to happen at the yard later that morning. He had the television on in his hotel room as he got up. He nearly fell over in his speed to get out of the bathroom to hear what the news presenter was saying.

"Officers from HM Customs and Excise have intercepted a large drugs shipment at Southampton docks this morning. Early reports suggest that it could be as much as £30,000,000 worth of heroin which has been discovered moulded into the front buoyancy tanks of two boats arriving from Turkey."

Two boats of the kind described were pictured. Xu looked on in horror.

"No more details are available yet, but we will keep you updated as further details emerge."

Xu froze and stared at the screen for a moment or two longer. How much did they know? He was probably being watched at that moment. He had to get out.

He packed as quickly as he could and walked down to the lobby. He would not bother checking out, they only knew him as Edward Lim. He went straight to the underground car park and jumped into his rented Ford Focus. He headed straight for Luton Airport, where he would get a plane out, anywhere, he did not care.

Xu was soon on an Easy Jet flight into Amsterdam. He had chopped up the sim card for his phone and dropped the pieces into a bin at the airport. The card was all that existed in the name of Edward Lim, and possibly the only way of tracing his whereabouts. Edward Lim no longer existed.

Xu Xiang flew into Singapore's Changi Airport on a Lufthansa flight late the next day. He would pick up is car and drive back across the causeway into Malaysia. He was sure he had covered his tracks well and was undetectable, but of one thing he was sure, heads would roll over this loss.

CHAPTER FORTY THREE

Linda and the others listened as Daniel's mother recounted the events on the earlier news broadcast. "That was probably old Han" said Daniel jokingly, not really believing it, but intrigued.

"Well if it was, we all had a close call" said Linda, who sensed that Daniel's comment was closer to the mark than they realised. At nine o'clock Daniel's mother put the TV news on again, but there was no mention of boats or drugs, nor did it feature in any other news bulletin that day. It seemed the story had vanished without trace.

The following day they headed back to Sussex, and the next morning Daniel and Luke went into the office while the girls tidied and prepared for the journey back to Singapore. The office was now functioning efficiently, with good staff. With the US boats on line they were looking forward to a good year.

They all headed for Heathrow that evening with the usual mixed emotions of sorrow at leaving and anticipation of the warmth waiting for them the other end. They were not held up at customs or immigration, and were soon on their way.

Grant received a call the following morning advising him that

Daniel Cassidy had left for Singapore the previous evening. This was no surprise. He and Gill thought the timing was suspicious, although it could just be coincidence. They decided to try to look for evidence about who else was involved. They knew Daniel would be back at some stage, and if they had reason to do so, they would speak with him then. He decided to ask the Singapore authorities to tell them if he left the country again.

In custody Han said very little, and gave no real leads to Grant and Gill's team. Eugene, on the other hand, squealed and told them everything he knew; unfortunately this was little more than customs knew already. He did however tell them of the existence of a Mr Lim, who he claimed was Han's partner. This, Gill and Grant realised, tallied with the Singapore mobile phone number, and led the trail back to Singapore.

When questioned about Edward Lim, Han remained silent. He would disclose nothing at this stage. It was becoming apparent that Gill and Grant would need to visit Singapore to talk to the Singapore authorities and interview the Cassidys and see what light they could throw on the situation. They would leave in a week. They would send Paul and Mike out to Istanbul at the same time to do some homework there with the authorities.

The Cassidys and the Oakleys soon settled back into their routine. Vera had, as expected, run the office in Beach Road with fastidious efficiency, and Sue Lee had kept the house immaculate, although Skipper was looking decidedly on the plump side. The bond between Skipper and Sue Lee was apparent as soon as they all arrived home. This was good news, but did not compromise Skipper's excitement at the arrival home of his family.

Two weeks after their return, Daniel's step-sister and brother-in-law, Diana and Garth, arrived in Singapore on the way back from Bali for a four-day stay. Linda and Daniel had invited them to stay at the house, but Diana had always wanted to sample the Raffles Hotel, so they stayed there.

Daniel collected Diana and Garth from the Raffles that evening - it was only a few hundred metres from his office - and took them home for a dinner party Linda was preparing. She had also invited their neighbours John and Tara. They enjoyed aperitifs round the rattan bar in the sitting room before retiring to the dining room for the meal. It was the first time Daniel and Linda had seen Diana and Garth for quite a while, as well as the first opportunity to catch up with John and Tara. The conversation turned to the Turkish trip, and Daniel ended up taking them all through the story piece by piece, leaving out no detail. They were all spellbound.

"Sounds like my worst nightmare" John said.

"Daniel, my god, I had no idea all this was going on!" said Diana. "I mean you could have been in jail now. And you could have done without all that stress. It's an amazing story and it could only have happened to you."

"Well, all I can say is thank God it's all over and done with and consigned to the history books" said Daniel.

They finished with a selection of cheeses and a fine port which Daniel opened specially for Garth's sake, knowing it was a weakness of his. A taxi arrived at 11.45 to take Diana and Garth back to the Raffles, and John and Tara made their way back next door, after they had all thanked Daniel and Linda for a thoroughly enjoyable evening.

CHAPTER FORTY FOUR

Daniel was in the office early the next morning. He had to get some urgent emails off. Surprisingly, Luke was the next to arrive at 8.30. He put the kettle on, made his way to his desk and started thumbing through the post.

Then the phone rang. Luke put down the post and picked the receiver up.

"Yes he is, who may I ask is calling?" Daniel heard him say. "Sorry, Who? Oh, Oh I see, hold on I'll put you through."

Daniel looked at Luke quizzically. "Who is it?"

Luke hesitated for a moment as if lost in thought, and then said "It's British Customs and Excise."

"Oh, yeah right, stop mucking about. Who is it really?"

"I'm serious, you'd better take it."

Daniel picked up the phone and pushed the button to put the call through.

"Daniel Cassidy speaking, how can I help?"

"Mr Cassidy, this is Gill Bordeman from Her Majesty's Customs and Excise in London, although I am speaking to you from Singapore at the moment. Can you please tell me what your involvement was with a Mr Han Atima."

Daniel swallowed hard and looked across at Luke, who had stopped dead to listen to the conversation.

"Er, well, we were going to buy some boats from him. Why do you ask?"

"Well, I have to advise you at this stage that he is being held at Her Majesty's pleasure and is awaiting a trial at the Old Bailey in London. Perhaps you would be kind enough to elaborate on these boats you were going to purchase from him?"

"What sort of things do you need to know?"

"Well for a start, what were they made of?"

"Glass fibre."

"I see. If it is OK with you a colleague and I would like to come over and see you and take a statement."

"OK, where do you want to meet?"

"At your home would probably be the most private I would suggest, and as soon as possible. How about 4 pm this afternoon?"

"Sure that's fine, do you want my address?"

"Not necessary, we already have it."

"Oh, I see, this sounds pretty serious."

"You could say that. We have apprehended Mr Atima with approximately thirty million pounds worth of heroin. That's the second largest drugs haul in the UK's history. I would ask you not to attempt to leave the country or make any arrangements until we have spoken with you."

"OK" said Daniel feebly and replaced the receiver.

At that moment Vera walked in with a big beaming smile. It vanished when she saw Daniel, who was as white as a sheet.

"Are you all right?" she asked.

"Well, what was all that about?" Luke asked almost simultaneously.

"You're not going to believe this."

"Go, on" said Luke. Vera just kept quiet, trying to assess what had just happened. She wandered over to her workstation and sat down.

"My intuition was right. Han has just been caught importing thirty million pounds' worth of heroin into the UK."

Vera's jaw dropped and her eyes widened in horror. Luke sat there dumbfounded.

Vera was the first to break the silence. "Where did they catch him and how?"

"I don't know yet Vera, but they're coming to see me this afternoon at home. He's apparently due for trial at the Old Bailey. It was the second biggest drugs haul ever."

"Typical" said Luke. "And you're in the middle of it. What does this mean?"

"I don't know yet Luke, I'll tell you when they let me know more later."

They sat in silence for a few moments longer, then Daniel said, "Can you cope without me today? I think I'd better go home now."

"Yes, sure" said Luke. "I'll give you a bell later."

"Could you just sign these before you go?" Vera said as she dug out some cheques that needed signature for sending out. Daniel signed the cheques and made his way back down to the car.

Linda was on the veranda with Sam when Daniel arrived home. She heard the car pull into the drive and got up to look through the sitting room window to see who it was. Linda was used to Daniel taking half days and odd days off, it was all part of the perk of running you own business, so it was no real surprise. She went and opened the door, took one look at Daniel getting out of the car and asked, "OK so what's wrong?"

"Put the kettle on honey while I change, and I'll tell you – you're not going to believe this."

"Now I am intrigued," she said as she disappeared into the kitchen and Daniel made his way upstairs.

Daniel got out of his work clothes and put on a pair of swimming shorts, then made his way back down to the veranda.

"So what's all this about?" she inquired.

"My intuition on the Turks was right. UK Customs apparently caught Han with thirty million pounds' worth of heroin hidden inside two boats."

"Oh my god!" Linda muttered, putting her hand to her mouth. She was wide-eyed with shock and just stared at Daniel. Sue Lee appeared at that moment and asked if they wanted drinks, as the kettle had just boiled.

"Er... what? Yes please," said Linda without taking her eyes off Daniel.

Sensing the awkward situation and seeing Sam's puzzled face, Sue Lee led the little boy away. Linda went to sit by Daniel.

"Well this is a turn up for the books" she said. "But surely we have nothing to worry about, after all you had nothing whatsoever to do with it. In any case, how do you know all this?

"They're coming to interview me this afternoon."

"Oh my god!"

They whiled away the time in the pool, discussing all that had happened.

At 4 pm they were ready and waiting for the customs officers. Daniel was pacing up and down between the sitting room and the hall and peering out at the drive every few minutes. At last Gill and Grant arrived, along with a uniformed Singapore Police officer and a member of Singapore Customs investigations unit. Sue Lee let them all in and showed them through to the veranda where Daniel and Linda were waiting. Friendly introductions were made and they all sat round the marble table. Sue Lee departed to the kitchen to make drinks for them all.

"I'd appreciate a decent cup of tea with fresh milk," Grant announced. "I have had nothing but UHT since I left England."

"We can certainly sort that out for you," Linda replied, and instructed Sue Lee accordingly. Gill launched straight into the reason for the call. She told them they had found Daniel's telephone number and details in Han's diary, hence the reason for wanting to question him about his relationship with Han.

"You mentioned on the phone that you were looking at importing some boats from this character" she said. "Can you tell us how this came about, from the beginning?"

Daniel started with the sacking of Gordon Burrage and the coincidental meeting with Edward Lim. He explained that Gordon had committed suicide shortly after being sacked, but that the police were fairly sure it was just that and not suspicious.

"OK, we'll make some inquiries with Surrey Police on that when we return," Gill said, making notes. "Now, tell us about this Edward Lim."

A torrent of further questions came forth about where Daniel had met him and how. What was his involvement as far as Daniel was concerned? Daniel mentioned Lim's office and the meeting with him in Istanbul and told the story of his whole Turkish experience, but did not mention his suspicions.

"Do you have any further information on this character, his wife, his home, his car, anything that we can link with him?" she asked.

"No nothing at all, only what I have told you."

"I do remember his car." Linda, who had been silent until now, cut in. All eyes at the table turned in her direction.

"It was a white Mercedes."

"Can you be a bit more specific?" one of the Singapore officers asked.

"Yes, it was one of the big saloons and it had black and white number plates."

"Malaysian registered, by the sounds of it."

"It also had a big dent down one side, and now I think about it, I had actually seen it sitting here in the park, in the drive over there when I drove home one day. It was not until I saw it when he came round here one day that I was sure I had seen it before, and yes I am convinced it was the same one."

"Well done honey, I didn't realise you were such a sleuth!" Daniel remarked. "Was it an old or a new model?"

"Oh, Daniel - it was one of the ones you like, like the one the Barratts drive, you know."

"Ah, that would be the latest S class if that's the case."

"Thank you Mrs Cassidy, that's most helpful. Is there anything else you can think of?"

"Not for the moment. To be honest it's such a shock to think we're involved with something like this, it has really shaken both of us badly."

"I'm sure it has" said Gill.

One of the Singapore officers asked if he could use the phone and rang one of his colleagues. He asked them to send someone to the Tanglin Club to get everything they could from there, including any footage from their car park cameras, if they had them. He also sent someone up to the Causeway to go through any film they had of vehicles of the Merc's description entering or leaving. After all, that was the only way in by car.

Grant then carried on from the British perspective and asked more in-depth questions about Turkey.

"Do you know where the factory was that he took you to?"

"Well, I know it sounds stupid, but no I don't, well not exactly anyway. He would never mention the name of the place to me at all."

"That doesn't surprise me, somehow."

"All I can tell you are the names of the signs we were following on the roads."

"Go on?"

"We went into the Asian side of Istanbul, then across a stretch of water on a ferry and then drove for about two hours. We came off the main road and on to a dirt track. The name we had been following was Burtha or Burka or something."

"Borsa perhaps?"

"Yes, that was it, Borsa. But we didn't go as far as the main town, we turned off before it."

"Can you give us any more information at all?"

"No I'm afraid not, I didn't have a map or anything."

"Excuse me a minute." Grant got up and pulled Gill aside to confer for a moment, then dialled out on his mobile phone. He phoned back to the UK and informed them of the approximate geographic location of the factory. This would be relayed directly to the authorities in Istanbul.

They sat back down.

"We are going to have to ask you to give evidence in London when it comes to trial at the Old Bailey at some stage in the near future. Will you be happy to do so?"

"Well, I'm not sure, would I be in danger?"

"As far as giving evidence is concerned I'm not going to beat around the bush" said Grant. "If you choose not to give evidence voluntarily you will be subpoenaed to do so. I hope that makes it clear?"

Daniel was silent for a moment and then looked at Linda.

"Yes, but can you assure me that my family and I are in no danger? I mean you must appreciate the position I am in!" Daniel said irritably.

"We fully appreciate the position you are in Mr Cassidy, but none of this is of our making," Gill responded. "However, while I would like to be able to say that you are in no danger,

I'm afraid that I cannot give you that guarantee. I'm afraid people who are crooked enough and greedy enough to carry out these sorts of operations have very little respect for human life. Unfortunately you were in the wrong place at the wrong time. The only thing we could arrange for you is to put you and your family in the witness protection programme."

"I have a business to run and family and friends. That is not even an option."

"Well, the choice is yours."

The true facts of what they were embroiled in were beginning to hit home. The more they did so, the less forthcoming Daniel was with any facts, as he realised he was between a rock and a hard place and could not get out of it.

"We need a statement from you" Gill said, getting out an official-looking pad. "I want you to run through the whole story again I'm afraid, leaving out nothing, while I write it down. I'm sorry for both of you, but the sooner we get these people behind bars the better, for a lot of people."

"Yes, I understand you're only doing your job, but I wish we weren't involved" Daniel sighed.

"Well you have got this Mr Lim and Han to thank for involving you I'm afraid."

"Yes, I know, I should have listened to my instinct."

"What makes you say that?" asked Grant.

"Well, if I'm honest, the whole thing appeared fishy from the word go, with the way they wanted to conduct the business, structure the deal and so on. I decided to ignore my gut feeling, thinking it was a good business proposition. How wrong I was! I'm sorry my love." He turned to Linda.

"Don't be so daft, you weren't to know."

With that the phone rang. It was Luke, so Linda brought him up to date while Daniel gave customs the statement they wanted.

Then a taxi arrived, with Diana and Garth. Daniel and Linda were supposed to be taking them to Jumbo Seafood that night, but in the shock and confusion of the day they had forgotten. Linda showed them into the sitting room, where she poured them all a gin and tonic and sat with them at the bar while they waited for Daniel to finish giving his statement. Then she brought them up to date with the day's events.

"I simply can't believe it," Diana exclaimed. "I feel awful now for having such a good laugh about it all only last night."

"Oh I shouldn't think twice about that. After all it is pretty comical in retrospect."

"Well, I only hope the rest of the saga turns out the same way! Poor old Daniel."

"Yes, I certainly hope you're right."

Grant and Gill were taking down the final words of Daniel's statement.

Grant asked Daniel when he was planning to get back to the UK again, and advised him he would have to spend some time there during the time of the trial. They would give him notice as to when this was likely to be. Fifteen minutes later they had wrapped everything up and Linda had joined them in the hall to see them all off.

"If you remember anything else at all, please ring me on this number, day or night" said Grant. "And remember if anything suspicious happens from now on in, if you're followed, or get any unusual phone calls or you're worried about anything at all, call this Singapore number, any time, or this number in the UK. The authorities here, as you know, are fully aware of the situation and are here to support you should you need it. We'll see you back in the UK later in the year."

Daniel took the two cards from Grant with the numbers and addresses on them, shook hands with them all and bid them goodbye.

"I think I need a drink" said Daniel.

"All in hand," Linda said as she produced an ice cold gin and tonic from the bar fridge and handed it to him.

Daniel sat down and let out a sigh.

"Sounds like you've had a hell of a day," Garth said, shaking his head. "You probably don't feel like going out this evening. We can make ourselves scarce if you like?"

"No. I won't hear of it. In any case it won't do me any good at all to brood on it. We'd be far better off sticking to our original plan and going to Jumbo Seafood. It won't take me long to have a quick shower and change."

The conversation at dinner that evening was dominated by speculation and intrigue about what had been going on, and what the outcome would be. At least they were sure of one thing, and that was that HM Customs knew Daniel was innocent of any involvement. The question that kept recurring was the whereabouts of Edward Lim, and the part he had had to play.

CHAPTER FORTY FIVE

Despite being meticulously careful down to the last detail, in Xu's ambition and greed he had overlooked one aspect of his anonymity; his car in Singapore. As far as he was aware, no one had seen it. Singapore immigration, with the help of Gill and Grant, had sifted through hours of video footage to try and spot the white Mercedes entering or leaving Singapore over the causeway. Over a month they were surprised to find that hundreds of white Malaysian-registered Mercedes had made the crossing. The vast majority were dismissed because they were the wrong models and some because they were too old, which finally left them with 12 possible vehicles. They met with one of the police commissioners in Malaysia, who agreed to arrange for the completion of that part of the investigation within the week. He assured them he would get some answers.

Xu's car was not registered to him directly, but to one of his many spurious companies, this particular one from a small office in Kuala Lumpur which was kept more or less as a mail box.

Some of the cars caught on the videotapes had been driven to Singapore on shopping excursions by women, and others by chauffeurs for their bosses to attend meetings, all of which had been established very quickly. They had narrowed the field down to three. The police had spoken to two of them, but had yet to talk to Xu, as every time they had been to his office there had been nobody there. They placed the office under observation to try to catch the owner for questioning.

Finally the white Mercedes had arrived with Xu at the wheel, on his standard post-collection run. They waited for him to enter the office and then went up to knock on the door.

On seeing the police, Xu looked most uncomfortable, something that had been noted by the officers. They spoke to him in Mandarin Chinese, asking him if he owned the car he had just driven up in. He told them it was owned by the company. He was now looking even more uncomfortable and would not look any of them in the eye.

They suggested that he had driven the car into Singapore recently. He initially denied this, saying that he had not been to Singapore, but they pushed him further, requesting a look at his passport which would show the stamp. Xu suddenly 'remembered' that he had visited Singapore to do some shopping, and stayed with some friends for a few days. How silly of him to have forgotten! The police took down all Xu's personal details and had them authenticated by their office before they left.

The police were sure that this was the man they were looking for and would report back to the Singapore and British authorities before taking it further. They now needed to find some evidence linking him to the drugs.

Immediately the police had left, Xu went back home and picked up the phone to one of his colleagues in Singapore.

He would stop this from going any further right now. He knew that Daniel and Linda were the only ones other than Han who could identify him. Han would certainly keep quiet - he knew only too well the consequences of not doing so.

Grant was delighted with their quick progress and the fact that they had someone under suspicion even before he had left Singapore. He suggested an identity parade with Daniel and Linda to identify him. This would at least allow him to be held while further investigations were made. The Singaporeans agreed and the Malaysians said they could set it up the following week, it would be held in Kuala Lumpur.

Gill rang the Cassidy house and spoke to Linda, informing them that they would need them to go to Kuala Lumpur the following week, Linda would let Daniel know.

"While you are on," said Linda, "Daniel and I remembered that he took some photos while he was at the factory in Turkey and we wondered if they would be of any help?"

"What are they of?" Gill enquired.

"They're of the different types of boats they were making, the ones they were offering to Daniel and Luke."

"They most certainly would, I'll hop in a taxi now and come on over."

Linda phoned Daniel to ask where the photos were, and let him know that Gill was on her way over to collect them.

Daniel had hardly slept a wink since the news had been broken to him. He was worried not for himself, but for Linda and Sam, and his thoughts kept on returning angrily to that fateful day when Han had arrived full of smiles on their stand in Earls Court.

Linda was the only one home that afternoon. Daniel was at work in Beach Road and Sue Lee had taken Sam down to the local shops, where she loved showing him off to all her friends. Sam, with his blond curls and endearing smile, was becoming quite a celebrity down at the market as well, where Sue Lee took him in his push chair most mornings, when she went to buy all the fresh vegetables for the evening meal. Sue Lee was working out extremely well and Daniel and Linda were delighted. They trusted her implicitly and by insisting on doing much of the food shopping she was saving both time for Linda, as well as an enormous amount of money by buying at the local market instead of the Cold Storage supermarket where Linda shopped.

This particular afternoon Sue Lee was quite oblivious to the fact that she was in fact being followed, and had been from the moment she had left home. The young Chinese guy was dressed entirely in black and surreptitiously followed her every move. He waited until Sue Lee had done her shopping and was on her own with Sam, pushing the push chair over an open but remote area of grass that surrounded the park of houses before he made his move.

He approached them from behind, and simply asked in a quiet even voice, in fluent Cantonese, "Are you the amah to the Cassidy family?"

Sue Lee turned round quickly, surprised that someone had managed to sneak up on her so quietly. She looked at him suspiciously, and noted his cold, humourless eyes. She knew he was trouble.

Gill Bordeman arrived at about 3.30 that afternoon. Linda invited her through to the veranda, where they sat down and discussed the merits of Singapore over a glass of Coca Cola each, before Linda went and fetched the photos.

Gill looked at the photographs carefully, inspecting each one at length and looking at every detail. She pointed out in one of the pictures the back section of one of the boats Daniel had captured on film, and told Linda that it was this model that had been used for the smuggling. Linda asked how the photos could be of any help, seeing that they had caught the people red-handed and surely had all the evidence they needed to convict them.

Gill apologised but said that she could not discuss things in any greater detail, but that it all went towards making up the larger picture.

It was as they were sitting talking that Sue Lee arrived home with Sam. Sue Lee walked through with Sam to where Gill and Linda were sitting.

"Sorry to disturb you Mem, but man give me this for you."

"Oh, thank you Sue Lee" Linda said with puzzlement, as she took the envelope "but which man, Sue Lee?"

"When we go out Mem. The man come up to me when we finish shopping."

Linda looked at the envelope. It was addressed simply to 'Casity', in bold type on the front. Linda looked at Gill. "How very odd," she said as she opened the envelope.

Gill noticed Linda go a sudden shade or two whiter, as

she read the note, which had been typed on lined A4 paper straight from a pad. The note simply said:

CASITY FAMILY

YOUR SON IS CUTE. HE WILL NOT BE FOR LONGER IF YOU SAY OR DO ANYTHING TO HELP A CONVICTION. YOU KNOW WHAT I MEAN. DO NOT MENTON THIS TO AUTHORITES OR YOU WILL REGRET. I HAVE PEOPLE WATCHING YOU SO YOU PLAY BY OUR RULES AND YOU WILL NOT SUFFER.

"What is it?" said Gill, noting Linda's distress.

Linda handed the sheet to Gill. Then she looked at Sam and went over to pick him up. "Did the man touch Sam?"

"No Mem, just give the letter."

As Gill read the note Linda picked up the cordless phone and called Daniel's office, where Vera put her straight through. At the sound of Daniel's voice Linda broke down.

"Please come home," was all she could say. Gill went over and took the phone from Linda and explained to Daniel what had happened.

Daniel, in his frustration, rounded on Gill. "This is all your bloody fault, if you had left us alone none of this would have happened. I'm on my way home and I hope none of your bloody lot are there when I get there."

Gill understood his frustration and did not bother to answer. She knew he would calm down and start to think rationally before he got home. Daniel slammed the phone down.

Gill picked up her mobile, rang Grant and told him of the latest development. He was disturbed by this latest piece of information, to say the least.

"Shit! Still, I'm glad you were there when it came to light, or we might never have known," he remarked. "Yes, it proves that we have touched a nerve somewhere. I can only assume that it is the people questioned in Malaysia. Actually, looking at it again it could be from Han's side of things, because the worry is of a conviction."

"I'll be there in 20 minutes" Grant said, and hung up. He arrived at the Cassidy house in a police car with the Singapore customs officers in charge of the case, at exactly the same time as Daniel.

Gill was right. Daniel had indeed thought about what he had said, and the first thing he did as he was walking in was to apologise.

"Where is Linda?" he asked.

"She has gone upstairs for a while" Gill responded.

Daniel dashed upstairs, where he found Linda sitting on the bed hugging Sam. Daniel went up and sat next to them and they sat in silence for several minutes drawing strength from each other as Linda sobbed quietly. They both now knew how real the danger was.

Sue Lee showed Grant and the others through to the veranda, where they all looked at the letter in turn, after putting on latex gloves. They did not want to put any more prints on it before the forensic boys had had their turn.

Daniel, Linda and Sam all came down after about fifteen minutes and Daniel read the letter. Grant watched him and gauged his reaction. He knew that the whole case both in Singapore and the UK hinged on Daniel's co-operation.

"We don't know at the moment who's behind the letter, Daniel. It could have been written on the instruction of Han, or from the elusive Mr Lim" he said. "Either way it's essential that we go forward and try to identify the person they're picking up for questioning on suspicion in Malaysia."

"Grant, it really is irrelevant to us which one of them is behind it. After all it was delivered to my amah and son not half a kilometre from our house. Now call me neurotic, but that leaves me feeling mighty vulnerable, because whichever part of their organisation it was, they're bloody well watching us!"

"Yes, that they may be, but the sheer nature of the letter is a shot across your bows to prevent you from saying anything or from giving evidence."

"Yes, and if I had my way I wouldn't give evidence, not under the circumstances."

"What the police will do for the moment is to keep you all in their sights at all times until we can think of something. They'll have a car outside at all times and you'll be escorted if you need to go out."

"Bloody marvellous, now we're under house arrest!"

"You are not under house arrest. It is simply a way of trying to secure your safety in the immediate future" Grant said forcefully.

"Daniel," Linda spoke for the first time, "let's just go

along with it for the moment, until we can think about it more rationally."

"OK honey, yes I guess you're right."

Grant and Gill said they would try and bring the trial in the UK forward and hold it as quickly as they could under the circumstances. They all departed with the letter, once another car had arrived to keep surveillance.

They all knew that time was of the essence now, and that they needed to get the identity parade done before anything else like this stopped Daniel and Linda giving evidence willingly. The Singapore police had already asked the Malaysians to arrest the man known as Xu for further questioning, and hold him until such time as the identity parade had taken place.

Xu received the phone call that afternoon, and was advised that the house had been swarming with police as soon as the letter had been delivered. Xu was steaming with anger and instructed the next move. He would stop this at all costs.

Xu's young Chinese protégé in Singapore had reacted quickly to Xu's request, and at 1 am the following morning he was heading back towards the Cassidy house. He left his car down on the main road, recovered a bag from the boot, which he carried, put a rucksack on his back and headed up the winding road into the park on foot. He rounded the bend and could see the house ahead of him with its porch and veranda lights lit, even though there was no sign of life. He had discussed the best way of carrying out his task with Xu and headed round the side of the house to the back door that entered the kitchen from the garden.

He had not spotted the unmarked police car that was tucked away in the drive opposite, but neither had the two officers seen him slip round the side of the house. They had the radio on and were busy smoking and chatting, with no inkling that something was going on under their noses.

The man tried the shutter and it was as expected, unlatched, although the security grilles behind it were firmly locked. He opened the shutter quietly and brought the bag up to the grille. He could faintly see the outline of Skipper sleeping against the far wall of the kitchen in the light that the full moon was casting through the open shutter. It was a particularly bright night.

He opened the mouth of the bag carefully and held it against the grille, making sure his hands were nowhere near the open mouth of the bag. He balanced his rucksack on his knee and brought it up under the bag, lifting the contents until it fell against the grille.

The bag came to life as a large black cobra slithered to freedom and threaded its way into the kitchen.

Once the snake had left, the man gathered the bag up, placed it in his rucksack and carefully closed the shutter and retraced his steps out of the garden.

One of the officers waiting in the car was in the middle of a story his colleague had heard many times before when he thought he saw something move near the side gate. He sat up and stared at the spot. His colleague followed the line of his gaze.

"There is someone by that gate, I'm sure of it."

"Probably just movement of the branches in the breeze."

"No, look there is someone coming out of the gate, Look, Look!"

"Ssh! Yes, you're right."

"Let him get past that next drive and then we'll get him, when there is nowhere for him to run."

They watched him walk past the next drive. He looked suspicious; he was looking up and down the road, eyes everywhere. They fired up the car and immediately the engine caught the car leapt forward out of the drive with blue lights illuminated.

As soon as he heard the engine the man turned round, and seeing the blue lights he immediately broke into a run. He tried to run up a steep bank on one side of the road and was nearly at the top when he lost his footing and fell heavily back towards the road, ending up in one of the large storm drains.

The two officers piled out of the car and were on top of him in no time. They had not really expected him to run despite their earlier comment, but by doing so he had shown himself guilty of something, and they showed no mercy.

Once they had him in cuffs and had searched his person, they radioed in to the station and gave them details from his ID card; a Mr Henry Ong.

"What were you doing coming out of the garden of that house Henry?"

No response.

"What were you doing coming from that house?"

Still no response.

The other officer was going through his rucksack standing at the open boot of the car.

"There is absolutely nothing in here. Seems a bit odd to be carrying an empty rucksack, doesn't it Henry?"

"I was just using their garden as a shortcut" he responded in a snarling, curt tone, now that he had had time to think.

The tone of his voice made them realise that they had caught him up to no good, and they summoned a second car from the station to come and take over surveillance of the house while they took him in for further questioning.

"And just where were you heading from and to that necessitated a short cut at one in the morning then, Henry?"

No response.

They bundled him into the back of the car and went back up to the Cassidy house. One of them stayed in the car with Henry while the other officer went round the house to see if there was any sign of a break-in or damage, but there was none, and all the security grilles were still locked.

"All appears OK," he reported back.

They continued to try and question Henry, but got nothing further from him. About 20 minutes passed before a second car arrived to relieve them from their surveillance duties. They headed back to the station to question the obstinate Mr Ong further. They would keep him until they had spoken to the Cassidy family the following morning to check all was OK. They had made the decision not to knock on the door or ring them when they had found Henry Ong, as all doors had seemed secure and there was no sign of any sort of wrongdoing or break in and they did not want to put the wind up the family any more than had been already.

CHAPTER FORTY SIX

Sue Lee was the first to enter the kitchen the next morning, opening the shutters and unlocking the grilles as normal. Skipper raised his head, took one look at Sue Lee, then rested his head back down and closed his eyes, deciding that sleep was still the best option at 6.30 in the morning; he was used to the routine by now.

Sue Lee wandered round the rest of the downstairs opening shutters and unbolting the security gates, then started her normal routine of sweeping the downstairs floor area. As she went back into the kitchen to get a mop she saw a policeman in the doorway and jumped. The police had watched from opposite and seen Sue Lee open up, so they had gone over to check that all was indeed OK.

Sue Lee advised them that everything was fine and he returned to the car. They radioed in to the station to let them know that all appeared normal. They would have to release Henry Ong. After all, all they had caught him doing was coming out of someone's garden.

Linda wandered down to the kitchen in her dressing gown to find a pot of tea ready and waiting for her to take back upstairs. This was the sign to Skipper that the day had begun, and he got up and greeted Linda with loud whines and a wagging tail. Linda put the pot and a couple of mugs on a tray and made her way back to the bedroom, leaving Skipper looking dejected in the kitchen at not being invited upstairs.

Unfortunately the noise Skipper had made greeting Linda had also awoken the other creature lurking in the kitchen. Earlier that night the cobra had headed for a dark corner of the kitchen, opposite to where Skipper had been fast asleep. It had slithered into the gap between the refrigerator and the wall, where it had coiled up, invisible to all - until now.

Sue Lee was walking back from her quarters, hotly pursued by Skipper, and had just entered the kitchen when she saw the snake stretching half way across the kitchen floor with its tail still behind the fridge. It was heading in her direction. She let out a scream, then turned and ran out of the house. Skipper keen to see what the fuss was about stood at the doorway and saw the cobra. He immediately put his hackles up and started barking at it.

The cobra, now fully visible, arched its body, raised its head and flared its neck, lifting its head two feet off the ground. The cobra stared at the dog, it's tongue licking the air menacingly. Skipper lunged forward, but still keeping his distance. The cobra let fly its deadly poison, striking Skipper right on the snake's intended target – his eyes. The dog recoiled and ran back out into the garden with deafening howls of pain.

Daniel and Linda had heard the scream from Sue Lee and were already making their way downstairs when they heard the noise from Skipper. They ran down, with no idea what to expect.

Daniel came to a sudden stop as he approached the kitchen from the dining room. He was faced with the sight of Sue Lee at the back door wielding the pole which normally supported the centre of the washing line, and using it to beat the cobra. She had obviously struck it a few blows as it was having difficulty moving. The next blow caught it on the head, and it collapsed to the floor. Sue Lee kept on whacking it until it was almost severed in two.

The two police officers then appeared behind Sue Lee and watched as she finished the snake off. Sue Lee saw Linda standing behind Daniel and shouted, "Mem, Skipper, please look!"

Linda darted out of the dining room doors to find Skipper lying on his stomach, desperately trying to wipe his eyes with both front paws. He was making spine-chilling noises of distress.

"Skipper! Skipper!" Linda said through a shaky tearful voice. At hearing her voice the dog stopped and tried to look at Linda, but it obvious that he could not see. His eyes had swollen to the size of golf balls. She stroked him and tried to calm him down, shrieking for Daniel. Sue Lee, seeing the situation and having had to confront snakes before, said "Water, get water Master!" Daniel duly obliged and quickly unravelled the hose and switched it on. Linda directed the water over Skipper's eyes while Sue Lee held him firm. He continued to whine, only even louder now, as he fought to free himself from Sue Lee's grip. They continued to do this for about ten minutes before Daniel noticed the two police standing there watching them. For some reason Daniel resented their presence.

"Shove off back to your car!" he shouted, and then continued in a quieter voice "you two useless lumps of lard."

"Daniel, that's not necessary!" Linda responded sharply.

The two policemen disappeared back to the car and left them to it. They had seen similar situations with snakes before. It was not uncommon in the tropics and Sue Lee seemed to have it under control. They did not report the incident, which seemed unconnected to their duties.

Linda left Daniel and Sue Lee hosing down Skipper's eyes and returned to the house to call the vet who could only advise them to continue doing exactly what they were doing. He told them that depending on how long the eyes had been infected, the swelling should go down and the dog's sight return to normal. However, they had to be sure that he had not actually been bitten. Sue Lee assured them that Skipper had not been close enough for that, and they all began to relax a little.

The idea of foul play did not enter the thoughts of any of them. They just assumed that the snake had entered through the kitchen door early that morning. It was not uncommon for them to find snakes in the garden; it was the down side of living with the view of a golf course.

Eventually Skipper started to calm down and then they led him to the veranda, where he lay with his head on Linda's foot. Daniel cautiously disposed of the snake, using a garden spade to chuck it into the undergrowth over the fence. Then he went to join Linda.

"I really can't stand the thought of being watched and chaperoned" he said. "It's going to drive me mad. I mean after all, if we're going to be shot what the hell are a couple of goons like that going to do to stop it? Absolutely bugger all, that's what."

"Yes I guess you're right. I can't say they make me feel that much more secure, but I did wonder about going to stay with the Van de Berghs in Hong Kong for a while. Nobody would find us there."

"I should think that so long as the authorities know where we are that wouldn't be a problem, but we shouldn't impose any danger on anyone else."

"I'll ring them and put them in the picture and see if they have any ideas, I would think they would be delighted to help."

"Well don't forget honey, we can't do anything until the identity parade in KL is over with."

"Yes, I know. Can you phone whoever is in charge of this charade and tell them to take their so-called protection off us?"

"Yes, I'll give Grant a ring before he leaves for London and talk through it with him."

The Kuala Lumpur police had been keeping track of Xu's movements since they had first visited him, on the realisation that this was quite probably the man the British and Singapore authorities were so keen to catch. They had also started to delve into the financial status and activities of each of the companies in which he was involved. They found they were unearthing quite a can of worms.

A day after the phone call from Henry in Singapore there

was a knock on Xu's door. He was asked if he would come down to the police station for questioning, as there was a lot they needed to ask him about. He was told in no uncertain terms that if he did not come with them of his own accord, he would be arrested.

He had, that day, written note number two to the 'Casity' family and that would now have been posted by a friend of his from a mail box in Kuantan. He was sure it would do the trick - it had to.

Daniel spoke to Grant that evening and they discussed the merits of police protection and what might happen next. Daniel made it quite clear that they did not wish to be followed and that the officers shadowing them were to be called off. He also let them know that they would probably go to Hong Kong for a while, until they were due to give evidence in London. Grant was leaving that evening for the UK with Gill to try and pull the trial forward and get things put to bed. Grant and Gill were leaving Daniel and Linda to liaise with the Singapore officers who would be taking them up to Kuala Lumpur for the identity parade in a couple of days' time.

The following day they woke up to a normal hot sunny morning. For some reason both Linda and Daniel felt a little easier about life and began to look forward to spending some time in Hong Kong. Linda was going out first with Sam, with Daniel to follow about two and a half weeks later. They would stay for a couple of weeks before heading back to London, where hopefully the trial would be sooner rather than later, although Daniel had been told it could be up to three months away. Daniel could not really afford that much time away from the business, but he had no option, and he had to put his life and that of his family first.

Daniel was flicking through the post at the breakfast table that morning, when an envelope made him stop in his tracks and stare at it. It was addressed, like the last, to the 'Casity' family. Linda saw Daniel freeze and looked over at the letter Daniel was holding. "Oh my god!" she gasped.

"Well I guess we had better see what our life expectancy is" muttered Daniel. "Just looking at the envelope won't help." He slid his finger under the flap and opened it along the seam, looking at the post mark as he did so.

"Kuantan" he read.

"If that's the case it's definitely Edward Lim who feels threatened."

"Yes, I would agree. Unless it's being done on behalf of Han."

Linda looked over anxiously as Daniel pulled the paper from the envelope.

The note simply read:

THE SNAKE WAS NO MISTAKE – YOU TALKED TO THE AUTHORITES – BIG MISTAKE. IF THE DOG IS DEAD, TOO BAD – YOU TALK AGAIN IT WILL BE YOUR SON. I CAN REACH YOU WHERE EVER YOU TRY TO HIDE.

"Daniel, now I really do feel unsafe" said Linda. "We've got to get straight out of here until the trial is over. I mean we're not only being watched, but they are getting snakes into our house, and that was with police protection. Don't you think we should tell them?"

"No, honey, I don't, after all what can they do about it? The threat is against us, not any of them. They'll just repeat what we've heard before. Have you mentioned going to HK to anyone?"

"No, why?"

"Well don't, because the fewer people know where we are, the less likelihood of the wrong people finding out. You had better advise the Van de Berghs of that as well."

They spent the next half an hour discussing what they should do next and the pros and cons of various actions.

"I think you and Sam ought to come with me today, I don't feel happy about leaving you here alone" said Daniel.

"We'll just get in the way. Can't you work from home today?"

"Yes, that makes better sense, I'll call Luke and Vera and put them in the picture."

Daniel went into the hall to phone Luke.

The next day was spent in much the same way. Daniel had cancelled all office appointments and Luke was looking after anything that was essential.

The following morning the police car arrived to collect them to take them up to Kuala Lumpur. Sam was an extra passenger; they did not want to leave him with Sue Lee in case someone came for him. In fact he had not been out of their sight since the second letter, and they had even moved his little bed into their bedroom.

They crossed the causeway and passed through immigration without having to queue, something of a novelty, and were soon on the new high-speed highway from Johor Baru up to Kuala Lumpur. Daniel and Linda were both visibly nervous as they approached the police station in KL, despite being assured by the officers accompanying them that there was no danger, and that at no time would they come into contact with any of the suspects.

They were driven straight in through some security gates at the rear of the building and away into the underground car park.

The building was not that old, of a good spacious design and centrally air-conditioned, but was already showing the signs of heavy wear and tear. They walked up two floors and were taken into a briefing room where they were offered a coffee. They were left alone for a while but did not discuss any of the matter in hand in case they were being listened to.

About an hour later the officers returned and asked Linda to join them first. Linda and Daniel had assumed that they would be asked to identify the person together, and it came as a surprise to be taken separately.

Linda was taken down one flight of stairs to the end of the building and shown into a room with one entire wall made of one-way glass looking into another room. She sat down and waited for the people to be brought in to the next room. Linda watched as each of them filed into the room and hid her recognition of Edward Lim well, as he entered as suspect number five.

The police waited until they had all entered the room before asking Linda to walk along the length of the glass and look at each of the suspects carefully before announcing if she recognised any of them. Linda got to the end of the row and announced that she did not recognise any of them. She was taken back upstairs, but to a different room to the one in which Daniel waited. Sam was brought in to join her.

Once Linda was seated in the waiting room, Daniel was asked to do the same. He gave the same verdict to the officers at the end of the parade.

Neither of them spoke on the way home in the car. They both felt guilty, but knew it was the only option that they had had in the circumstances.

They arrived back in Singapore hoping that this would be the end of the threats, but knowing they had a long way to go yet with Daniel still to give evidence at the Old Bailey. They sat down that night with large gin and tonics after putting Sam to bed, but the drinks did little to alleviate their mood.

The Malaysian police were disappointed at the outcome of the ID parade, but would be charging Xu anyway with other counts of fraud and embezzlement they were uncovering. He was not out and free yet. He was advised that the charges against him were now of a financial nature and would be dealt with in Malaysia. Xu knew his threats had worked.

The Singapore authorities were continuing to make inquiries as to the nature of Mr Lim's activities in Singapore and had visited the Tanglin club armed with photographs of Xu, but while they had sparked a vague recognition with some of the staff, none of them could be sure. They had done the same for the neighbouring offices in the Shaw centre, but the result was the same. The Singapore Customs phoned Grant and Gill in London and let them know the outcome. They too were disappointed that that line seemed to be going nowhere, but they were concentrating on getting Han and Eugene put away.

CHAPTER FOURTY SEVEN

Linda and Sam were to fly out to Hong Kong in two days' time. Linda had spoken to Kate in Hong Kong and they were delighted to be of assistance; after all nobody would know they were there. They could relax for a few weeks. Linda was assured that they were welcome for as long as they liked.

Keanu and Kate Van de Bergh were Americans, originally from New Jersey, who had lived in Hong Kong for about seven years. They had no children and adored Sam, spoiling him rotten whenever the opportunity existed. Keanu was in his late thirties, dark haired, fit and good looking, helped by the permanent tan from the water skiing he did each weekend. He was with one of the American banks, while Kate was a socially active housewife, with natural blond hair and a superb figure. Kate was naturally attractive, and when dressed up for an evening out she was stunning.

The couple lived in Stanley on Hong Kong Island, in a beautiful four-bedroomed house set high in the hills with its own pool and spectacular views over the bay below and the ocean beyond. A red Ferrari F360 Modena and a Silver Range Rover graced the drive. They were well paid and led a good life, and were the envy of many.

They had first met Daniel and Linda while water skiing

in Singapore many years before, and had hit it off with them immediately. From that time on they had met up at least four or five times a year, usually while Keanu had been in Singapore on a business trip and Kate had gone along for the ride. They always stayed with the Cassidys, much preferring the home life to that of hotels, and had become the closest of friends.

Linda spent the next couple of days packing up all they were likely to need for the following few weeks. She was standing looking at the packed cases the evening before they were due to leave when Daniel walked in from work. Linda looked at Daniel, and her eyes welled up and she started to sob uncontrollably. Although they had both decided there was very little risk now, she did not want to leave Daniel alone in the house for the next few weeks. She was worried, angry and upset that this turn of events had been forced upon them.

Daniel just held her and stroked her head until she finally stopped. "Look at the mess you've made of my shirt," he said light-heartedly. Linda looked at the wet patch covered with mascara and lipstick and started to giggle.

"You know I can't come with you straight away" he said. "There is too much to do in the office and I can't leave Luke to do it all. The sales side would be a disaster with Luke in charge, you know how undiplomatic he is. Besides there is no danger now."

"I wish I could believe you on that, but Han is not going to go down quietly is he?"

"I don't think he has an option. After all it wasn't me who

caught him with the drugs, and he was caught red handed, there must have been other witnesses."

Daniel looked at the luggage. "Bloody hell, I think we'd better charter a jet of our own if you've got that lot to go!"

Linda looked at the luggage and the tears returned.

"It's only going to be a few weeks honey, and we'll be at home in Sussex before long" said Daniel. "I'm sure you don't need that much, it'll cost us our life savings in excess luggage!"

This criticism pushed Linda her over the edge. She had coped with the situation extremely well up until now. "Right!" she said as she unlatched and picked up one of the cases. "You can pack the bloody things yourself!" The first case fell open and the contents distributed themselves all over the floor. Daniel watched in disbelief as Linda repeated this with each packed case and the entire contents of Sam's wardrobe fell to the floor, followed by most of Linda's lifetime collection of clothes.

Daniel turned to walk away and leave her to it.

"And if I'm missing something when I get to Hong Kong, don't bother following me there!" she bellowed after him through the tears.

Daniel was almost in tears himself at the sight of Linda so distressed, but he decided he had better leave her to it and get it out of her system rather than try to sort it out now. She needed the release, to blow off steam after all the tension build up.

The fact that Daniel was turning and walking away only made Linda worse. She was furious that he wasn't going to stay and argue the point.

"Did you hear me?" she shouted.

Daniel muttered "Yes, perfectly" under his breath.

"Did you bloody well hear me? Don't bother coming!" came the shout from the bedroom. Then she collapsed on the bed in a mixture of rage, frustration and fear. Daniel continued to the bottom of the stairs and things went quiet upstairs. He told himself she would soon get over it.

Daniel poured himself a stiff whisky and sat out on the veranda. He wasn't in the mood to watch television or read, so he just sat there and stared at the pool and out onto the golf course.

"Everything OK sir?" came Sue Lee's voice from behind him.

Daniel turned, " Yes thank you Sue Lee, Mem just a bit upset with the naughty men making threats, she be OK later."

"You want me make supper, sir?"

"Yes, please, if you would, and can you get Sam ready for bed for me?"

"OK sir." And she duly disappeared back in the direction of the kitchen.

Daniel crept back upstairs and peered through the bedroom door. Linda was lying on the bed curled up with her eyes closed, silent and exhausted. Daniel closed the door quietly and returned downstairs to his whisky.

Sue Lee appeared with Sam from the playroom and took him up for a bath. Daniel went up and read his son a story before returning downstairs to have his own supper. He sat alone and ate, having decided to let Linda sleep. She was obviously in need of it.

The next morning Linda nestled up to Daniel and whispered an apology to him. They held each other very tightly for a long time.

Daniel got up shortly afterwards and started to repack the suitcases, but even halving the number of clothes, there were still going to be plenty. Linda and Sam said goodbye to Sue Lee and they got into the car to head for the airport. They had told Sue Lee and all their other friends that they were going back to the UK for a few weeks and would be there until the trial was over. The fewer people knew they were in Hong Kong the better.

They drove in near silence to the airport only being interrupted by Sam. Neither of them wanted to talk about what might happen. They checked the luggage in and the three of them went to have a coffee, staying until the last minute before Linda and Sam had to head down to the gate for boarding. They again went over the merits of not disclosing the snake attack to the authorities and of pretending not to recognise Edward Lim – they were convinced it had saved their lives, for the moment. Linda was in tears once again as they said goodbye, but Daniel told her to be strong.

"Ring me as soon as you get there, I'll be in the office." Daniel said, as he wiped the tears from round her eyes.

"OK honey I will, I miss you already though." Sam sat in his pushchair sucking his thumb, completely oblivious to the turmoil their family had been thrown into.

As soon as Linda had gone through immigration she

turned and took one last wave to Daniel, who was by now choking up himself. When she had disappeared from sight, he turned round and walked back towards the car in the knowledge that at least his family was going to be safe.

Linda's mood soon brightened as she concentrated on getting to the boarding gate, stopping briefly for a bottle of Gordon's to take to the Van de Berghs. She was already focusing her thoughts on Daniel coming over to join them in Hong Kong and for the moment dismissed any danger he was in from her mind.

The flight to Hong Kong was only a few hours, nothing compared to the European long hauls, and Sam behaved perfectly for the entire flight, much to Linda's relief. She was looking forward to getting to the Van de Berghs and settling in for a few weeks.

Their flight landed at 1:20 that afternoon at the recently-completed Hong Kong International airport. Having collected their cases, they wandered through customs and the glass doors beyond to the throngs of people waiting for friends and relatives. They saw Kate immediately, waving wildly and making her way to the gap in the barrier through which Linda and Sam would exit.

They greeted each other as if they had not seen each other for years before making their way to the car park and loading the cases into the back of the Range Rover before heading off on the journey that would take them at least an hour and a half through to Hong Kong Island and across it to Stanley. Kate had even gone to the trouble of buying a child seat for the back of the car, knowing Sam would be with them for a few weeks, Linda was embarrassed by this and had offered to pay for it, but Kate would not hear of it. She could not wait to hear about what had been happening and listened intently for the entire journey as Linda unravelled the story.

They finally arrived at the house and the electric gates swung open. Kate took one of the cases and showed Linda to her room and then on to Sam's room. In Linda's room a large bouquet of flowers lay on the middle of her bed with a large bow and the words 'Dearest Linda, welcome for as long as you need us. All our love Keanu and Kate xxxxx', written on a large card attached to them. The card brought a tear to Linda's eye, but she held herself together and gave Kate a hug.

In Sam's room they had bought covers and curtains covered with Pooh bear pictures which, to Kate's delight, Sam immediately recognised and pointed at. A large soft toy of Pooh bear sat in the middle of his bed and he could not conceal his delight.

After Linda had phoned Daniel to tell him she had arrived safely, the three of them went down to the beach and Kate continued to question Linda on the events that had driven her to seek refuge with them. Kate agreed with their decision about the ID parade and their failure to report the snake incident. She too was sure it had probably saved their lives. This was something that Linda had needed to hear from someone other than Daniel, and it made her feel much better having told someone.

When they returned to the house that afternoon Keanu was already home. He had made the effort to leave the office early that evening, knowing they had house guests. He too was delighted to see Linda and they all sat round the pool overlooking the wonderful view of the bay drinking champagne while the maid prepared the dinner.

Linda went through the story for a second time, with Keanu listening carefully but stopping her every now and again to ask probing questions about the situation. He too endorsed their line of action and said they would have done exactly the same thing in their shoes.

"Well that is quite a story," Keanu concluded, "it seems unbelievable."

"It's the sort of thing you read about every now and again, but you never expect it to happen to you" Kate added.

"Poor old Daniel. How's he coping with the pressure?" asked Keanu.

"Oh, you know what he's like, nothing really seems to faze him, but I think this is beginning to take its toll on him. He's really trying to forget it until the trial."

"Not an easy thing to do, to be mixed up in something like this and try to forget it."

"Particularly as Customs have told him he's their number one witness. As you can imagine, that will bring a lot of pressure."

"I only hope that the guy in prison doesn't know he's their number one."

"Well this is part of the worry. We may well be out of the woods as far as Mr Lim is concerned, but what is the one who's about to get life in jail going to try?"

"I wouldn't think that they will try anything in the UK,

they know that the authorities will be watching Daniel like a hawk."

"I hope you're right."

"I'm sure I'm right, and besides you needn't worry about that yet, you'll be fine here and you can stay for as long as you like, you know that."

"That's very sweet of you both. I really don't know what we would do without you."

Before dinner was ready Linda got up to go and feed Sam and put him to bed. Kate had insisted on reading him his bedtime story, something Sam was equally happy about.

Over dinner Keanu was on good form and determined that Linda would enjoy herself while their guest. As Linda laughed at some of the banter, Kate could see the signs of stress through the laughter and wondered how long it was since Linda had actually felt relaxed enough to laugh.

Daniel had driven straight from the airport to the office that morning and had immediately settled in to the work routine, to the extent that he had almost forgotten about the threats to his life. He was pleased to hear Linda's voice, and even more cheered by how happy she had sounded.

That evening he and Luke went to the Tanglin Club for a drink and a meal, during which he had put Luke in the picture with all the latest developments. Luke thought they had made the right decision on the ID parade, but warned that the worst was possibly to come in the UK with Han. Daniel rationalised this with the view that if Lim had been the mastermind, Han was possibly just the puppet and a disposable asset without the real contacts.

"In any case," Daniel said, "we won't go back until just before the trial, because after it, whatever the result, the danger has gone."

"It's only gone if you're not the one to put him away" Luke suggested.

"Yes, I've been thinking about that. I'm just going to answer the questions directly without any elaboration or insinuation."

"I think that's all you can do really. In any case, if you ask me this guy deserves to go down for life."

"Yes he does, and I'm sure he will anyway, with or without my testament. I mean, after all they caught the guy red-handed, and they must have got their intelligence from somewhere about the haul, so why do they really need me?"

By the end of the meal and after a couple of bottles of red wine, Daniel, with Luke's help, had decided that in reality there was no danger at all and that the whole ordeal would pass without event. They left the club in a taxi that night, planning to return for their cars the next morning.

Luke had asked if he could come and stay at Daniel's that night, as he was not on the best of terms with Michelle at that moment. Daniel had been only too happy to oblige and although he didn't admit it, he was actually relieved at the thought of having someone else in the house. Sue Lee always kept the guest room ready for visitors and Daniel told Luke he could stay as long as he liked.

They had a nightcap at home before retiring to bed and it was now Luke's turn to tell Daniel about the problems he and Michelle were having. Daniel listened carefully and sympathized. He was going to have to advise Luke that he ought to be more attentive towards her, or lose her.

Daniel did not sleep particularly well for the next few nights, but as time went on and no more notes were forthcoming he relaxed a little and began to sleep better. Luke stayed for three nights before venturing back home, only to return again the following night having had a blazing row during which he had turned and walked out.

Michelle had phoned Daniel on his mobile. She was lost without Linda around, and needed someone to turn to. Daniel felt awkward and stuck in the middle but was good at listening, so he let Michelle get it all out of her system. What he heard did not come as a surprise, but he told her to make allowances because of the pressure Luke was under at work and said this was the root cause of it all. He assured her that Luke was not having an affair and that he had been staying with him all the time.

The next few weeks seemed to fly past. Grant was in touch with Daniel twice a week, keeping him abreast of the likely trial dates, which were being put back each time they spoke. Daniel had a feeling that in reality he was just keeping tabs on his key prosecution witness.

Linda spoke to Daniel daily and was extremely happy in her new surroundings, although she missed Daniel desperately. He had delayed his trip to Hong Kong due to work and the fact that the trial was delayed, so it would have meant being away from the office indefinitely if he had left now. Linda had not been happy, but understood.

Eventually, five weeks after Linda had departed for Hong Kong, Daniel followed. The trial date had been confirmed. Daniel would spend a week with the Van de Berghs before he, Linda and Sam went back to the UK, to arrive a week before the trial.

Daniel touched down in Hong Kong to a rapturous welcome from everyone. When they arrived home Kate took charge of Sam while Linda and Daniel disappeared upstairs to unpack and have a little time to themselves. It seemed as if they had been apart forever.

That evening they gathered outside for the usual evening ritual of drinks by the pool before dinner, followed by a superb roast turkey which Kate had prepared specially for the occasion. After dinner, as Kate and Linda sat and chatted, Daniel and Keanu stood out on the pool veranda, looking out at the sea.

"So how are you really feeling at the moment – no pretence?" Keanu asked.

Daniel continued to look out to sea with his glass of whisky in hand as he thought about the answer. He really wasn't sure.

"I think I'm OK, but it really is a case of up one minute and down the next. I guess I'm all right until I think about the trial, and what could be in store for me prior to it. To be honest, I've never dreaded anything so much in my life. The whole thought of being at the Old Bailey fills me with dread. I mean, I've only ever seen it on the television, but the thought of being there as a key witness in the second largest drugs hoist in the UK - well, yes, it does fill me with complete and utter dread."

Keanu was a good listener. Daniel continued. "Keanu, you know I've never run from anything in my life, I've always confronted things head on, and God knows there have been enough things to confront, but in this instance if I could run right now I think I'd do the minute mile! I feel as if I've had enough stress to last me my entire lifetime."

"Well why don't you stay here until the day before the trial? At least that way you know you're safe."

"That's kind, but I've been in touch with Tom and Mary, some friends who have a boat in the marina in Chichester, which they have kindly offered us the use of should we wish. We may take them up on their offer, you know, make it a bit of a holiday and stay on their boat touring the Solent for a week. It'll keep the mind occupied anyway."

"It sounds like a good idea to me. Does Linda know this yet?"

"No, I only spoke to them a couple of days ago. I'll see how Linda feels about it when we get back. She loves the house over there and she may just want to stay at home, we'll see."

They stood and chatted for a further 20 minutes before joining the ladies and ultimately retiring to bed. The next day they all went to the beach, where Daniel and Keanu spent most of the time taking it in turns water skiing from Keanu and Kate's speedboat. It was the first day of pure leisure that they had had in a long time.

That evening Keanu and Kate decided they were going to take them to Lamma Island for a seafood meal. The maid would babysit Sam. They got a taxi to Aberdeen, where they jumped on a sampan, and after a couple of minutes of negotiating between Keanu and the lady at the helm they were on their way out of the harbour and across to the island. The sea was slightly more choppy than would have been ideal and at some stage Daniel muttered to Keanu that perhaps for the girls' sake they should have taken the ferry, but they all arrived without incident. The sampan nosed its tyre-fendered bow up to the concrete jetty and the woman kept it against the jetty by applying throttle while they all alighted. They could not help but notice that Linda looked remarkably relieved to get off the sampan.

Lamma Island was an unusual place with only a couple of thousand inhabitants and no cars at all. They walked up the concrete jetty, remarking on how quaint the bay looked with the lights of the restaurants and bars lining its shore, their reflection lighting the ocean and all set against the backdrop of the hillside behind.

"This looks like perfect stress-free living to me," Daniel remarked. Linda squeezed his hand, as if in agreement.

"It's a great place if you don't have an office on the other side of town to get to" said Keanu.

"And I think I would be lost if I had to rely on ferries and taxis every time I needed to go anywhere, I just couldn't imagine it without my car" Kate added.

"I'm sure you're right" said Daniel. "It's just that we feel like being recluses at the moment, and this seems like a dream."

After a superb meal of prawns, crayfish and other seafood, they caught the last ferry of the day back to central Hong Kong and took a taxi back to Stanley. Linda and Daniel felt more relaxed than they had for a long time.

The rest of the week in Hong Kong with their friends seemed to go in much the same vein. It had done them both good. The Van de Berghs offered Linda the option to stay on while Daniel went back to the UK, but she insisted that she was going to go back as moral support for Daniel. They were leaving on the Virgin Atlantic flight for Heathrow at 10.40 that evening, but that left the whole day to enjoy the beach and some more skiing.

The journey to the airport in the Range Rover that night was quiet, in great contrast to the journey a week previously when they had collected Daniel. Keanu and Kate offered to take some leave and come back to the UK with them both to give them some moral support during the coming weeks. Daniel and Linda thanked them, but suggested that they come over when they were back there later in the year and they could all truly enjoy themselves.

Daniel called Grant the day prior to leaving to ensure that all was still going ahead as planned; it was.

The flight took off on schedule and as soon as the 'FASTEN SEAT BELT' signs had gone off Sam was fast asleep. Linda and Daniel waited until the meal had been served before they too fell asleep.

CHAPTER FOURTY EIGHT

Han was determined not to spend the rest of his life in jail, which under the current circumstances was almost a certainty, barring a miracle. He had been caught red-handed by HM Customs. The proof was undeniable, it was a major haul and a very serious crime. He was rightly a very worried man. His barrister had advised him of the gravity of the situation and had advised him of his best line of defence. Even so he knew he was likely to be in for the long run, but he would try every trick in and out of the book first.

Maya had been staying in London for the weeks following Han's arrest, along with his mother. Han had given Maya a couple of phone numbers of friends in Istanbul and asked her to contact them and get them to come to London as soon as possible. He was going to need their help. Maya had not heard of these friends before, and was suitably suspicious. She had been playing the loyal wife, thinking that Han needed her in his time of need, but she doubted his innocence and if it was indeed proven that he was guilty, this would be the last she would have to do with him. He had always known her views on drugs. As a nurse she had seen first hand the damage that they could do, and she could not believe the level to which he had lowered himself. Han on the other hand had fallen out of love with Maya a long time ago, if indeed he had ever truly loved her. Before the arrest he had made other plans with his new-found fortune. They did not include Maya. However, since the arrest he knew that his best plan was to play the loyal, loving family man. He needed Maya now, but not for the reasons she would have wished.

Han, unsurprisingly, had not heard a word from Xu and did not expect to now, except possibly to warn him about what he should say in court, but no such messages had yet filtered through. He knew Xu was going to be seriously angry that the deal had gone wrong, although Han was at a loss to know where it had gone wrong and did not know how he would explain it to Xu if he did get out. Han was also aware how cheap life was in Xu's mind, and although it was not of immediate concern, it was something that was nagging at the back of his mind.

Han was surprised at the depth of knowledge the customs officials had, and even more surprised at how long they had been tracking him. He was determined that Eugene would be made to take the heat off him and do the time, but his barrister was not convinced.

Han wondered whether Customs knew about Daniel and whether they had told him of his fate yet, a question that was soon answered when it was announced by his barrister that Daniel Cassidy was to be one of the witnesses for the prosecution. Han, for a moment, felt humbled and humiliated and wondered what Daniel had thought when he found out the truth. He assumed he would be angry at being dragged into something like this.

Han spent a lot of time giving thought to what Daniel could say that could harm his defence. He had to think of everything Daniel knew, and let his barrister know so that the best defence could be prepared. His other option was to ensure that Daniel did not say anything out of turn. He would continue to think about the best way of dealing with the current situation and would talk to his two colleagues when they arrived from Turkey in a few days' time. They might look on it from another perspective.

Daniel, Linda and Sam's flight touched down half an hour early that morning at Heathrow, and after retrieving their luggage they made their way straight to the car rental desk. They were too tired and emotionally drained to catch the bus to Gatwick, and they were at some stage going to have to rent a car anyhow because the BMW needed to be put through the MoT and taxed before it was road legal. They decided to go to the house for the first half of the week before going down to their friends' boat in Chichester, which after much discussion they had decided was a good idea. This was as much as anything to keep their minds occupied, apart from the security aspect.

As they were standing at the car rental desk Daniel's mobile rang.

"Hi, Daniel, it's Grant. Welcome back to the UK."

"Thanks Grant, How is it all stacking up?"

"Very well. We've built a fairly cast iron case against both Han and his colleague, Eugene, and you'll be pleased to hear it is all going ahead on schedule."

"Oh yeah I'm ecstatic" Daniel responded in a droll and sarcastic manner.

Grant ignored the sentiment and carried on.

"Look, we have to meet, where are you staying? At your place in Sussex?"

"Well that's where we are heading right now, yes, but we won't be there every day until the trial, we have other plans for the week."

"OK, I'll meet you down at the house this afternoon. There are several things I need to run through again with you to finalise our case."

"Oh - yes, I suppose so" Daniel replied in a hesitant manner.

"Good, I'll see you at what, four o'clock?"

"OK, see you then."

"What was that all about?" Linda asked, realising that they were back in the thick of it again already. Daniel told her about the meeting that afternoon at the house as they made their way to find the rented VW Golf.

It took them 25 minutes to get the car, during which time Daniel commented a number of times on how it would have been quicker on the bus. He was tired and irritable as he was reminded that his predicament was all too real. He had managed for the past few weeks to tell himself that the worry he faced was a thing of the future, a problem to face tomorrow, and until now a problem on a different continent. Unfortunately tomorrow had now arrived and it was time to face facts again, a reality that Grant's phone call had jolted them back to.

It took them just over two hours to navigate the distance between five of the junctions on the M25 that morning in a chilly drizzle. Daniel knew he should have insisted on a car with an automatic gearbox and commented more than once on how he could not do this every day. To make matters worse Sam was now wide awake and almost as if he sensed the feeling of his parents, was unhappy, fidgety and tearful, only causing more stress to them all.

They finally left the motorway and the atmosphere became a little more relaxed as with the momentum of the car Sam finally fell asleep. They arrived at their house about three and a half hours later, having stopped briefly for some bread and milk and a few other essentials.

Linda was the first inside as Daniel removed the cases from the boot. They would leave Sam until last, leaving him to sleep for as long as possible.

Although nothing was immediately obvious, the moment she stepped through the door Linda stopped. Her sixth sense told her that something was amiss. The house seemed cold, but there was something more than just that.

Han's friends had arrived from Istanbul and had visited him on a number of occasions in prison. They would indeed do all they could to help their colleague and they both conferred with each other after the meetings with Han to discuss the most effective way of achieving the goal. They had all decided that Daniel was a threat, but that the circumstances would put Han away before anything that Daniel might say. However they needed to let Daniel know he was under observation, and that a wrong word would be unwise. They would find him somehow and apply the pressure.

They eventually located the Cassidy home, and after a couple of days of general observation decided that it was uninhabited. They had a closer look and it was apparent that nobody had been there for quite a while, which they reported back to Han.

Daniel and Linda had only to move from the hall to the sitting room to have their worst suspicions confirmed. The room was in turmoil, with drawers turned out, debris everywhere and the window to the side of the sliding doors into the garden broken. Daniel phoned Grant immediately and told him that they had been apparently burgled, although he and Linda had convinced themselves it was a warning sign.

It was too much for Linda. She was tired after the long flight, and now finding her home had been infiltrated by strangers, she was scared once again. She sat on the sofa and burst into tears. Daniel looked after Sam, but would not touch anything until the police had done their bit.

Grant told Daniel to phone the police straight away and said he would leave immediately to get down to the house and join them. He advised Daniel not to touch or move anything until the police had been and did not hide his worry about the situation. He called Gill to join him as soon as he had put the phone down.

Grant made a call from his mobile to the Sussex police senior duty officer as soon as he and Gill were in the car. He made a brief explanation of the situation and the possible dangers involved. Armed police arrived at the Cassidy home within minutes.

Daniel's next call, was to a glazier to fix the broken glass, as the wind and rain were blowing straight through the open hole. Judging by the amount of water on the carpet, it had been doing so for some time.

Linda and Daniel went upstairs, hardly daring to look, for fear of what they may find. All the drawers had been pulled from their runners and lay on the floor with their contents strewn about the floor. They sat on their bed as the police took fingerprints from every object that had been handled downstairs.

"This has just got to be a sign to say they can get to us" Linda said, looking earnestly at Daniel.

"It's either that or a hell of a cruel coincidence" Daniel replied. "On the face of it there doesn't seem to be anything missing."

"Luckily most of our valuable stuff is in Singapore."

"Yeah, but even the video is still here."

Linda let a small smile come to her face "That's probably because it's a vintage model."

"You're probably right honey, but if nothing is missing, they were either disturbed or our friends have paid us a visit. I don't like it either way."

"Let's see what Grant makes of it."

They decided that they would tidy up and secure the house, see what was missing, then go straight down to Chichester to Tom and Mary's boat just as soon as Grant had left. Daniel phoned Tom and Mary to see if it was convenient for them to go to the boat straight away that evening. Tom was horrified to hear about the break-in and told Daniel that the boat was ready as soon as they wanted it. Tom would phone the harbour office, where he left a spare set of keys in case of an emergency, and ensure they would be available to Daniel at any time from then on.

Shortly after putting the phone down from Tom, Grant and Gill arrived on the scene. They introduced themselves to the officer in charge, who was sitting in the open tailgate of a Volvo T5 estate car outside. They chatted for some while before heading in to the house.

Daniel and Linda made their way downstairs and met Grant and Gill in the hallway, and they all headed for the sitting room. The policeman who had been fingerprinting the room advised Linda that he had finished and if she wanted to start clearing up she could do so.

They all sat down and one of the officers asked if he could help by making them all a hot drink.

"Yes, thank you, that would be very kind. The milk is still on the floor of the Golf, and you'll find tea bags in the right hand unit above the hob," Linda advised him.

Gill got straight to the point. "I'm so sorry for what has happened here. It must have been an awful shock to have got back to find this."

"You could put it that way" Daniel muttered.

"Anyhow," Gill continued, "having spoken to the officer in charge here, they have got a lot of prints, but at this stage until they finish and take all of yours they don't know if they have any prints from the culprits. So in a nutshell we don't know whether this break-in is related to the trial or not. The fact that there appears to be little if anything missing is suspicious."

Grant then cut in, "We are basically going to have to keep an eye on you, for your own safety until the trial next week. I know you won't like this, but it has just got to be done. We cannot take any chances in the light of what has happened."

"Well, don't worry about us, because of this we did not feel comfortable staying here, so we've arranged to stay on a friend's boat on the Solent until the trial. We'll have the mobile." He told them of their tentative plans for the week.

Grant and Gill would have been happier with them in a safe place of their choosing. In the end they conceded that they were probably just as safe moving around, but insisted that they would have to check in every evening and morning and let them know where they were.

As Daniel and Linda were giving their fingerprints for elimination, the glazier arrived and was given the OK to fit the new glass.

Grant then continued with some further questions that would hopefully help their case, and while doing so he touched on what had happened in Singapore and Malaysia with the identity parade. Daniel and Linda said very little, although by the way the questions were put they felt the officers knew that they were holding back. They really did not care. At least they were alive.

Grant was soon on the phone arranging an unmarked car to tail Linda and Daniel down to Chichester. It would follow at a distance and ensure that no one else was following them.

As he did this Daniel sat with Sam, Gill and Grant while Linda went upstairs to get hold of some bedding to take down to the boat. Everything else would either already be on the boat, which was completely kitted out, and they could buy food down there. Their suitcases were still in the car from the airport.

Daniel then spent half an hour on the phone to the UK office. He had spoken to them and Luke in Singapore before leaving Hong Kong

It was 6.30 that evening before they finally locked the house up and started on the 45-minute journey down to the marina. It had not been the afternoon of rest they had expected, and Daniel had to admit, once they were on the way, that he was on the verge of being too tired to drive.

It was on the A27 near Worthing that Daniel first noticed the red Vectra following them. He hoped it was Grant's tail and not someone else.

"Can you just ring Grant on the mobile, honey, and check that it's a red Vectra they have following us."

Linda looked up and then dialled the number. "Hi, Grant, it's Linda Cassidy, just quickly, can you confirm what type of car is supposed to be following us please, is it a red Vectra?"

"I'll find out and ring you right back."

"He's finding out and ringing us back," Linda repeated to Daniel as she put the phone back in the car door pocket.

"How on earth can he not know?"

"I suppose the car is from the police and not from customs, so he can't be expected to know them all."

"I guess you're right."

"Do you think we're being paranoid, honey?"

"Quite possibly, but I reckon we've a right to be after what has happened to us in the past few weeks."

Grant rang back within two or three minutes.

"Linda, don't panic it is ours, but you did the right thing to ring. If you have any suspicion about anything, you must let us know."

"OK Grant, thank you. We'll see you next week, all being well."

"Don't worry so much, you'll see us all right, now have a good time."

CHAPTER FOURTY NINE

They continued their journey to the marina, where they first went to the harbour office to collect the keys, then straight on round to the other side of the marina to find the Lady B. They located the correct pontoon, parked the car as close to it as possible and got Sam out of the back and put him in his pushchair. They did not take any luggage with them, but would locate the boat and open up first. Tom had told them she was moored on the finger against the end of the pontoon, so they walked slowly to the end, looking with interest at the various types of craft moored on either side on the way.

Daniel pointed at one particularly sorry-looking little speedboat moored at one of the fingers. It was half sunk and covered in mould, and its cockpit cover was so full of water that it was like a paddling pool.

"That is what Luke would refer to as firewood," he remarked with a smile to Linda.

"I have to say I'm inclined to agree with him. I mean it costs a lot to keep something in here, so what an earth is that here for? It doesn't look like its been moved in years."

"I actually don't think it's capable of moving."

They walked on and looked up. They were nearing the end of the marina and there straight ahead of them was the

Lady B. She was a Trader 41+2, only a couple of years old, and Mary and Tom had kept her immaculately. She was not a sleek boat, but more of a civilised gentleman's motor yacht with fabulously practical luxury accommodation. She was ideal for entertaining, which was after all what it was mostly used for, as were many of the other large yachts around her.

They climbed aboard and entered her beautifully teak-lined main saloon; she was a truly lovely boat. Daniel turned on the main electrics and they had a quick look round before going back to the car to collect the cases and the bedding. They spent the next hour organising themselves, before feeding Sam and putting him to bed in the forward cabin. He was asleep before Daniel had finished reading him his story. Daniel then went off to get some fish and chips for supper. They would eat and then probably just pass out due to tiredness.

Linda made the bed up and had a shower while Daniel was off getting the food from the chip shop in East Wittering. As he drove out of the marina he saw the Vectra sitting on the side of the perimeter road from where it had a good view of the *Lady B*. He found it faintly comforting to know someone was close at hand, although the other side of him was annoyed that it was necessary and found it an invasion of his privacy and freedom. He longed for the following week, when it would all be over.

The following morning they awoke to the sound of the creaking of their mooring warps, the clatter of the halyard on the neighbouring yacht and the faint slap-slap of the wind-whipped waves against the hull.

"Sounds like the wind has gained strength overnight" Daniel muttered to Linda as he got up to make them both a cup of tea.

"Should be fun" Linda said with a smile, as she glanced out of the porthole. Seeing the dark clouds, she instinctively pulled the duvet further up until it was round her neck.

If the weather permitted they would head out to Cowes on the Isle of Wight that day and spend a couple of days there. They had a full English breakfast that morning, after which Daniel phoned Luke while it was still an acceptable hour in Singapore. He then spent time on the phone to the UK office and finally, once he had sorted out one or two urgent business problems, he phoned his mother and brought her up to date with the latest situation. He played down any danger they might be in.

Later that morning they wandered over to the marina shop with Sam to buy some papers and a few provisions. The weather was not desperately bad, but considering they did not need to be anywhere in particular, they decided to wait until the following day before setting sail.

It had stopped raining, but it was damp and the wind coming in off the coast was bracing. They were half way back to the boat when Daniel's mobile rang. He picked it from his pocket and noticed that it just said 'call' with no caller ID.

"Hi, it's Daniel" he said. Then he stopped in his tracks, glanced at Linda and then looked around him.

Linda sensed something was wrong and stood motionless, staring into Daniel's eyes for a clue.

Han had been uptight about the fact that his 'colleagues' had been unable to locate the Cassidys. They were obviously not staying at their house. Maybe they were still in Singapore?

He would have to get them to phone Daniel on his mobile. Although customs had his Filofax with all his numbers in it, he knew he also had the number at home. He would get Maya to get hold of it for them.

The next time Maya visited him, Han asked her to get the mobile phone number for Daniel from the Istanbul house. She could get her mother to go in and find it and ring it through to her.

"Why do you want this number?" Maya had asked him.

"I want you to give it to the two friends who have come over."

"Yes, but what for, Han?"

"That's none of your business, just do as I say."

Maya picked up her handbag and left. She had nothing further to say to him, but knew she had to do as she had been asked. She made the call to her mother in Istanbul, who was looking after the children for her. Her mother would ring her back with the number. Maya had an uncomfortable feeling about what Han was planning, but if her fears were correct she would make sure they were thwarted. She had to do it so that Han would know nothing about it, as she was quite sure of the consequences for her if he thought she was behind anything.

The next call Maya made was to David Armstrong, the defence barrister defending Han.

"Please don't let on to Han that I have contacted you, but

there is something you should be aware of" she said. She told him what she had been asked to do.

"OK, thank you Mrs Atima, I think I get the picture" he replied. "Leave it with me, I'll talk to your husband and advise him that Daniel is no threat to him. Don't worry, I'll be diplomatic, he won't know we have spoken, but if he's intending threatening people, we must put him off because that is unacceptable and it will get him banged up permanently, as quick as a flash."

Armstrong immediately went across town to the prison where Han was being held. He had formulated some thoughts and had to convey them to Han in a subtle way before he did something stupid. David was seated in the meeting room when Han was brought in. Han sat down opposite David.

David opened the dialogue and got straight to the point. "As I mentioned to you, this chap Daniel Cassidy will be testifying for the prosecution. Now, this is going to be an uphill struggle because you're telling me there was a money man who you won't identify, but we have other information suggesting that you had a partner in all this. Quite frankly the prosecution are going to rip you to threads and prove that you did it willingly, and that you were in it from the start out of sheer greed."

An officer brought in a couple of cups of tea for them both. As soon as he had left David resumed.

"As you know, Daniel is one of the key witnesses for the prosecution and having visited you out in Turkey, he has put in his evidence about a partner he was dealing with as well. I think we can use him to your advantage in all this. Because he has met your partner he could help in your case, although he won't know it and neither will the prosecution, until the time."

Han looked at David quizzically. "What do you mean? How?"

"Believe me, he could be your biggest ally. It's actually good news that he will be testifying. I mean, there is very little he can say or do that is detrimental."

"But I don't understand, he is going to testify against me?"

"I know, but you'll have to leave this one with me and I'll run through the final plans for the trial with you nearer the time, probably at the end of the week. Believe me, he is probably the only person that can save you from rotting in jail for the rest of your life."

David left Han looking a little bemused, but fairly sure that he had understood what he had said. He only hoped that he had made it clear that they needed Daniel and that this would save any threat to him. David knew that Customs were monitoring every move and phone call to do with Daniel. Surely Han could not be so naïve as to try and interfere with a witness?

David called Maya to let her know that he thought he had got the message across, but did not elaborate on any of the detail. She just hoped he was right.

When Maya went in to visit Han the next morning, the first thing he asked was whether or not Maya had given the phone number to his friends.

"Not yet, I have only just had the call back from my mother with the number."

Han was not happy. "Well get out of here now, go and phone it through to them straight away!" he shouted.

Maya knew that David's message had probably fallen on deaf ears, but then she thought to herself that Han always did think he knew better than anyone else. She left the prison and wandered back to the hotel. She was in no hurry to give them the number, but knew that she had to do it, and it had to be the correct number. The consequences of doing otherwise did not bear thought.

About an hour later she got through and gave one of them the number. They wasted no time in finding a public phone box and making their call.

"Mr Daniel, you don't know me, but I know you and your family very well. You are a witness at my friend's trial next week. You be careful about what you say, you know he is innocent. By the way, we know where you are. We are watching you all the time."

The line went dead. Daniel repeated it word for word to Linda. They both looked around them. They were not far from where the Vectra had been parked the previous night, so they walked briskly in that direction. As they did so Daniel's mobile went again. It was Grant.

"Daniel, don't worry about the call you just received, they are bluffing."

"How do you know about the call, I haven't told anyone yet? And how do you know they are bluffing?"

"Daniel, we have got all calls to your mobile being

monitored, it is for your own good. We're sure nobody knows where you are, we've had people on the marina gates all night. It is just a bluff to frighten you into perjuring yourself in court. I cannot stress enough - don't listen to it."

Daniel was furious, more about the fact that his mobile was tapped than about the previous call. He switched it off and put it back in his pocket.

"Come on honey, we'll go out today, stuff the wind, we need a change of scenery" he said. With that they turned back round again and started walking back towards the boat. As soon as they were on board Daniel double checked the tide times, as there were certain times at low water when they would be unable to get the *Lady B* through the channel on the other side of the lock. They were fine for another hour.

Daniel put the keys in for both Volvo Penta engines and without wasting any further time, fired up the port engine. He waited for it to settle into a steady idle before he fired up the starboard engine. He would let them both warm up for five minutes before slipping the mooring.

"We're going to have to lock out honey, so can you put some more fenders down the starboard side" he said.

"OK."

He went back on deck, released the spring line and neatly coiled it into a locker on the aft deck. The wind was pushing them on to the pontoon, so after a few more minutes when both engines were registering a temperature on the gauges, he let the bow line go and asked Linda to hold the stern line and jump on when he asked her to do so. They left the pontoon without incident, as if Daniel did it every day.

As they approached the lock, Daniel looked at the boats surrounding him and then back at the lock again. He had to admit he was worried about the lock for fear of putting a scratch in the gleaming hull, and the lock looked as if it would only just take the boat. He carefully and slowly coaxed her into the lock, using both engines separately to keep her straight in the crosswind that was blowing. It took every ounce of his concentration, but she was finally in place and the lock keeper threw the bow line down to Linda, who was waiting on the deck. Daniel then darted out to the back of the boat to catch the stern line. The water was released from the lock gates and the *Lady B* tugged at her restraining lines as the water level dropped until finally the gates opened fully.

As Daniel was going back to the helm he noticed a couple of men standing at the railings of the lock watching them. The lock keeper asked in a cheery manner where they were going. Both Linda and Daniel ignored him, assuming he would think that they had not heard, and within seconds the *Lady B* was roaring out of the lock.

Daniel looked back and saw one of the two men who had been watching them in the lock talking into a mobile phone as he watched them disappear. He knew then that they were Grant's men and wondered where they would catch up with them.

Daniel wanted to get out of the area as soon as he could, in case Han's men really did know where they were. He nudged the throttles forward, knowing he was exceeding the speed limit through the moorings at Itchenor, and waited until he was past them before he opened her up a little more.

About forty minutes later they reached the Chichester Bar beacon and open water. He opened the throttles of the two 360 HP engines to the stops and waited as the *Lady B* gradually increased her speed. Once she was beyond her normal optimum cruising speed he reduced the throttle settings to about 85% and they settled on their course through the old wartime forts, past Portsmouth and onward to Cowes.

Linda had been with Sam down in the saloon, but she was finding it a little difficult below now that they were under way, particularly as she had just had to change Sam, so they both joined Daniel on the helm seat. It was too rough to make drinks. They would have to wait until they were in the lee of the Isle of Wight before it would be smooth enough for that, so they sat and enjoyed the passing scenery, waiting for smoother waters.

"I wish we could just go to France and forget the whole thing, as if it was a nightmare" Linda suggested.

"Don't tempt me honey. If only!"

They arrived in Cowes late that afternoon and were directed to a visitors' mooring' where they made sure the *Lady B* was secure before sorting themselves out. As they sat in the saloon and looked about them, Daniel saw two men standing at the railings looking in their direction. It was the same two who had been in Chichester.

"That didn't take long. Grant's boys were here before us."

"Why does that not surprise me" Linda said sarcastically.

"I thought they would track us. Anyway, only another few days to endure."

Han was getting more and more frustrated by the day, as his friends were getting nowhere in their efforts to locate Daniel. He wanted them to be seen, to emphasise that he, Han, could reach them despite being locked up. They had staked out the Cassidy home, but had seen no movement in or out. They now did not know where to start looking and now couldn't even phone him to threaten him.

Han was more pissed off by the fact that they could not find the family than anything else, because in reality some of what his barrister had said had sunk in. However he still wanted them to know that he was in charge. He told the boys to keep looking.

Robin, one of the two plain-clothed police officers tailing Daniel and Linda, walked down the pontoon. He had seen the *Lady B* come in to the marina and had waited for them to settle in before disturbing them. Daniel saw him walking towards the boat, and sat up to see out of the window. Robin knocked on the hull of the boat. Daniel got up and went on deck to talk to him.

Robin introduced himself and they shook hands.

"Mr Cassidy, I have a formal request from my boss, asking if you could please contact Grant at customs, as he needs to talk with you urgently."

"Does he indeed? OK, thank you, I'll give him a buzz." Daniel turned to go back into the boat.

"Er, Mr Cassidy - it is urgent sir."

"It always is, Robin, but don't worry, I'll ring him now."

Daniel went back aboard, grabbed his mobile from the dashboard and switched it back on.

"What did they want?" Linda asked.

"Grant wants me apparently."

Daniel dialled out.

"Grant, its Daniel, I gather from our accompanying convoy that you wanted to talk to me."

"Yes, thanks for ringing. The police are continuing with their investigations into your break-in and they have come up with several other prints. So if we're going to prove whether or not it was you-know-who and his merry band of men we're going to need to fingerprint any guests you may have had staying to eliminate them."

"I see, well actually you may be in luck because Luke and Michelle have been staying and they are due over here next week again, so you can ask them then."

"That is I assume your partner in Singapore?"

"That's it, him and his other half. If they're still together next week."

"Oh, I see – OK. And by the way, I understand you're in Cowes at the moment. Please keep us abreast of your movements, it is so much easier than us having to guess and work it out, and it's for your own sake after all."

"Well, all being well we will probably stay here until the day before the trial, when we'll head back to Chichester. Linda is not a great lover of the sea."

"OK Daniel, and if you're talking to Luke before he arrives, can you let him know what we need?"

"Yes, will do."

"All being well we'll see you Monday then, at ten sharp. You're happy that you know where to go?"

"I'm not happy exactly, but yes I know where to go, I've had a look at an A to Z."

"Excellent, don't worry, it'll all be over by next week. See you then."

"Yes, bye Grant."

That evening, early, Daniel and Linda wandered up through the steeply sloping street of the town centre, Sam in his pushchair. They stopped at a little pizzeria for a spot of supper. They had passed Robin and colleague en route and had nodded in recognition, but that was the extent of the communication.

Sam was beginning to get irritable toward the end of the meal so they left and made their way back to the boat. They bathed Sam and put him to bed before retiring on to the aft deck, where they sat in the evening sun which had shown its face about an hour previously, at the same time as the wind had abated. They had a couple of drinks, which helped to relax Daniel, and ended up chatting at length to a doctor and his wife on the yacht moored next to them on the other side of the finger pontoon. They watched the evening news at 10 before showering and going to bed at 11.

Linda heard the creaking of the mooring warps and the slight jolt against the *Lady B*'s hull first. She opened her eyes and sat half upright in bed. Daniel was still fast asleep. There was no further noise for a few seconds, although in the early hours of the morning it seemed like hours, so she put her head back down. Just as she had done so she heard the thud of someone in soft soled shoes on the deck above her. She nearly screamed in fright, but managed to catch herself, she leaned over and rocked Daniel hard.

"There is someone trying to get in."

"What, what are you on about?"

"There is someone trying to get into the boat."

"You sure?" Daniel said. He sat bolt upright, all his senses suddenly on maximum.

"Yes, listen."

With that Daniel too heard movement up above. He threw the duvet off and was on his feet in milliseconds. He got his bathrobe off the back of the door and quietly made his way to the galley, where he picked up a kitchen knife. He continued quietly, his senses all functioning at 110%. By the dim gloom of the lights on the main pontoon he could see someone on the aft deck of the Lady B. He crept out of the side saloon door and made his way down the deck on the opposite side of the cockpit and came round behind the person, who was bending down at the corner of the deck. All the time he was looking for a second intruder.

"What are you doing?" he challenged in an aggressive tone, more out of fear than anything.

The intruder turned, saw the knife that Daniel was yielding and let forth a shrill scream. A woman's scream.

Linda, who had been following closely behind Daniel, rushed up and out on to the deck. At the same time a man's voice from a boat alongside them rang out.

"What in bloody hell's name do you think you're playing at?"

With that, without any further notice, the man on the next boat jumped over the guard rails of his boat and on to the *Lady B*, where he launched himself fully at Daniel and rugby-tackled him to the deck. This caught Daniel completely unawares and he fell backwards heavily against the structure of the fly-bridge, the knife flying from his hand as he did so.

Linda, seeing the fight developing, quickly made her way back into the cockpit and locked the door. She went straight to the boat's helm position and blew the horn five or six times to try and alert help. Within 30 seconds people from boats all around were raising their weary heads out of hatches and portholes to see what was going on.

Andy, the man from the Southerly with whom they had chatted earlier in the evening, came straight across as Linda shouted to him for help. Daniel meanwhile was finding his strength and fighting back hard against his aggressor, while the first intruder stood and screamed her head off. Andy came up on deck with the stealth of a cheetah and soon had Daniel's male attacker in an arm lock.

It was then that Linda saw the two police running down the pontoon as fast as their sleepy legs would carry them. She released the door and shouted to them that they were being attacked. They leaped straight up on deck and went to the aft deck to sort the situation out. One of the police officers restrained Daniel, while the other seized his attacker. The woman who had boarded the *Lady B* still screamed and now fought to get at Daniel, who had been fighting her husband.

Once he had his breath back the man shouted "What the bloody hell is your game, are you just a fucking idiot or what?"

"What did you call me?" Daniel shot back, attempting to lay another punch at him.

"All right, all right, we're police officers. Now how about someone telling me what is going on here?" said the policeman holding Daniel.

Linda was the first to speak. She began to explain, but the male boarder, who was still being held by the other officer, kept interrupting. "I've never seen anyone make such a fuss about anyone boarding their boat to tie off before."

The officer, PC Thompson, knowing the situation, jumped to the defence of Daniel and Linda.

"Well sir, it is the early hours of the morning, which is a hell of a time to be creeping about on someone else's boat. I'm not surprised they were alarmed, I would have been."

"Well excuse me, but you're obviously not a yachtsman yourself. It happens all the time. We boarded so that we could tie our boat against theirs" the man shot back at the officer.

PC Thompson was trying to conclude the incident quickly. He did not want to go into the whys and wherefores of the Cassidy family situation.

"Well, let me put it this way sir. You were on their property when this incident occurred, so I suggest you make your way back to your boat and we all forget this little incident occurred. I would however like to see some form of identity from you both first."

"Are you having a laugh? What sort of police state are we living in now?"

"I'm not going to argue with you, will you please produce some identity."

The man pulled his wallet out from his inside pocket and produced some credit cards and a membership card with a photo on it. PC Thompson examined them. The man was the Labour MP for a London Borough, so he would not be looking for any negative publicity.

"OK, now please go back to your boat and forget this ever happened" said PC Thompson. The man muttered something under his breath, shook himself free from the officer holding him and walked over to where his wife was standing. They made their way back over the guard rails to their own boat.

"I am sorry," Daniel said turning to PC Thompson. "I thought - well, I don't know."

"I know what you thought and I fully understand," said the officer.

"I guess we owe you an explanation."

"Well, not really, I just can't understand why they attacked you."

Later, when Linda went to make a drink to take back to bed, she glanced out of the window to see that the boat that had caused the trouble the previous night had already untied and was quietly making her way out of the harbour. This was a relief, as they had not known how they were going to face them that morning.

"They've gone!" she shouted down to Daniel.

"Thank God for that" was the reply back from the cabin.

They decided that they would not go on anywhere else, as it was blatantly obvious that they were not going to be able to turn this into a mini holiday, as they had anticipated; they were simply in hiding. They would head back to Chichester the next day. Daniel also wanted to return while the weather was good, as it would have been typical of their recent run of luck if Daniel had been unable to make it to the trial because they were stuck in a little harbour to avoid bad weather.

Early on the morning of departure, Daniel went up to see the duty police who had done shifts with PC Thompson and his partner. He told them they were heading back to Chichester.

The voyage back was uneventful and smooth. They did not see the Southerly yacht again, and before long they were navigating up the Channel to the Chichester marina. Once again the butterflies entered Daniel's stomach at the thought of taking the *Lady B* through the lock. But Linda ensured they were fully fendered and again they locked through without incident and were soon tied up at their berth.

Just as they switched off the engines, Daniel's mobile rang. It was Luke. Daniel sat at the helm seat and brought him up to date, and Luke told him what was happening at work. Luke was travelling back from Singapore that evening and was just about to leave for Changi Airport with Michelle. Daniel told him to ring when he got back and they would arrange to meet at the office. Daniel was pleased they were both coming over, as they would be able to keep Linda company while Daniel was at the trial.

Again that evening they ate on board, having taken Sam to the beach for a long walk in West Wittering. The sea air and the building tension of knowing that the trial was the day after next had worn them out, and they were in bed by ten. The alarm went off at 6.30 the following morning and Daniel was out of bed far quicker than he would normally have been. He had hardly slept, despite the tiredness.

Today was the day he had to go to the office to sort out a few things, and the day they would go back to their house. They did not mind going back so soon, particularly as Luke and Michelle would be there for moral support and they knew the police would be outside until further notice.

At seven o'clock the phone went. It was Luke, already at the office. Daniel told him they would be there by 11. It took them twice as long as they had anticipated packing up the boat, and it appeared twice as much was coming off as had gone on a few days earlier. They cleaned and polished every surface, vacuumed and swept until the *Lady B* looked like new. They eventually left after 11 am and did not reach the office until 1 pm.

Daniel, who had told Luke about the fingerprinting, called Grant that morning and he in turn was arranging for someone from the local constabulary to go to the office that afternoon to take the prints. They could then probably draw some conclusions as to who had broken in to the Cassidy family home, something that would either put Daniel and Linda's minds to rest or unsettle them further.

CHAPTER FIFTY

When Linda and Daniel finally arrived at the office, the police had just finished and were on their way out. "Nice of you to make it" said Luke with a slightly sarcastic smile. Linda went in first and gave Luke a kiss, followed by Michelle.

"Nice to see you too," remarked Daniel as he carried Sam and followed Linda in to the office. They all shut themselves off in the top office as the General Manager's secretary made them all a coffee. There was much to catch up on. Luke suggested that the girls took one of the rental cars and went down to the house with Sam, but Daniel interjected and said that it was not a good idea for them to go on their own. He told them about the latest situation, and said they had not actually stayed at the house yet. Luke agreed that it was probably better for them to all go at once, but Daniel could tell that once again he thought they were overreacting.

The girls decided to go off to the pub for lunch with Sam. They would try to bring back a burger for Daniel and Luke. They started by discussing the situation in Singapore; Luke had not worried Daniel with it previously, but business was booming and it was becoming apparent that things were getting difficult without Daniel's presence. The business needed them both. Vera was looking after things admirably from an admin point of view but there were many decisions only Luke or Daniel could make, and things were definitely stretching at the seams.

In the UK things were all under control, with the management looking after it well, and Daniel had been in daily contact to advise on any queries, as had Luke, but his desk was still full of paperwork that needed clearing. Daniel would go through each customer's business with Luke that evening at home and they would fax Vera to compile replies and quotes for each that required immediate attention. Daniel did not mind. He reflected that it would help to take his mind off the following day's events.

By the time the girls arrived back with burgers Daniel had gone through most of the post on his desk, as had Luke, and they had managed to bin 90% of it as junk mail.

They all headed back to the house at 4 pm that afternoon and it was with a certain apprehension that Daniel and Linda turned in to the drive.

"I wonder if it will ever feel the same again. Coming home, I mean" Linda said with a sigh.

"Of course it will honey, just as soon as this is all behind us."

Parked outside the garage was a blue Ford Focus with two plain-clothed police aboard. They got out to greet Daniel and the family.

It was only really at this point that the penny dropped with Luke as to the seriousness of the situation confronting his colleague. He had until now been sheltered from the whole series of events and had almost scorned Daniel's concerns, but seeing the police sitting outside the house for their protection brought the reality home to him. Daniel noticed a marked change in his attitude towards things that night - he even started asking relevant questions regarding the trial - but Daniel tried to guide the conversation away from that, as he was trying to forget it.

Michelle and Luke helped them both to get the house straight and they all spent the first couple of hours thoroughly cleaning every inch of the house. It was still covered in fingerprinting dust and had not been touched since the break in. Once they had completed that it all felt much better, it was home once again.

It was not until about 9 pm that Daniel and Luke sat down to go through the paperwork, but Luke announced that he was simply too tired after the flight, so they both agreed to leave it until the following day.

The police changed shifts during the night. Daniel heard the car approach on the gravel drive and heard the muted conversations outside before the original car drove off. He was wide awake by 5 am and was in the kitchen making a tea when Luke walked in and joined him. He too was wide awake, but due to jet lag, not as in Daniel's case, nervous apprehension.

One of the police officers was going to continue to guard the house while Daniel was in court, and while Daniel had insisted to Grant that he would make his own way to the Old

Bailey, Grant had insisted that he should be at least accompanied there, if not back. Luke was going to take Daniel and the officer to the station that morning. Daniel had not wanted any family or friends to accompany him. He would rather go and get it over with on his own.

Just before Daniel walked out of the door, the phone rang. He looked at it, wondering whether or not to answer it. He decided he had better, in case it was Grant or Gill and that the whole event had been postponed, so he picked up the receiver slightly apprehensively, but to his relief it was Keanu calling from Hong Kong to wish him all the best at the trial that day.

CHAPTER FIFTY ONE

They left the house at 8 am. Daniel's train was leaving at 8.25 and would get into Victoria by 9.30. Daniel said goodbye to Luke as the policeman bought two tickets, and they awaited the arrival of the train. When it arrived it was already full, and Daniel had to stand for the entire journey. How did people do this every day, he wondered to himself. He could now see why people suffered the misery of the M25 commuter traffic each day, if this was the only other option.

As the train gathered speed out of the station, Daniel looked around him to see if there was anyone suspicious nearby. There was no one, but in his mind he could have made up a story for every one of them. He held on to the grab rail and his mind started to think about what he had in store that day. He wondered if the Old Bailey would be as daunting as it looked on the television. He thought about all the cases he knew of that had been held there, all the notorious criminals that had passed through its doors.

He did not communicate with the policeman during the journey, as he was not in a talking mood, but the officer seemed to understand and did not try to force conversation.

The train came to a halt between stations. All the commuters had their noses in books, magazines or the daily papers, and not a sound could be heard. Daniel looked at his watch; it was already nine o'clock, only 30 minutes to go.

The train started forward again with a lurch and a creak and, in what seemed no time at all, they were passing Battersea Power Station, a huge square dinosaur of a brick building with a huge chimney on each corner, ugly and bland, but not without a certain charm. As they rattled over the Thames and on into Victoria, Daniel's nerves were becoming more apparent to him. He noticed his palms were moist.

He made his way down to the tube station, accompanied by the policeman. He already knew he had to take the Circle Line to Liverpool Street and then change to the Central Line for a couple of stops to St Pauls. The tube was packed and when the doors opened on the platform, it was as much as the people on board could do to save themselves from being pushed out, but that did not stop the odd person still trying to board, unsuccessfully, to the fury of those already on the train.

Daniel waited patiently. He knew another train would be along shortly.

Daniel got off and joined the queue at the escalators to take them up to ground level. As he got on to the street he looked for a street name so he could get his bearings. They were on Newgate Street. After consulting his A to Z and conferring with his companion they set off down Newgate Street in the direction of the Old Bailey, arriving at ten to ten exactly. Daniel stopped briefly on the pavement and looked up at the imposing building ahead of him.

"I didn't think I'd see the day when I had to enter this place" Daniel commented to the policeman.

"I must admit you have beaten me to it" he responded with a smile.

They went in through the main entrance and approached the reception counter. He told them of the purpose of his visit and was told to go through the doors to his right where he was confronted with a clear glass swivelling door. Having thanked the policeman who had accompanied him, he was asked by security to step inside. The door closed behind him, leaving him standing enclosed in what looked like an upright torpedo tube. After a few seconds the door ahead of him opened and he stepped through to the waiting security guards, in an area not dissimilar in size and layout to a customs hall at an airport. Once through, he was asked which case he was connected with. Then he was shown along a stone-floored corridor with tall ceilings, lit by unwelcoming fluorescent tubes, with large wooden doors every 15 feet or so on the left and small half glass-fronted waiting rooms on the right hand side. He was asked if he was for the prosecution or the defence and then guided to one of the small waiting rooms, where he took a seat and was told that the prosecution council would be down to see him shortly.

About half an hour later, as Daniel was becoming more and more anxious and wondering if he was in fact in the right area, Gill arrived.

"Sorry to have kept you waiting, it's been one of those mornings."

Daniel stood to shake her hand. "Oh, don't worry," he said gallantly, trying to hide his apprehension, as if he did this sort of thing every day of the week.

"I am afraid it may be another hour or two until we can bring you in, but I'll pop back and see you shortly to let you know how it's progressing."

"I see, well I'm not going anywhere," said Daniel meekly, still in awe of the unfamiliar surroundings. He sat back down on the wooden bench.

He was the only one in the room, and with nothing to read or look at the time dragged and the following hour seemed like an eternity.

Finally Grant appeared round the door.

"Hi Daniel, I'm sorry for the delay, we've been having right fun and games upstairs. The jury still has still not been agreed after some last minute objections from the defence."

"So, where does that leave us then?"

"Well it's unlikely to be resolved today now as we have got to go through the business of swearing in the jury. All I can suggest is that you return home today and we see you back here at the same time tomorrow. I'm really sorry."

"Ok, if that's the way it is, then that's the way it's got to be, I'll see you in the morning."

Grant shook hands with Daniel, then hurriedly disappeared to go and sort things out. Daniel sat back down again and took out his train timetable from the pocket of his coat. He decided he would be unable to catch the train that left Victoria Station in 15 minutes, but would aim to get the one that left Victoria in an hour.

As he walked through the foyer of the court house he looked for his police escort, who was nowhere to be seen. He had been told that Daniel would be in the building for a while and was off getting a sandwich. As Daniel turned out of the entrance of the Old Bailey he took his mobile from his pocket and called home, Linda answered.

"Hi, hon, it's me. Guess what, they have only postponed it until tomorrow now!"

"Oh Daniel, I am sorry darling, after getting yourself all geared up for it. What a pain."

"Yeah, you could put it like that, I've now got to go through the whole palaver of not knowing what to expect again tomorrow. Anyhow, do you think one of you could pick me up at the station an hour and three quarters from now?"

"Of course we can."

"Actually, no, I tell you what, I'll give you another call when I'm 15 minutes away, so please make sure someone is in."

"Will do darling. See you later."

Daniel continued down the street a few paces further where he stopped at a newsagents and picked up a *Daily Telegraph*. Next door was an Italian coffee shop, and as he had half an hour to kill he decided to stop there for a drink before going on to the station.

The coffee shop was small with a couple of tables and chairs outside on the pavement. Inside there were a few tables down the left hand side with the serving counter running a quarter the way down the right hand side, opening up to a larger seating area at the back.

Daniel approached the counter and ordered a Cappuccino. He thanked the waiter, paid, and carried on to the back of the shop, where there was an empty table on the right beyond the counter. All the other tables were full.

He placed his coffee and paper on the table and removed his coat, hanging it over the back of his chair before sitting down with his back to the wall, from where he had a view of the rest of the café.

He tore open the sachet of sugar, emptied the contents into his coffee and started to stir it. As he did so the people at the next table were leaving. Daniel looked up as they left and as they moved towards the door it gave Daniel a better view of the tables beyond.

He froze for an instant, hardly daring to believe what he was seeing. Then he grabbed his *Telegraph* and opened it at eye level, at the same time sinking down in his chair. Once he had settled he allowed himself to glance over the top of the paper as he turned a page, just to ensure he had not been mistaken in what he had seen. He had not. He slowly raised the paper and turned in his seat to a height and position where he could not be seen from that direction.

Daniel could not believe the predicament in which he now found himself. He was sitting in a café opposite the court where he was about to be a key witness against Han, an alleged drug baron, while opposite him sat the accused's mother, the woman he had met in Istanbul, along with two black-haired, moustached, swarthy-looking characters who Daniel knew he had also seen before. Where was his police escort, now he needed him?

Daniel stared at the same spot in the page of his paper until it became a blur as he wondered how he was going to get out of this one. He thought and thought about where he had seen the other two before, and then it came back to him.

It was as he had been walking to the toilets, across the foyer of the hotel in Istanbul on the night of Han's mother's birthday. He had seen Han talking to these men then.

They could only be there for one reason. He was sure it was one of them who had phoned to put the jitters up him when they had been in the marina at Chichester. They had probably been looking for him everywhere. It was probably they who had ransacked his home and now, having avoided them so far, he had walked straight into them just before the trial was due to start.

Daniel looked at his watch. He had about 25 minutes to kill. In that time he hoped they would leave and that he could exit rapidly in the other direction.

He did not read a word of the paper or even turn a page during the next 25 minutes, but he began to sweat more and more as the coffee shop emptied and he realised he was going to have to move.

He had switched off his mobile so as not to draw attention to himself. He knew Han's mother would recognise his voice if she heard it.

It was becoming more apparent to Daniel that they had settled in for the day. After all, the court case was not being heard yet, so what else was there for them to do?

Daniel thought they must have given up on finding him before the trial and that they must now be resigned to the fact that he was going to testify, but that hopefully could say nothing to put Han away. However he did not want to take the chance of being seen now, as he was sure they would have a go at him.

He had to move, or not only was he going to miss the train, but it was increasingly likely he would be recognised.

He turned round to face the wall as he stood up and placed the paper on the table, not looking in their direction. He spent a while putting his coat on and doing the buttons up, then slid out from his table, still with his back to them as he faced the service counter.

"Goodbye sir" the waiter said as Daniel sidled past. Daniel raised his hand and half-smiled in acknowledgement, then slowly turned towards the door. He turned right out of the shop, the opposite way from which he had come so as not to expose himself to their view. He did not look in, but gazed firmly over the road until he had casually passed the window. He then looked straight ahead, increased his pace and headed for the tube station.

He did not look back until he had reached the end of the road. Then, just before he turned the corner on to Ludgate Hill, he allowed himself a quick glance back.

The three of them had left the café and were heading in his direction.

Daniel increased his pace and reached the next turning into St. Pauls Churchyard. When he again glanced back, to his relief, there was no sign of the trio.

Daniel now found himself glancing back every few hundred yards as he walked up to Cheapside and then left again to the tube station. He walked down towards one end of the platform, where he stood and waited for the train that would take him towards Victoria. The train arrived and as he was boarding he glanced toward the platform entrance and saw a man heading rapidly in his direction. The train doors closed before his pursuer had time to board.

Daniel was pleased to see that the train was fairly empty. He jumped on, walked to a series of empty seats and sat down.

As he arrived at Victoria he realised he had only four minutes to catch his train, as the transfer at Liverpool Street on to the Circle line had taken longer than anticipated. He bolted up the escalators, then on up the stairs into the main station. He looked for his platform number. Typical - it was down the far end to the right. He jogged across the station, glancing at his watch unnecessarily often, until he reached the platform, where the guard had just reached the end of the train and about to blow the whistle.

"Wait!" shouted Daniel as he ran up to the end carriage.

"You'll have to wait for the next one son" The guard shouted at him as he then continued to blow his whistle.

"Like hell I will!" said Daniel. After all the train was not yet moving. He was the only one on the platform and he could have waited three more seconds before blowing his whistle. He yanked open the door closest to him and jumped on. He closed the door as the train started to shunt forwards. He heard some shouts of annoyance from the guard outside, but he did not care. The train was on the move and he was on his way.

Han had stayed in daily touch with his friends. He had gradually resigned himself to the fact that whatever was said in court was going to have to be.

His barrister had also reiterated on each visit how necessary it was to let it run the course.

Maya had gone back to Istanbul and would return for the trial, but not before. She could not be bothered to visit her self-centred villain of a husband until then. She had had enough of him.

Han, in light of the fact that his friends had given up looking for Daniel, had asked them to make sure his mother was all right. She had already visited him soon after his arrest, when she had given him a real dressing down. She had found it difficult to subdue her anger and disappointment with him, and he had felt thoroughly ashamed. She and Maya were close to each other, and when it came to the crunch Han's mother was firmly on Maya's side. She deplored the way Han treated his wife.

Fifteen minutes from home, Daniel phoned the house and let them know where he was. Luke offered to come and pick him up, so Linda said she would make sure he left immediately.

Daniel spent that afternoon with Luke going through various aspects of the business that needed sorting out, sending at least 22 emails and 15 faxes. It was all long overdue. Without Daniel's undivided attention, things were beginning to slip. The company was growing and there was more than Luke could cope with alone.

As they sat eating roast lamb at the kitchen table that evening they were all keen to hear what the court hearing had been like, but sadly all that Daniel could communicate to them at that stage was the décor of the waiting room. They were however intrigued and concerned to hear that he had come across Han's stooges in the café.

Daniel had a fitful sleep that night with visions of the Old Bailey and his images of what the main court room must look like filling his thoughts. He was dreading facing Han in court.

CHAPTER FIFTY TWO

The next morning they followed the same pattern and duly arrived at the Old Bailey at ten to ten again. Daniel once again thanked the policeman who had accompanied him on the journey, and was duly shown into the same waiting room.

Within three minutes, and just as Daniel had retrieved a book from his case to settle in for a long wait, Gill appeared, bid him good morning and asked Daniel to follow her upstairs to the courts.

They arrived in an enormous hall with a high ceiling and entrances to the different main courtrooms down one side. There was a series of airport departure lounge-style chairs with central coffee tables arranged about twenty feet away from each door, and outside court No 2 a couple of other witnesses were waiting for the same case.

"You are the first witness for the prosecution, so you should be called in about fifteen minutes or so" Gill advised Daniel, who nodded his acceptance.

Gill then disappeared through the door to court no 2.

Daniel sat down and once again retrieved his book. He had been asked not to confer with other witnesses and he duly started to read, although he found concentrating difficult, and he found himself trying to imagine what lay behind the great doors to Court no 2. Was there a small briefing room before you got to the main court?

Yes, surely there must be. They must tell him the form before he went in. Who is who, how to address everyone, wouldn't they? Surely they must. Oh well, he'd soon find out.

Such were Daniel's nerves that he found himself regretting that he had had the second cup of tea that morning and now needed the toilet badly, but there was nobody to ask if he had enough time. He would wait until someone of authority came back out through the door to the courtroom and see if he could disappear for a minute or two.

After a few minutes, when nobody appeared, he decided to go anyway, so he advised the other witnesses that he would be back in a couple of minutes if he was needed.

He wandered off in search of the gents. He saw a man in the black robes just about to enter one of the other courtrooms so Daniel asked him directions to the closest wash rooms. The chap pointed to the end of the corridor adjacent to them.

"Just down the end there."

"Thank you" Daniel said as he wandered on down the corridor. It was a surprisingly long way.

Daniel was remarkably calm as he made his way back down to the waiting area, until as he was in sight of it, he saw Gill standing there, obviously waiting for him. He increased his pace, almost to the trot, having visions of being responsible for holding up the entire court proceedings.

"Ah, there you are." Said Gill, looking at her watch, "I'm afraid you're on."

"Oh well, let's get it over with," said Daniel. His legs were turning to jelly and there was a churning sensation in his stomach. He followed Gill through the doors to court no 2. As he walked in he was startled to find all eyes were upon him. One of the clerks spoke.

"Would you step into the witness box?" said a clerk. Daniel started to look around him, working out who was sitting where. It was a daunting place. His line of vision eventually landed on the back row to his left, opposite the judge, where he saw Han sitting, head bowed, eyes closed. Daniel quickly averted his gaze, in case Han opened his eyes. Daniel looked up at the judge to his right, then across at the jury directly opposite him, then at the barristers. He had had no idea that there would be so many lawyers involved. He could not work out who was working for who, but was sure it would all soon be made clear.

He spotted Grant and Gill sitting at one of the tables, so he assumed that the prosecution barrister was the one in front of them, with his entourage sitting behind. The clerk came up to Daniel and having confirmed which religion he was, handed him a bible and told Daniel to hold it in his right hand and repeat the words on a card he held up.

"Please speak clearly into the microphone Mr Cassidy."

"I hereby promise to tell the truth, the whole truth…" Daniel spoke clearly and concisely into the microphone. As he had finished he heard from somewhere above him the sound of a woman crying. He looked up, but could not see anything as it was coming from a balconied area above his head, obviously the public gallery. Who was it crying, he wondered? It could only have been Maya, and at that moment he felt awful for being there.

He was asked to confirm his name and address for the records, and did so. Three of the barristers in the row closest to him then introduced themselves.

Daniel had got the prosecution barrister right, but was thrown by the fact that two people were actually on trial, Han and Eugene. The centre barrister was representing Eugene. Eugene was a new face as far as Daniel was concerned and someone about whom he knew nothing.

The prosecution barrister started with a lot of general questions.

"How did the accused initially make contact with you?"

"At the boat show in Earls Court, London, via information from a colleague of his in Singapore."

"And for the benefit of the jury, could you please explain the nature of your business at the boat show?"

Daniel duly explained briefly about the boat business.

"What was the nature of his enquiry?"

"Well, he initially wanted to see if we could build boats for us in Turkey, but the nature of the inquiry changed and he then wanted to know if we wished to purchase sports boats."

"How did he propose that the business be conducted?"

"He wanted to supply the boats free of charge, and for the profit to be split when they were sold on."

"Was this unusual, in your opinion?"

"Yes, it is certainly a way of business that is new to me. If anything, most suppliers normally insist on full payment up front, even before the goods are shipped."

"Tell us about your trip to Istanbul?"

Daniel continued to tell the story of his visit. He kept it to fact and did not go into the detail of his inner feelings or suspicions. When he glanced up from the barrister asking the questions he saw Han, who was in view just above the barrister's head. He was staring at Daniel with a cold, unmoved expression. It was an expression that said it all to Daniel. It said: If you say a word out of place son, you'll regret it. It sent a shiver down Daniel's spine and from that moment on he made sure he did not regain eye contact.

"Why did you insist on going to Istanbul?" The prosecution continued.

"We had to know what the quality of the boats was like. We could not just buy blind, even if they were being supplied free of charge."

"And what were your findings when you got there?"

"Well, quite frankly the quality of the boats was nowhere near good enough."

Questions kept on coming from the prosecution for a further two and a half hours, when the judge then intervened and suggested that they all broke for lunch. Daniel would have to be in the witness box for the afternoon as well.

Gill told Daniel that he could go to the restaurant on the top floor for some lunch and that he should be back ready for court at 2 pm sharp.

Daniel wandered up to the top floor and found the restaurant. He looked around him wearily the whole time, aware that some of Han's relations could be in the vicinity, and knowing he would have to avoid them at all costs. He was not sure whether they would have access to this part of the court building or not, but he would keep an eye open anyway.

He sat alone for a lunch of Irish stew and pondered the morning's events. He felt the afternoon would be easier now he knew the ropes. The vision of Han in the dock staring coldly and deliberately kept coming back to him.

He finished the stew, went to collect a coffee and then sat back at his table and called Linda. Linda picked up the phone almost before it had rung. She had been eagerly waiting for the call.

"How's it going sweetheart? Have you finished?"

"No, unfortunately it looks like I'm in for the afternoon as well."

"I've been thinking about you all morning, are you OK?"

"Yes honey I'm fine, not much to it really. Just standing there answering questions."

"Can you see *him* from where you are giving evidence?"

"Yes, I'm sad to say I can. Anyhow I'll bring you up to date in full this evening. I'd better get back down there for the next session."

He rang off and made his way back down to the court, where he once again sat outside. At ten past two he was asked to re-enter the witness box.

The prosecution continued for a further half an hour. It was then the turn of the defence. David stood and began asking his questions, pausing occasionally to refer to the notes he had taken while the prosecution had been questioning Daniel.

The first questions were really a re-run of the questions that had been asked by the prosecution, only phrased slightly differently, but after a few minutes the tack changed.

"I put it to you Mr Cassidy that your dealings with this whole business were held predominantly not with my client, but with a gentleman in Singapore who was the real person behind all this."

Grant looked at Gill. "Here we go" he murmured.

"No" said Daniel, "In fact nearly all my dealings with reference to the boats were held with Han. The other guy knew nothing about boats whatsoever."

"Well, I would suggest that the fact he knew nothing about boats at all was really irrelevant, considering it was his intention to smuggle drugs, not boats. Could you just confirm that you did in fact deal with someone else regarding the business of buying boats?"

"Yes, we dealt with both of them."

"Thank you Mr Cassidy. I would now like to move on to the way in which you do business normally and to establish why this offer of business from my client was so different, in your opinion. Are you familiar with the shipping terms FOB and CIF?"

"Yes I am."

"And how do you normally conduct your business?"

Daniel spent the next half hour explaining to the jury the different types of shipping terms and methods of payments they used for different products from different places. In the end Daniel had made his point clearly and concisely and shown what an odd offer of business the Turk had made.

David spent the next hour trying to persuade Daniel that in fact his trip to Turkey had been entirely normal, but Daniel more than persuaded the jury otherwise.

Han had not taken his eyes off Daniel for the entire period, and Daniel could almost feel his glare burning into his skull.

At 4.30 the defence had finished with Daniel and the judge announced that the trial would adjourn until tomorrow. Grant and Gill caught up with Daniel in the large foyer.

"Thank you so much, Daniel" Grant said, as he shook his hand.

"Yes, thanks" Gill added.

"I don't think there will be a requirement for you again, but you're staying in the UK for a while anyhow I understand?"

"Yes, that's right. Unfortunately an aunt of Linda's is not too well, so we'll be staying to give a bit of support to her mother. We'll see how it goes, but we'll be here for a couple of weeks or so."

"OK. Well, we'll be in touch if there's any news, but as far as you're concerned I think the answer is to try and forget the whole ordeal."

"OK Grant, thank you, but I really would appreciate knowing what happens."

"Don't worry, you'll be one of the first to know, but this could go on for a month or two."

"I am sure you won't have any trouble finding me" Daniel said with a grin.

As Daniel turned and walked from the Old Bailey he felt as if an enormous weight had just been craned from his shoulders. He felt like a new man, contented. As he sat on the train he suddenly was overcome with tiredness. The stress had lifted, and it was a real struggle to stay awake, but he managed. He once again phoned home as the train was approaching, and Luke came to collect him from the station.

CHAPTER FIFTY THREE

Linda and Michelle had put a couple of bottles of Moet on ice. That evening the four of them sat at home and drank a great deal too much of it. They were delighted that the trial, for them at least, was over, and they could regain their lives once again.

The following morning they phoned Hong Kong. Keanu answered, and was delighted to hear it was all over. He said he would arrange for he and Kate to visit Daniel and Linda in Singapore as soon as they got back there.

Daniel and Linda spent the next few days with Daniel's parents, and a week later Linda's aunt died peacefully. They stayed for the funeral, then headed back to Singapore a couple of days after that. They talked on the plane at length about the fact that Edward Lim was probably still at large, but they knew Daniel had nothing to fear. He had not put him away and they were sure that they could resume normal life once again. Linda rested her head on Daniel's shoulder as she sat with a glass of red wine which the stewardess had just given her, and happened to mention that life was probably going to be a little dull after the recent excitement

"Yes, and I'm looking forward to every dull moment of it" Daniel responded.

"So am I."

Daniel spent the next week catching up with the office work, although he left at four each afternoon to ensure he would spend some time with Sam before his bed time. Linda started to resume her normal social activities and both she and Daniel were in great demand because of what they had been through.

Two weeks later Keanu and Kate came to stay for the week. It was a week of total relaxation and leisure with water skiing, tennis and dining top of the agenda, mixed of course with shopping for the girls, who must have known every paving slab in Orchard Road by the time they had finished.

Daniel only went in to the office for three days that week, Vera was once again handling things beautifully, now that things were back on track, and Luke had gone away for the week with Michelle up to a little resort on the East Coast of Malaysia called Desaru.

It was during that week, after discussions with Keanu, that out of sheer curiosity Daniel phoned the officer who had been in charge of the operation in Singapore. He asked if they had found anyone in connection with the drugs running.

"No, not directly" the man replied. "However the character we picked up in Malaysia who was at the identity parade in Kuala Lumpur proved to be quite interesting and has been put away by the Malaysian police for a long time. Once they started delving into his past they found fraud, embezzlement and host of other illegal practices. I have to say I wouldn't be surprised if any drugs connections with Mr Lim stopped when he went away, but that is purely, as you say in England, a hunch. There has been so much money running through his hands that is unaccounted for. Anyhow I'm pleased it is over for you Mr Cassidy, it was not a pleasant thing to have been involved with."

"No, you could put it that way. Anyhow, thanks for your support."

Daniel and Keanu discussed at length the latest revelations over a drink, sitting round the pool. The girls were out shopping in Holland Village.

Keanu and Kate had to leave at the end of that week, as work beckoned back in Hong Kong. The next two weeks saw a return to normality and routine started to set back in. The socialising was even busier than it had been before the event. Both Daniel and Linda were hot property.

A month after returning, Daniel rang Grant to see if there had been any news on the trial. He was told that it was still ongoing.

"What on earth is that costing the taxpayer?" Daniel asked incredulously.

"You don't want to know," was Grant's response. "But it will be worth it when he's put away and out of action."

"Oh well, I will be back in London in a couple of weeks' time, so maybe I'll give you a ring then."

"Yes, do that. I should be in a better position to estimate

the end of it by then."

"OK Grant, speak to you then."

Daniel and Luke set off for London on the Saturday evening flight for a short week-long visit, most of which was taken up with meetings at the UK office. They were due to talk to a number of importers in various European countries who were keen to become sole agents for their products.

On the Tuesday morning at about 10 am Daniel's mobile rang; it was Grant.

"Daniel, hi, it's Grant. How are you doing?"

"I'm fine thank you Grant, You've obviously got some news."

"Yes, I have and I wondered if Gill and I could buy you a drink, perhaps this evening and let you know how it all worked out?"

"I'm sure that would be fine, where do you suggest?"

"I would say at that little pub close to your office."

"The Hatch, OK that's fine. I'll be finished here at about six, so shall we say 6.15 at the Hatch?"

"See you then Daniel."

"OK Grant, but can you tell me the final outcome?"

Grant had already hung up. Daniel toyed with the idea of ringing him back, but decided it was only a few more hours, so he'd wait until the evening.

He left the office with Luke at exactly 6 pm and they duly arrived at the Hatch at ten past. Grant and Gill were already there, standing at the bar ordering their drinks.

"Ah, Daniel!" Grant said, offering a hand. "Hi, Luke. How are you?"

Daniel thought he detected a false happiness in their voices, and that the smile was definitely not telling the real story, but let the thought go.

"What can I get you both?" Grant offered.

"Half a Strongbow for me please," Daniel replied.

"And a pint of orange juice for me," Luke added.

The barman poured the drinks and they wandered over to the nearest table, the same table at which Xu's accomplice had sat those many months previously to see to Gordon. Once they were all seated Grant initiated the conversation, "Right, where shall I start?"

Gill then suggested that they take up the story from the time that Daniel gave evidence.

"All I really need to know is how long he's gone down for" Daniel suggested helpfully.

"We'll get to that" said Gill.

"Well, he put in a plea for duress" Grant started.

"That doesn't mean a thing to me," Daniel responded, giving Grant his undivided attention.

"What it basically means is that he knew he had been caught red-handed and that there was no avenue of escape from that point, so he did the only thing he really could do and pleaded duress. This simply means that he claimed that if he had not done the drug smuggling, the lives of his family as well as his own life were under threat."

"But under threat from whom?" Daniel quizzed Grant.

"Well, this is where it gets interesting, because he denied he had a partner in the operation but said he had no option to do it because the supplier was forcing him to."

"Surely if that's the case, he would have to prove it?"

"Logic would say yes, but unfortunately he did not have to prove duress and we couldn't disprove it. So it's an easy out for him - provided the jury believe him."

"Wait a minute, are you telling me what I think you are telling me? Someone who was caught with thirty million pounds worth of heroin in his hands, and who obviously masterminded the whole thing, has just walked free?"

Gill answered Daniel. "I can assure you that we are as upset about it as anyone. You can imagine the months and months of work and man hours that it has taken to put this whole case together and our devastation at the end verdict by the jury."

"I certainly can."

"Unbelievable!" Luke said, shaking his head.

"Yes, Luke, it is." Grant replied. "We're completely gutted by it. It makes you wonder why we bother. The only positive side is that we did stop a large consignment of drugs hitting the streets and I should think the other people involved in the drugs deal with him will be pretty pissed off with him, but no, it's not the result we would liked to have seen, or indeed the one we expected. He really got off on a technicality, because if he had had to prove from whom he was under duress and he had not done so, he wouldn't be free now."

Daniel was dumbstruck. Eventually all he could say was "Well I guess if it's that easy to get away with a stunt like that he's probably engineering the second attempt right now."

"I don't think we'll be seeing any more of our friend, I

think the shock of it all will put pay to that. In any case there will be people in Turkey who will want their pound of flesh from him" Grant remarked.

Daniel nodded in half-hearted agreement, thinking he knew what Grant meant. The four of them sat in silence for a few seconds as both Daniel and Luke let the latest information sink in. They were genuinely confused.

Grant and Gill knew only too well why they felt as they did. The outcome of the trial had been a complete shock to Grant and the team, and indeed had caused a wave of murmured disbelief throughout court number 2 when the jury had read out the verdict. This had been followed by sheer disappointment, and a feeling of months of wasted work.

Daniel quietly wondered to himself whether in fact Han's two friends had achieved more than they were all aware of. Had they perhaps managed to intimidate the jury? He mooted the point with Luke, who said he had been wondering exactly the same thing.

Han walked out into the grey, dreary light, tears of relief in his eyes. Thank goodness, he thought, for the British justice system. He was free.

Han, Maya, his mother and his two colleagues all shared a celebratory meal at their hotel that evening. His room was a far cry from the prison cell of the previous night. He had never appreciated a hotel room so much in his life.

The following day, having flown back to Istanbul, Han and Maya drove out to their home on the outskirts of the city. It was a good feeling to be back. There had been a time when he had thought he might never see his home again.

He walked out on to the patio and drew deeply on his cigarette, looking out over the garden in the fading evening light. It was a glorious evening. He saw that the lawn needed cutting; well, that was a job he would be more than happy to do himself on the morrow. He had learned his lesson. Had it not been for the lawyers his mother had engaged, he might never have had the chance to cut that grass again. He only wondered where Xu had vanished to.

Just then something glinted briefly in the shrubbery at the foot of the garden; a piece of glass, perhaps? He stared at the spot. Something was moving...

Han turned to throw himself sideways, but he was a fraction of a second too late. A sharp crack echoed across the garden. The high-velocity bullet caught him in the middle of the chest. Han collapsed across the edge of the patio, his mouth agape, his eyes in a frozen stare of shock. His cigarette fell from his fingers, rolled off the edge of the patio and dropped, still glowing, into the rich, green grass.

ND - #0065 - 270225 - C0 - 203/127/21 - PB - 9781861510761 - Matt Lamination